‖‖‖‖‖‖‖‖‖‖‖‖‖‖‖‖‖‖‖‖
D0451687

**He pulled on a pair of gloves,
then opened the knapsack.**

An apple, a peanut-butter sandwich in a plastic bag, a small container of blueberry yogurt and a plastic spoon. Shorts, socks, a T-shirt with a penguin on it. A set of keys, a pair of sunglasses, a cheap wristwatch. A paperback copy of *Oliver Twist*. He found her wallet stuffed into one of the shoes— why did anyone ever think that was a good hiding place?—and the face smiling at him from the driver's license photo was the same as the one he'd seen on Alexx's autopsy table.

He opened the book at random and read aloud the first line his eye fell on: "There is a passion for hunting something deeply implanted in the human breast."

Very true, he thought. *Even if that something is only a little time on a beach to read a good book and maybe go for a swim. And out there, in the water, you became the focus of someone else's hunt.*

He put the book back into the knapsack, turned and stared out over the water.

And that hunter, in turn, has now acquired some hunters of his own . . .

CSI: MIAMI™

RIPTIDE

DONN CORTEZ

CSI: MIAMI produced by CBS Productions, a business unit of CBS Broadcasting Inc.
and Alliance Atlantis Productions Inc.
Executive Producer: Jerry Bruckheimer, Carol Mendelsohn, Ann Donahue, Anthony E. Zuiker, Jonathan Littman
Series created by Anthony E. Zuiker, Ann Donahue, and Carol Mendelsohn

POCKET **STAR** BOOKS

New York   London   Toronto   Sydney

The sale of this book without its cover is unauthorized. If you purchased this book without a cover, you should be aware that it was reported to the publisher as "unsold and destroyed." Neither the author nor the publisher has received payment for the sale of this "stripped book."

An *Original* Publication of POCKET BOOKS

A Pocket Star Book published by
POCKET BOOKS, a division of Simon & Schuster, Inc.
1230 Avenue of the Americas, New York, NY 10020

This book is a work of fiction. Names, characters, places and incidents are products of the author's imagination or are used fictitiously. Any resemblance to actual events or locales or persons, living or dead, is entirely coincidental.

Copyright © 2006 by CBS Broadcasting Inc. and Alliance Atlantis Productions, Inc. CSI: Miami in USA is a trademark of CBS Broadcasting Inc. and outside USA is a trademark of Alliance Atlantis Communications, Inc. All Rights Reserved.

CBS and the CBS Eye design TM CBS Broadcasting Inc. ALLIANCE ATLANTIS with the stylized "A" design TM Alliance Atlantis Communications, Inc.

All rights reserved, including the right to reproduce this book or portions thereof in any form whatsoever. For information address Pocket Books, 1230 Avenue of the Americas, New York, NY 10020

ISBN-13: 978-0-7434-8058-1
ISBN-10:   0-7434-8058-9

This Pocket Star Books paperback edition August 2006

10 9 8 7 6 5 4 3 2 1

POCKET STAR BOOKS and colophon are registered trademarks of Simon & Schuster, Inc.

Cover design by Patrick Kang.
Front cover photographs by Getty Images.

Manufactured in the United States of America

For information regarding special discounts for bulk purchases, please contact Simon & Schuster Special Sales at 1-800-456-6798 or business@simonandschuster.com.

For Spider and Jeanne Robinson:
for love, inspiration and support over the years.

1

BISCAYNE BAY GLEAMED aquamarine in the late afternoon light, the sky above as clear and blue as a musical note. From his seat in the stern of the police boat, Horatio Caine could look one way and see the shining, skyscraping outline of downtown Miami; if he turned his head a few degrees, he was treated to an ocean view dotted with the low, dark-green bulk of mangrove islands, occasionally crested by a barrel-sized seabird nest. It struck him just how often he was treated to gorgeous vistas like this one on his way to viewing something unspeakably ugly.

Payment, of sorts, he thought, then corrected himself. *Not payment—compensation. A consolation prize, at best.*

Detective Frank Tripp killed the engine as the boat glided up to the shore, crunching its way onto a narrow white-sand beach. "There you go, Horatio,"

Tripp said. "Go do your thing. I'm gonna stay in the boat for now—not a lot of room in your crime scene."

"Thank you, Frank," Horatio said.

The hummock wasn't large, maybe a few hundred square feet of dense foliage, fifteen or so feet high, with a narrow strip of beach. Horatio stepped out carefully, then gave Doctor Alexx Woods a helping hand as she joined him.

"You all right?" he asked.

"Damn mosquitoes," she grumbled, swatting at one on her arm. "I don't know why they never seem to bother you."

"After the first hundred thousand bites or so, you develop an immunity," he said absently, but his attention was already focused on the reason they'd come out to this tiny mangrove island just south of Miami: the corpse of a young woman.

It wasn't a pretty sight. She lay on her back, wearing only a snorkeling mask. One of her arms was outstretched, tangled in the spiderlike roots of the red mangroves that covered the small island. The mask was completely filled with a white foam that obscured her face, and a mass of raw pink and red flesh protruded from her mouth.

Alexx stepped carefully over the body. They both crouched down, one on either side.

"Fisherman found her," Horatio said. "Looks like the tide washed her up."

"She should be on the bottom," Alexx said. She

reached out with a gloved hand and gently moved the jaw back and forth. "Temporomandibular muscles aren't in rigor, but—" She took hold of the body's right wrist and lifted it slightly. The entire body rocked, the arm obviously stiff. "—major muscle groups are. Skin is bluish and rigor is starting to break, meaning she's probably been dead around fourteen hours or so. Belly isn't distended and she wasn't obese, so refloatation shouldn't have occurred."

Carbon dioxide, sulfur dioxide, ammonia, hydrogen sulfide, methane; Horatio knew that the gastrointestinal tract of a decomposing body produced all of these gases, and that when enough of them had been produced the body would rise to the surface like an inflated balloon. But it was a process that generally took at least twenty-four hours and produced a bloated corpse.

"That's not the only odd thing," Horatio said. "She's wearing a mask, but no flippers or snorkel. Not even a swimsuit."

Alexx was examining the mass of flesh protruding from the mouth. "What's really strange is this . . ." She grabbed the body by the hips and gently rolled it to one side, exposing the back. Another mass of raw flesh extended from between the buttocks. "There's been some anthropophagy, probably by crabs and sea lice," she said, "but I can still identify these as parts of her alimentary canal. Horatio, something tore her insides . . . *out*."

"And whatever it was also placed the body here," Horatio said. "Any ideas?"

"Well, I can tell you that the parts of her esophagus and colon I can see are inside-out. That suggests that she literally blew up."

"Explosive decompression?"

"To this extent? If somebody shoved her out an airlock on a space shuttle, maybe."

"I was thinking more along the lines of deep-sea diving. Fish from extreme depths sometimes explode if they're pulled rapidly to the surface . . ." Horatio shook his head. "But this whole area is shallow water, no more than ten feet." He picked up one of the corpse's hands and examined it. "Fingernails are torn, indicating a struggle. And there's something stuck beneath one of them . . ."

He extracted a dark blue sliver with a pair of tweezers and slipped it into an evidence bag. "And what about these marks on her legs?"

There were several deep wounds on the lower calf of one leg. Alexx studied them, then frowned. "Look like bite marks," she said. "Not sure from what, though. The pattern's the wrong shape to be human, and not jagged enough for a shark or barracuda. Deep bite, too—whatever it was, it was strong."

"So what we have," Horatio said, "is nonhuman teeth marks, explosive decompression and a body that shouldn't be where it is."

Alexx looked down at the body sadly. "None of them should be where they are, Horatio," she said.

He slipped on his sunglasses and looked toward the mainland. Another boat was approaching—Delko and Wolfe, on their way to process the scene. "Then we'll have to make sure," he said, "that we find out where she's been."

"Water recovery, huh?" Wolfe said. The young CSI had to speak loudly over the sound of the boat's motor. "Guess you've done a lot of those."

Eric Delko nodded, his face serious. "Yeah, they can be pretty gruesome," he said. "Boat props hack them up, everything from shrimp to sharks chew on them, and decomp gets real bad real fast. And in Florida, the climate can work for you or against you."

"How so?"

"The more bacteria in the water, the quicker the body breaks down. In a warm, wet environment like a swamp, there's a *lot* of bacteria. I've seen bodies that have only been in the water for twenty-four hours turn black from putrefaction . . . but sometimes, the opposite happens."

"What, it turns white?"

"Kind of. It's called saponification—only happens in warm, wet, anaerobic environments. Subcutaneous fat combines with calcium and ammonium ions to form adipocere, this waxy, white-gray stuff. Basically, it's—"

"Soap," Wolfe finished. "Right, I read about that. You ever see it?"

"It's not common, but yeah, I've seen it," Delko said. "It slows down decomposition, kind of like mummification. Conditions have to be just right, though."

They approached the mangrove island. The beach was no more than a strip of sand maybe twenty feet long; Alexx had already climbed back in the first boat to make room as Wolfe and Delko's craft landed.

Horatio, wearing a dark blue linen suit without a tie, his shirt open at the collar, managed to look just as comfortable and in charge as he did on a Miami street. "Mister Wolfe, I want you behind the camera," he said as his CSIs splashed through the shallow water and on to shore. "Eric, get suited up. This key is looking less like the original crime scene and more like a dump site, but we still might find something of value underwater."

"On it," Delko said. In fact, he was already wearing his wet suit; as Wolfe grabbed the camera equipment, Delko started putting on scuba gear.

"We have an ID on the vic?" Wolfe asked. Horatio moved aside to let him start photographing.

"Not yet," Horatio said. "I've got Calleigh checking missing-persons reports for the last forty-eight hours."

"Any theories?" Wolfe asked. He zeroed in on the wounds and snapped several pictures.

"Nothing that makes sense," Horatio admitted. "It just doesn't add up . . . I think we might be looking at a staged scene. Look at the way her arm is wedged between two of those roots."

Wolfe leaned down and took a good look. "Yeah," he said. "Like someone didn't want her drifting away on the tide. And what's with the condition of the body? It's almost like . . ." He trailed off.

"Like something reached inside her, grabbed hold of her internal organs and *pulled*," Horatio said. "From both ends . . ."

Diving was a dangerous pasttime. Nobody was more aware of that than Eric Delko, the Miami-Dade crime lab's resident diver; he had pulled more corpses out of sunken cars or boats than he cared to count, and every body was a reminder of the hostile environment he now glided through. The ocean off the Florida shore was much like Miami itself: Warm and inviting, filled with sparkling beauty and flashes of brilliant color, it could still kill you in an instant.

Some parts were prettier than others, of course. In the shallow, brackish waters of Biscayne Bay, mangrove islands and human traffic meant water filled with sediment, plankton, and detritus, some of it natural, much of it man-made. Delko moved through the murk cautiously, hovering just above the bottom, scanning the swaying bed of seagrass for anything out of place. The problem was, there was too much; beer cans and rusting pipes and old plastic milk crates, sometimes so encrusted with barnacles or muck they were identifiable only by their shape.

He moved in a circular route around the island, dropping weighted flags to mark his progress. He had plenty of company; green and loggerhead turtles, bonefish, pompano, black and red grouper. Crabs and lobsters scuttled out of his way, and swarms of shrimp flurried past in rippling pink waves.

He was hoping to find one of the vic's flippers or maybe her snorkel, since neither would float. What finally caught his attention, though, was a tiny scrap of white. He thought at first it was another plastic shopping bag, too many of which he'd seen drifting along the bottom like ghostly tumbleweeds, but it was too small and the wrong shape.

On closer inspection, it turned out to be the top of a bathing suit. The straps looked like they'd been cut.

Being a forensic investigator, Horatio found, eventually produced a kind of Zen philosophy toward life. Not a detached, nirvana-aimed approach, but an acute awareness of the fact that everything was connected—again, not in a vague, metaphysical way but in a direct, pragmatic one. Locard's Principle stated that any two things that came into contact transferred bits of themselves to each other, and Horatio had discovered that the twin concepts of *transfer* and *trace* applied to almost every area of life. There was a network of connections between physical objects that remained invisible to most people, but Horatio had developed a heightened sensitivity to it, one that had subtly changed all his perceptions: He couldn't watch a woman take a sip of wine without noticing the lipstick she left on the glass, couldn't look at a piece of furniture without noticing fibers left behind on the upholstery. Privately, he thought of it as Sherlock Holmes syndrome, but didn't share that insight with anyone else. They'd probably assume he was talking about Holmes' cocaine habit, this being Miami . . . and considering what had happened to Horatio's brother Raymond, the last thing Horatio needed to do was start a rumor involving himself and drugs.

Transfer and trace. They applied to reputations, too.

Of course, sometimes that was a good thing. Horatio was surrounded by people who were very good at their jobs, and he tried to learn from them at the same time he passed on whatever expertise he had. Ideally, his whole team worked like smaller parts of a larger organism, with knowledge and skills being the commodity transferred from cell to cell.

Leaving traces of what? Horatio wondered as the elevator doors opened and he walked into the foyer of the Miami-Dade crime lab. *Ourselves, I suppose. Shreds of dignity, stains of honor. Bits of moral fiber* . . .

"You know, Horatio," Calleigh Duquesne said, falling in step beside him, "every time I see you with that little smile on your face, I try to figure out what's on your mind."

"Any results so far?"

"No, you remain inscrutable. But I've had better luck with that DB you found in Biscayne Bay."

"Oh?" Horatio stopped and turned. "You have a name?"

"I do," Calleigh said. She wore her straight blond hair long and loose at the moment, and pushed it back behind one ear as she flipped open a file folder and consulted the contents. "Gabrielle Maureen Cavanaugh. Reported missing yesterday—according to her roommate, she sometimes goes on hikes alone, takes a picnic lunch."

"We know for sure it's her?"

"Roommate confirmed the ID a few minutes ago. She's pretty shook up, but willing to talk. I was just heading down to the interview room—want to join me?"

"I believe I will," Horatio said.

The roommate's name was Stephanie Wheeler. She was a short, plump woman with a mass of spiky, purple-tinged dark hair and eyeglasses with thick black frames. She wore a pair of knee-length denim cutoffs, sandals and a loud Hawaiian shirt;

despite the dichotomy of having to identify a body while dressed for the beach, Horatio could see by the pain on the woman's face that clothing was the last thing on her mind.

Horatio introduced himself and Calleigh, and took a seat on the other side of the table from where Stephanie sat. Calleigh sat down beside him.

"I'm sorry for your loss," Horatio said. "I'll try to make this brief."

"Thank you," Stephanie said. Her voice was calm, but every now and then a tear would bulge out from her lower eyelid and slide down one cheek.

"You say that Gabrielle liked to go hiking alone," Horatio said. "Did that include swimming as well?"

"Sometimes," Stephanie said. "She'd bring along a diving mask and snorkel so she could see underwater. No flippers—she didn't like them." Stephanie blinked rapidly. "Too much trouble to carry on a hike, she said. And she just didn't like them."

"I see. She was a good swimmer?"

"Oh, yes. I told her she shouldn't go swimming by herself, but—she was very independent. You couldn't make her do anything she didn't want to." Stephanie nodded, as if confirming something more to herself than Horatio. A tear dripped, unnoticed, from her chin.

Horatio and Calleigh exchanged a glance. "Stephanie," Calleigh said, "did Gabrielle have anyone in her life who might have wanted to harm her? An ex-boyfriend, maybe?"

A slight frown crossed Stephanie's face. "Why? I mean—my God, are you saying she was *murdered*? I—I thought that the body looked that way because it had been underwater—"

"We're just checking every possibility," Horatio said. "Is there anyone like that you can think of?"

"No," she said flatly. "Nobody like that. Everybody loved Gabrielle. She was stubborn, but you couldn't stay mad at her. I don't know of a single person who would dream of hurting her."

"Anyone she might have met recently who seemed to be paying a lot of attention to her? Maybe even someone online?" Horatio prodded.

"Not that I know of. She hardly ever used the computer, even for email. She doesn't have a boyfriend, not right now . . ." She trailed off. "I guess she won't, either," she added quietly.

They had a few more questions, but learned nothing that seemed significant. Gabrielle had been young, pretty, well liked; she didn't do drugs or hang around with dangerous people. She worked in one of Miami's many hotels, at the front desk. Horatio planned to ask Calleigh to run the vic's prints through AFIS once they were through with Stephanie, but he strongly suspected Gabrielle Cavanaugh's only crime was that she liked to spend time alone.

Unfortunately, Horatio thought, *there are plenty of*

places where that's enough to get you killed. And Miami is one of them . . .

"Well, Alexx?" Horatio said, pulling on a pair of gloves. Gabrielle Cavanaugh's body lay on the stainless-steel autopsy table before them, looking somehow more alive with the diving mask removed and the protruding flesh removed from her mouth. "What can you tell me?"

"Cause of death was drowning," Alexx said. "When a drowning victim can't hold her breath any longer, the respiratory center of the brain takes over—it makes her breathe in, whether there's any air to be had or not. The water irritates the trachea, triggering a cough reflex. This expels air from the lungs, which is replaced on the inhale by water. The cycle gets more and more forceful, sometimes producing vomiting. Lack of oxygen produces unconsciousness, but doesn't stop the cycle; it progresses to more vomiting, convulsions, and what's called agonal gasping. During this phase, the aspirated water irritates the tracheal and bronchial glands into producing mucus, which gets mixed with the water and any remaining air into a froth. Rupture of alveoli cells in the lungs also contributes and will keep on doing so for several hours after the body is out of the water—that's why her mask was filled with white foam. But when I tested her blood, I got a surprise. Horatio, this girl didn't drown in salt water."

"You're sure? Even without the lungs present?"

"Absolutely. Fresh water is hypotonic compared to plasma—osmosis transfers it into the bloodstream through the alveoli at an extremely rapid rate. It can add up to fifty percent to blood volume within a minute—hers was just over forty-two. She drowned somewhere else."

"The area where she was found is brackish," Horatio said. "Fresh water does enter the bay from canals, though . . . what about the extrusion of her internal organs?"

"Condition of the thoracic cavity indicated they were *pushed* out—and I think I know how."

She pointed to a tiny red mark on the abdomen. "This is a puncture wound—so small I didn't notice it until I got her on the table. I think she was injected with something under a lot of pressure. The thoracic cavity is a sealed unit; you pump enough gas or liquid into it, something has to give."

"And something did," Horatio murmured. "But this had to have been done postmortem, right?"

"Definitely. Her lungs would have to have still been in place to produce the foam. I can't tell you much about the condition of the lungs themselves, though, because wildlife predation removed them—and the stomach—while they were exposed. But I did a blood gas test and found elevated levels of carbon dioxide—even though she was already dead, some of the gas made its way into her bloodstream. Somebody pumped her full of CO_2, Horatio—blew her up like a balloon."

"And the gas escaped once the externalized organs were chewed through," Horatio said. "What about sexual assault?"

"Vaginal tearing and genital ecchymosis."

"Indicating she was raped . . . did you recover any semen?"

"No. Either he didn't finish or he wore a condom."

"What about the bite marks on her leg?"

Alexx shook her head. "Like I said, nonhuman. There's something strange about the wounding pattern, too."

"What do you mean?"

"Look at this," she said. "The bite is almost down to the bone, and the flesh is torn—but if it was that strong, it should have just ripped her calf muscle right off. It started the job, but for some reason didn't finish. I took a closer look and found a fleck of foreign material in the wound, might be a tooth fragment. I sent it to Trace."

"Good. I'll check our animal database, see if I can ID the marks. Maybe we'll even get lucky and get a DNA match."

"This is an odd one, Horatio. Whatever this poor girl went through, it wasn't pleasant."

Horatio took a step back from the table. He studied the still face of Gabrielle Cavanaugh, tried to imagine her on one of her solitary hikes. She probably brought a book along, a snack, maybe some sunscreen so she could lie in the hot Florida sun without burning. And if it got too hot, she could always cool off with a swim . . .

"Whatever she went through," Horatio said quietly, "we'll find out."

"What we're looking for," Horatio told his team, "is a weapon known as a Farallon shark dart."

They were assembled in the layout room. Delko stood with his arms crossed over a tight black T-shirt, looking serious and broody; Wolfe, in a grey suit jacket and light blue shirt, was studying the diver's mask and bathing suit top on the table, the only physical objects they'd recovered from the crime scene. Calleigh, in a loose-fitting white blouse and black slacks, sat with an open notebook in front of her and a pen in one hand.

"Uh—I don't think I'm familiar with that one, H," Wolfe said.

"It's a shark-deterrent device," Delko said. "A canister of compressed CO_2 with a long, sharp needle on one end. Sharks have up to thirty-six percent fewer nociceptors than a human does—basically, they don't feel pain. In order to stop one, you have to do a massive amount of damage all at once. The shark dart injects gas into the body cavity of the shark, causing its internal organs to be forced out the mouth and rectum."

"And somebody used one on Gabrielle Cavanaugh," Calleigh said.

"Postmortem," Horatio said. "Before that, she was raped."

"The way the body was mutilated suggests rage," Wolfe said. "So does placing the body—somebody wanted us to see his handiwork."

"I'm not sure the body was placed," Delko said. "Before the CO_2 escaped, the body would have floated. It might have gotten entangled in the mangrove roots naturally."

"There's also the matter of the bite marks," Horatio said. "Calleigh, have you made any progress on that?"

"I have," Calleigh said. "The key was the spacing between the teeth—point-four-five inches. Believe it or not, they came from a bottlenose dolphin."

"A dolphin?" Wolfe asked. "That's rare. They hardly ever attack humans."

"Actually, dolphins are a lot more dangerous than people believe," Delko said. "They are predators, after all—a killer whale is really just an overgrown dolphin. Dolphins frequently attack sharks, and even porpoises."

"This is true," Horatio said. "And even though the use of a weapon indicates human involvement, dolphins can also be trained."

"Well, that would certainly be a first," Calleigh said. "Flipper as assassin."

"You know, it might not be as far-fetched as it sounds," Delko said. "There was a rumor going around the dive community a few years ago about dolphins being used by the Navy to kill enemy divers during the Vietnam War. And not to be indelicate, but dolphins are highly sexual creatures—there've been a number of reports of them directing that kind of behavior at people, especially menstruating women."

"You're suggesting she was molested by a dolphin?" Calleigh said, raising her eyebrows.

"I suppose that's a possibility," Horatio conceded. "But let's concentrate on the human angle for now . . . Eric, I want you to check the shoreline along Biscayne Bay—concentrate on outflow areas from canals. Calleigh, you follow up on the dart, get us a list of distributors. Mister Wolfe, I want you in the lab—we found transfer under the vic's fingernails and in the wound, and I want to know what they are and where they came from."

"What about you, Horatio?" Calleigh asked. "Heading up to SeaWorld to interview a few suspects?"

"If that's what it takes," Horatio said mildly. "Because whoever or whatever did this to Gabrielle Cavanaugh, they're still out there . . ."

2

THE DRIVE UP HIGHWAY A1A was, as always, filled with tourists. It was a road with one purpose, to connect the Keys to the rest of Florida, and they were strung along its length like pearls on a necklace. Except this necklace wasn't a loop; it stopped dead at Key West, the last and gaudiest pearl of all, filled with eccentric locals and tourist traps that would sell you everything from Ernest Hemingway's favorite cocktail to live hermit crabs.

Horatio wasn't going that far, however. His destination was one of the smaller keys, and a research facility called the Aquarian Institute. He turned his Hummer off the highway and onto a narrower paved road, following it as it wound its way deeper and deeper through dense, lush vegetation until the very last turn, where it ended abruptly no more than fifty feet from the shoreline. A white shoebox of a building on pilings jutted out over the surf, with a dock extending out from that. Two small boats were moored there, an older cabin cruiser and a rigid-frame Zodiac.

Horatio parked and got out. The building had a lot of windows, and all of them were beaded with water. It was a phenomenon Horatio thought of as the Budweiser effect, and he saw it a lot in Miami; high temperature and humidity outside plus an air conditioner cranked to maximum inside equaled glass covered with condensation, just like a cold mug of beer.

Personally, he thought people should try harder to adjust to the climate. There was something distinctly off-kilter about a place where you had to go outside to warm up.

He strolled along the short walk and up to the front door, also glass. Decals proclaimed allegiance to PETA, the Humane Society, the International Fund for Animal Welfare. He pulled it open and stepped inside.

The foyer was small, no more than a glassed-in porch, with a beat-up wooden desk holding a computer and a few plastic chairs along one wall. A stack of dog-eared magazines sat on a low table in the corner, the one on top featuring an underwater shot of a scuba diver and a stingray. Framed photos of dolphins, killer whales and belugas adorned the walls.

There was a chair behind the desk, but no one was in it. "Hello?" Horatio called out, but got no response.

He noticed a yellow Post-it note stuck to the front of the desk, which read: IF YOU HAVE A DELIVERY, I'M OUT BY THE PEN. DOWN THE HALL TO END, LAST DOOR ON LEFT.

He followed the directions, down a short hall and through an unlocked wooden door that led outside to a covered deck. A long, sloping ramp led down to a three-sided concrete pool, the fourth side a tall mesh fence that separated the pool from the ocean. Some sort of wheeled apparatus with a padded top stood at the pool's edge.

Horatio made his way down the ramp. When he was halfway, a face wearing a diving mask and snorkel popped up at the edge of the pool. The woman wearing it pulled the mask off and called out, "Yes?"

Horatio walked up to the edge of the pool. "Good afternoon. I'm Lieutenant Horatio Caine. I was wondering if I could take a moment of your time."

The woman looked up at him suspiciously. She had high, Slavic cheekbones, a full-lipped mouth and black hair streaked with grey. "What do you want? I'm very busy." Her accent was Russian, her tone dismissive.

"I left a message on your voice mail, but I'm afraid I couldn't wait for you to get back to me," Horatio said. "I have a few questions—"

She cut him off. "Of course you do. Cops always have questions, it's in their DNA. Well, I have questions, too. And not to be rude, but my questions matter to me more than yours do."

"I wouldn't be too sure about that," Horatio said calmly. "You haven't heard any of mine, yet."

She rested her arms on the edge of the pool and glared at him. "So go ahead, ask."

"I'd be more comfortable if we could do this face-to-face."

She pursed her lips and considered this, then shrugged. "I doubt that," she said, "but if you insist . . ."

She placed her palms flat on the concrete and pushed herself out of the water, flopping onto her belly then rolling onto her back and sitting up so she was seated at the edge with her calves dangling in the water. Horatio got only a brief glimpse of her legs when she turned over, enough to see that she was wearing flippers—and there was something unusual about her lower limbs.

As she reached down and undid the buckles, he saw what it was. They were artificial.

Both legs ended just above the knee. Her prosthetics made no attempt to imitate the appearance of an actual leg—they were made of matte-black metal, with several curving pieces flanking what looked like a hydraulic piston. She set the prosthetics down side by side, the flippers holding them upright; they looked like some kind of bizarre web-footed sculpture.

She favored him with a hostile smile. "Can you

help, please?" She indicated the device Horatio stood beside with a nod, and he realized it was some sort of wheelchair he'd never seen before. "I'm still getting used to it," she said. "Tricky to get into, you know?" She held up her arms like a beseeching toddler, but the glint in her eye told him she wasn't the one being embarrassed.

Horatio crouched down, met her eyes, and put both hands firmly around the waist of her one-piece black bathing suit. He straightened up, lifting her easily with her arms resting lightly on his shoulders, and placed her carefully on the padded surface. Neither his grip nor his gaze wavered, and he saw the look in her own eyes shift slightly from malicious enjoyment to amused appreciation.

"*Spaseba*," she said. "A moment." She fiddled with the controls, and an electric motor whirred as the posture of the machine changed to form a backrest. She settled herself against it and fastened straps around her waist and shoulders, then used the controls again. The shape of the frame changed again, tilting up and straightening out, bringing her to a fully standing position.

"There," she said. "Face-to-face—though not, I am afraid, toe-to-toe. I hope your questions are worth all this trouble."

Horatio smiled. "That depends. How do you feel about dolphins attacking people?"

She snorted. "Disappointed it doesn't happen more often," she said. "Damn tourists paying money to swim with Flipper. They think animals are what you see in a zoo or on TV—they see a bear, they spread peanut butter on their child's hands so they can take a picture of it getting licked off. Damn dumb morons."

She twitched a joystick on the arm of the chair and it spun around and took off. Horatio had to hurry to keep up.

"What's this about?" she said. "Some new animal rights group complain about my bottlenoses? How I'm keeping them prisoner and doing terrible things to them? Tell them I'll buy one of their damn stickers and put it on my door."

"Excuse me," Horatio said, taking a few quick steps and cutting her off before she reached the ramp. "But this is a bit more serious than that, Doctor . . . ?"

"Zhenko," the woman said. "Doctor Nicole Zhenko. So, what happened and why should I care?"

Horatio took a deep, slow breath before answering. "A woman is dead, Doctor Zhenko. Her body was found with bite marks from a bottlenose dolphin on one of her legs—"

"Hah! Ridiculous," Zhenko snapped. "You must have made a mistake. Dolphins don't scavenge from corpses."

"There's no mistake," Horatio said patiently. "And the bite was made prior to death, not afterward."

"So you're saying this dolphin actually killed somebody?" Her tone was less confrontational, but not by much. "Chewed her up like a shark?"

"Actually, death was caused by drowning. There was only a single bite mark—a deep one, on her leg."

"Then it was not a dolphin. There are cetaceans that will attack and kill a human through submersion—there was a case a few years ago where an orca drowned a trainer at an aquarium—but a dolphin would not attack like that. Was there extensive bruising on the body? The torso, the belly?"

"No. Why do you ask?"

"Because if a bottlenose wants to kill something he isn't going to eat, he rams it. Over and over, *wham wham wham*." She steepled the fingers of one hand together into a crude cone and smacked the tips into her other palm for emphasis. "With the fulcrum, its nose. That's how they kill sharks—a bunch of them attack, all at once. Like your American thing, with all the beat-up cars trying to kill each other."

"A demolition derby," Horatio said with a smile.

"Yes! If a dolphin had killed this woman, you would have found round bruises all over her body. But you didn't, so you must be wrong." She charged forward in her chair and then changed direction abruptly, going to Horatio's right. She stopped in front of an old, off-white refrigerator sheltered by the overhang of the deck and pulled open the door.

"I'm not saying a dolphin was to blame," Horatio said. "I'm just telling you what we found. The bite mark was unusual, but not as unusual as what was done afterward." He told her about the condition of the body as she rummaged in the fridge and pulled out a large green plastic bag.

"A shark dart?" she said, frowning. She folded out a tray from the side of the chair and put the bag on it. "I don't believe it . . ."

She hesitated, then grudgingly said, "Well, maybe. I always thought they were just stories, paranoid fantasies—but there were people who swore they were true, said they'd seen them with their own eyes. Maybe they did."

She rolled back toward the pool, and Horatio fell into step beside her. "Seen what, exactly?" he asked.

She reached the edge of the pool and stopped. "Dolphins, trained by the Navy to kill. They had a device like a shark dart strapped to their fulcrum, so they could ram an enemy diver. The swimmer nullification program, it was called. Your government has always denied there was any such program." She grabbed the plastic bag, reached into it and pulled out a fish about a foot long. She tossed it into the air over the pool, and suddenly there was a streamlined grey body arcing through the air. The dolphin caught the fish neatly and sliced back into the water.

"I understand you've worked with Navy dolphins yourself," Horatio said. He stared down at the water and the sleek shape gliding through it. "As a matter of fact, isn't *this* a Navy dolphin?"

"Ah, you've done your homework," she said, throwing another fish in the pool. "Does poor Whaleboy need an alibi? I promise you, he hasn't been in open ocean in a year. Before that the Navy had him, and I don't know what the hell they had him do. Maybe he was waiting for Osama Bin Laden to go snorkeling."

"Maybe," Horatio said. "The Naval officer I spoke to on the phone said you're in charge of preparing dolphins for release into the wild once the Navy retires them. Is that difficult?"

She gave him an appraising look. "Difficult? Think about this: You have a dog. A smart dog, very well trained. You have this dog for most of its life—ten years. Then, one day, you say, 'I am done with you. Time for you to go live in the forest. It's okay, though, this nice lady will teach you how to be a wolf.'" She shook her head. "It's insane. But better they have some freedom before they die. And freedom, it's no picnic."

"No," Horatio agreed. "No, it isn't . . ."

"I see you are admiring my transportation," Zhenko said. "Nice ride, no?" She made a gesture with her hand, and Whaleboy responded by standing up on his tail and moving backward with rapid beats of his flukes, making it look like he was walking backward on the water. She rewarded him with another fish.

"I appreciate effective technology," Horatio said.

She chuckled. "Effective and expensive. Custom-made Levo with V-track thoracic and head support. If you want a good piece of technology, go to the Swiss, that's what I say. Cuckoo clocks or wheelchairs, they make the best."

"Are your prosthetics Swiss, as well?"

She gave him a quick, flat glance, and he wondered if he'd made a mistake. When she replied, though, she didn't sound angry.

"No. American and German. The feet are made by Otto Bock, the socket by Hanger. Carbon-fiber composite, with titanium polycentric swing phase control." Her voice was clipped and efficient. "Waterproof, of course. I would like to upgrade to one of the newer systems, like an Endolite Adaptive—hydraulic/pneumatic hybrid cylinder, third generation microprocessors, time, force, and swing sensors—but they're expensive. I'll probably settle for a modified Lord RD-1005; cheaper, but the knee has an MR fluid damper and a millisecond response time. So they say."

She made a twirling motion with one hand, and Whaleboy leaped into the air, doing a somersault at the same time.

"For a Navy dolphin, he seems like quite the performer," Horatio said.

"He's a big show-off," Zhenko said, affection in

her voice. "The Navy taught him all these tricks. He loves the attention, so I indulge him. I'm trying to wean him off the dead fish, but he won't eat live ones yet—the stubborn bastard is too lazy to catch his own, now. But he'll learn, sooner or later."

"I'm sure he will," Horatio said with a grin. "What else can he do?"

"What, besides finding mines in the Persian Gulf? Here, I'll show you. Take this fish." She thrust one at him imperiously. Horatio took it.

"Now, do this," she said. She made a fist and raised it over her head, then brought it down sharply, like she was chopping with an imaginary axe.

Horatio did as he was told. Whaleboy immediately dove and came up a few seconds later with a bright orange Frisbee in his mouth. He tossed it at Horatio with a flick of his head, and Horatio caught it reflexively with a laugh.

"Here you go, pal," Horatio said, throwing him the fish. "I'm sure you'll appreciate it more than I would."

"That's all you get today, you greedy torpedo," Zhenko called out. Whaleboy opened his mouth and chattered at her in return, then dove beneath the surface with a slap of his tail.

"Doctor Zhenko," Horatio said, "I can see you have a lot of experience with dolphin behavior and training. I have to ask—"

She didn't let him finish. "If someone like me could train a dolphin to be an assassin? To kill on command?" She shrugged. "Maybe yes, maybe no. The Navy says they use them for detection and retrieval—like guard dogs, yes? To patrol and to fetch. Dolphins can dive up to five hundred thirty-five meters deep and they don't get the bends, so they can recover things from the bottom faster than a human diver."

"The thing about guard dogs," Horatio noted, "is that many of them also bite."

"True enough," she admitted. "The Navy trainers show me the hand signals for 'throw' and 'jump' and 'tailwalk,' but how do I know what else they've taught him? Maybe I scratch my nose in the pool one day and he rips my throat out."

"You don't seem terribly worried about the possibility."

She snorted. "What is the point? Death comes to all of us, and worry only gives you wrinkles. Besides," she said, indicating the stumps of her legs, "after this . . . nothing else seems so bad. The worst, it's already happened, so the hell with it. You know?"

"Not really, no," he said. "And I wouldn't presume to pretend I do."

The hard look on her face softened, ever so slightly. "No. You don't. At least you don't try to lie to me about it. Hah! How about that, an honest policeman."

"I do my best," Horatio said.

"Okay, so I will be honest with you. The Marine Mammal Program—that's what the Navy calls it—they have lost a few dolphins over the years. Nothing they will admit to, but it happens."

Horatio studied her intently. "Lost how?"

"Misplaced, not there, no longer present. *Ffftt!* Gone. They send them out for a mission and they don't come back. Maybe they got caught in a tuna net, maybe they just got tired of taking orders. Who knows? But I tell you one thing, Mister Honest Cop; those dolphins, they never should have been caught in the first place."

She dug in the plastic bag on her lap and threw another fish into the pool. "He shouldn't be here," Zhenko said. "Not him, not any of them . . ."

The northern part of Biscayne Bay abutted Miami Beach. It was heavily industrialized, dealing with marine traffic that ranged from shrimp boats to cruise ships. Though much of the Bay was shallow—no more than a dozen feet—deeper channels had been dredged to facilitate larger vessels.

Hopefully, the police diver flags on the surface would prevent any of those vessels from cruising through Delko's search zone. He'd seen bodies that had been through the props of a big ship, and had no desire to wind up on the bottom in several pieces.

The garbage in the deeper channels was more

prevalent, not to mention bigger. Shopping carts, tires, old stoves, with the ever-present coral and barnacles growing on them giving them a surreal kind of beauty. *It may be a junkyard,* Delko thought, *but at least it's an interesting one.*

He wasn't looking for flippers anymore—according to her roommate, Gabrielle Cavanaugh hadn't used them—but he was still hoping to find the bottom of her bathing suit or the snorkel.

The absence of the snorkel bothered him. Most snorkels were attached by sturdy rubber rings to the side of the mask itself; it was almost impossible to lose one without losing the other. The roommate was sure Gabrielle had taken it with her, but it hadn't been found with the body. It was possible she'd simply gone diving without it, leaving it on the shore with her towel and picnic lunch, but then why bring it at all?

What he was really hoping for was the shark dart. The models he'd seen had the dart mounted at the end of a four-foot pole, and the canister of CO_2 was good for only a single shot. The pole or the canister might have been discarded or lost after the attack . . . depending on who or what had used them in the first place.

A dolphin. Delko just didn't believe it.

It wasn't that he saw dolphins as some sort of highly evolved, peaceful, smarter-than-man beings, either. Male dolphins were known to kill dolphin calves; such infanticide occurred in other species, too. Male lions often killed the offspring of their rivals to ensure their own genes would be passed on instead.

Dolphins had also been observed to kill porpoises—the only reason for which seemed to be that the smaller animals resembled dolphin calves. *Homicide and stupidity,* Delko thought, *are not necessarily reserved for the human race.*

No, Delko had no problem with the idea that a dolphin could kill a human being. What bothered him was the use of the shark dart.

Delko had seen many a staged crime scene. People tried to make a crime of passion look like a burglary gone wrong, a homicide look like an accident. And, almost always, they overdid it. A real crime scene was messy, confusing, contradictory; it took time and persistence to decode and understand the evidence. The logic of a staged crime scene leaped out at you: *Look! A gun! Look! An open safe! Look! The scene of a struggle!*

Horatio had taught Delko to immediately distrust such obvious setups. "If it looks obvious, it's probably not," Horatio would tell him, and usually he was right. Once you took a really close look at the scene, all sorts of discrepancies would emerge.

For instance, a shark dart struck Delko as an absurd choice of weapon; a blade would be just as effective and far simpler. He supposed a dolphin with a needle attached to its nose could ram multiple times, but there was always the chance the needle could break off, too.

Plus, the sequence of events didn't quite make sense, either. The shark dart was used after the vic had already drowned—why? It just didn't quite line up . . .

And then he found the rope.

Calleigh decided to take a closer look at the puncture wound itself, or at least pictures of it. If the dart had been used antemortem, it might have left some sort of impression of the base of the needle, similar to a muzzle stamp or hilt mark—but there wasn't one.

She took another look at the pictures of the bite marks. Or maybe *mark* was more accurate; there appeared to be only one. That was odd in and of itself; since most animal attacks left multiple bite marks. This just looked like something had clamped on and refused to let go.

She picked up a magnifier and scrutinized the photo in closer detail. After a moment, she noticed something she hadn't before: The tearing of the flesh was unidirectional, toward the ankle.

Now, that's odd, she thought. She knew some cetaceans killed their prey by shaking it—killer whales could worry a seal back and forth so hard it would literally shake to pieces—but this didn't indicate that.

She tried to picture the scenario in her mind.

Shallow, murky water, glowing with sunlight from above. Something fastens on to Gabrielle Cavanaugh's leg. It pulls her under. She struggles to get back to the surface, to the air. It doesn't let her. She kicks, desperately, frantically, her lungs running out of oxygen . . .

"That's why the flesh is torn in one direction," she murmured. "You tore it yourself, trying to get free. You were trying to go up, but it was keeping you in place . . ."

The whiteness of the rope stood out in the murk like a serpent's ghost. It was coiled around a rod that jutted from the bottom like a periscope from the remains of a submarine . . . which, Delko saw as he swam closer, was exactly what it seemed to be. He could even see the outline of a conning tower, complete with guardrail and hatch.

On closer inspection, though, it turned out to be an illusion. The conning tower was rusting sheet metal, the periscope only an old pipe; the hatch was made of ancient plywood. Somebody's idea of a joke, Delko guessed. The whole thing had probably been mounted on a motorboat and piloted around the Bay by drunken college students making loud jokes about "submarine races," until its inevitable sinking by accident or booze-fueled impulse. It looked like it had been there for decades.

But the rope was brand new; it hadn't been underwater long enough to acquire so much as a layer of algae. Delko unlimbered his camera and took a few careful shots from different angles, especially where it was knotted around the pipe, before finally grabbing the loose end. There was a steel carabiner tied to the end, a big metal latch you could snap to something else easily.

Delko unwrapped the rope from the pipe and swam upward holding the end. It was around a dozen feet long, which at this depth meant it only reached halfway to the surface.

Couldn't be a tether for a boat.

But it might have been used to keep a drowning woman submerged . . .

3

CALLEIGH DUQUESNE WASN'T having much luck. She'd quickly discovered that the Farallon shark dart hadn't been manufactured in years, though she did find a few for sale on eBay. Australian law enforcement seemed to have had a problem with them at one point, going so far as to specifically list them by name as a legally prohibited weapon.

She swiveled her chair away from the computer screen and sighed. Even if they found the dart, it would be difficult to match something as small as a puncture wound to the needle—and she couldn't perform ballistics tests on a gas.

She could, however, track down all the distributors in Florida that had at one time carried the Farallon. She spent the next few hours on the phone, talking to stores that sold dive equipment and compiling a list of customers who had bought one. It was a time-consuming and frustrating process; dive shops in Florida were one of those businesses that sprang up and then went under all the time. Half of them didn't keep accurate records and some were unwilling to divulge any information unless she had a warrant—she alternated between using her Southern charm to cajole and her cop voice to threaten.

It was, she realized after several frustrating hours, going to be one of those days.

The first person Horatio ran into when he got back to the lab was Delko, who was studying the length of rope in the layout room.

"So you found this on the bottom?" Horatio asked.

"Yeah, attached to a fake periscope. Some kind of U-boat mockup, looked like it had been lying there rusting for years."

Horatio picked up the neat stack of photos on the table and looked through them. "I see . . . but the rope is obviously new."

"Multifilament polypropylene," Delko said. "Twelve-strand braid, no core. I've found the company that makes it—it's used in a lot of places, from the military to the industrial. Trying to narrow it down, but it's a pretty big field."

Horatio studied one of the photos intently. "How about the knots?"

"The steel carabiner on the end is tied with a buntline hitch—common boating knot. The one attached to the pipe, though, was a lot more intricate—it's something called a Turk's head. Gets used more for nautical decoration than anything practical."

"And it looks like it would take a while to tie, too . . ." Horatio mused. "Which means our guy is either very good at holding his breath, or was using scuba gear."

"That makes sense," Delko said. "The shark dart is a diver's weapon."

"Good work, Eric. I think you've found our primary crime scene."

Delko sighed. "Yeah, for what good it does us. No prints, no trace, no witnesses except turtles and fish."

"Well, we know at least one thing for sure," Horatio said. "No matter how smart they might be, a dolphin didn't tie that knot . . ."

"So, Ryan," Calleigh said. "You have a good weekend?"

"Not bad," Wolfe said, not looking up. He adjusted the focus on the microspectrophotometer; he was studying the scrap of material found under Gabrielle Cavanaugh's fingernails.

"Do anything special?" Calleigh was on hold, trying to reach a scuba shop in Coconut Grove.

"Not really, no," he murmured.

"Ah. I went out, caught a movie—that new Will Smith one?"

"Uh-huh."

"Had to leave halfway through, though. My head caught on fire."

"That's nice . . ."

"But the men in the UFO put it out. With their ice-cream ray."

"What flavor?" he asked absently.

"Pistachio?"

"Good, good," he muttered. "Pistachio has excellent fire-retardant qualities."

"Okay," she sighed. "So you're paying attention. You could at least try to *sound* interested."

He looked up. "I'm sorry," he said. "I'm—well, I'm just not good at small talk. Never have been. It balances out though—like hockey."

"Hockey?"

"It's something I suck at but have no interest in. I'll never be a great hockey player, but I don't care. It works out."

Calleigh frowned. "Not really. You can't spend all your time in the lab, Ryan—fieldwork requires people skills, too. You were a beat cop, you know that."

"Well, yeah, of course," he admitted. "But there's always an objective when you're talking to a witness or a suspect. Casual conversation is usually kind of . . . well, pointless. I've always felt that way, even when I was a kid."

"You must have been fun at birthday parties."

"I never had many friends. Books always

seemed more interesting to me than people—my parents were actually worried for a while I might be autistic. During my robot phase, anyway."

Calleigh blinked at him. "Excuse me? *Robot* phase?"

He looked slightly embarrassed. "It was my grandmother's fault, really. See, she had this huge stack of old *Reader's Digest*s, and whenever we visited I used to read the articles. I loved that anatomic series they ran—you know, 'I Am Joe's Brain' or 'I Am Joe's Kidney'?"

"Sure, I remember those. My doctor used to keep a few lying around his waiting room— *Reader's Digest*s I mean, not kidneys."

"There was this article in one of the issues about an actual autistic boy who thought he was a machine. He acted like one, referred to parts of his body as mechanical, insisted he be treated like one. I—well, I thought it sounded pretty neat, so I figured I'd give it a try."

"How old were you?"

"Eight. After a week of taping batteries to my body and making a lot of beeping noises, my parents got pretty worried. They took me to a shrink, who figured out I was obsessive-compulsive, not autistic."

"Must have been hard on your folks. I have a cousin who has Asperger's syndrome."

Wolfe nodded. "Yeah, they thought I might have that for a while, too. I had a lot of the same symptoms—social awkwardness, highly developed vocabulary, obsessive focus on certain subjects. You know, all the things they used to just label you a geek for."

She rolled her eyes. "Tell me about it. But being a geek doesn't have the stigma attached it used to; these days, it's actually kind of trendy. All those dot-com millionaires shook up the social strata."

"Sure. With that much money, even Bill Gates becomes a sex symbol."

"You know," Calleigh said thoughtfully, "I read recently where the cases of Asperger's in Silicon Valley have shot through the roof. Apparently the gene that causes it is reinforced when both parents have it."

Wolfe grinned. "So two socially inept people meet, fall in love and have little geek babies?"

She shrugged. "Evolution in action. Can't argue with success, right?"

"Argue? Hey, I may wind up moving to Silicon Valley myself."

Calleigh sighed. "I'm starting to feel like this phone is attached to my ear . . . you know, Ryan, you're not a bad talker. You just need a little practice in more mundane conversations."

"If there was a class in that, I'd sign up," he said, only half-joking.

"Well, I've been told I'm a sparkling conversationalist on almost *any* subject," Calleigh said. "Even when I'm on hold. So come on—let's play some hockey. I'll even drop the puck."

"Uh—okay," Wolfe said.

"So, Ryan—what did you do this weekend?"

He thought about it for a second before answering. "Not much, really. Cleaned my gun, caught up on a few forensics journals. I read about this really interesting case in Texas—"

"No shoptalk," she said politely but firmly. "Not that I wouldn't find it interesting, but our work isn't exactly cocktail party material. Didn't you do anything fun?"

"Well—I did go to a barbecue."

She brightened. "Really? Oh, my dad used to make great barbecue when I was growing up. What did you have? Ribs? Steak? Good old-fashioned burgers?"

He hesitated. "Actually, it didn't turn out so well. The host used too much accelerant getting the charcoal going and the grill hadn't been cleaned in a long time. There was a massive grease fire."

"That's too bad—was anyone hurt?"

"No," he said. "Fortunately, this UFO showed up and put out the fire. With their ice-cream ray."

She narrowed her eyes and tried to glare at him, but he just looked back at her seriously. After a second she gave up and grinned.

"You," she said tartly, "as Daffy Duck used to say, are *despicable*. I wash my hands of any attempt to civilize you, and banish you back to the socially inept pit you came from."

"He shoots," Wolfe murmured, "he scores . . . You know, I think I have a match on this material."

Calleigh's bantering tone disappeared instantly. "What is it?"

"Some kind of latex. There are some very fine, white grains on one side, though. I've isolated a few—going to take a closer look at them with the SEM."

The scanning electron microscope could magnify an image up to a hundred thousand times through the conversion of emitted electrons, as well as providing data on a substance's composition. Calleigh, phone still cradled against her ear, came closer to study the monitor with Wolfe.

"Hydrated magnesium silicate?" she said.

"Talcum powder," he said, nodding.

"Surgical gloves?" she suggested. "They put talcum powder inside some brands to make them easier to put on and take off."

"Yeah, but it's a weird color," he said. "I think this came off of something thicker—a wet suit, maybe."

"Rubber instead of neoprene? Old school," Calleigh said.

"I'm going to see if I can narrow it down further," Wolfe said. "Maybe we can match this to a particular manufacturer."

"Well, I hope you have better luck than I'm—Hello? Yes, I'm still here. Well, when will the boat be back? Yes, I *know* cell phones don't work underwater—"

Wolfe smiled. "Go for the slap shot," he advised.

"According to Trace, the material found in the vic's leg was ethyl cyanoacrylate," Wolfe told Horatio over the phone. Wolfe was still in the lab, while Horatio was in his Hummer.

"Super glue," Horatio said.

"Not just any super glue. The materials database says this particular glue is a specialized formula made by a company called Cyberbond. It's called polyzap—designed to be used with man-made materials like Lexan, delron, nylon and polycarbonate, or natural substances like rubber or leather. It's marketed primarily for taxidermy."

"Meaning our animal bite probably came from an animal just as dead as our vic," Horatio said. "Mister Wolfe, tell Calleigh and Delko I want to see all of you as soon as I get back. Meet me in the conference room."

"Sure. What's up, H?"

"If I'm right," Horatio said, "our workload."

Horatio was headed to the beach.

He appreciated the ocean. It managed to be vast and timeless and soothing while also being immediate and dangerous. It reminded him, he supposed, of death itself; it projected the comfort of the inevitable.

After Delko's discovery of the rope, Horatio knew where Gabrielle Cavanaugh must have been when she decided to go for a swim: Oleta River State Park. The mouth of the Oleta River was no more than fifty yards from Delko's phony sub. Horatio had radioed ahead and gotten the area evacuated and sealed off, and gave specific instructions making sure anyone on the beach took their supplies with them when they left.

He pulled into the parking lot, empty now except for a patrol car. Two officers were waiting, leaning against the hood of the car. They straightened up as he got out of his vehicle and walked over.

"Afternoon, gentlemen," Horatio said, showing his badge. "Everyone out?"

The first cop, a short, barrel-chested man with a grey mustache, nodded. "Yep. There were only about twenty or so. Most didn't mind, a few were grouchy about having their sunbathing interrupted. Everybody took their stuff with 'em, just like you wanted."

The other cop, a skinny, blond rookie with a too-serious expression on his face, added, "You didn't want us to detain anyone, did you?"

"No," Horatio said. "What I'm looking for isn't going anywhere—unless the tide gets to it before I do."

He walked out onto the sand. There was an eerie stillness to a completely deserted beach in the middle of a hot, sunny day.

Like the shore of the Styx, he thought. *The whiteness of bone, not sand. Maybe I'll run into a few ghosts playing volleyball.*

He found what he was looking for on a little grassy spit that jutted out onto the beach like a peninsula, shaded by a date palm. A large blue towel, its corners weighted down by a pair of sneakers, a small blue knapsack and a half-full Nalgene water bottle.

He pulled on a pair of gloves, then opened the knapsack. An apple, a peanut-butter sandwich in a plastic bag, a small container of blueberry yogurt and a plastic spoon. Shorts, socks, a T-shirt with a penguin on it. A set of keys, a pair of sunglasses, a cheap wristwatch. A paperback copy of *Oliver Twist*. He found her wallet stuffed into one of the shoes—why did anyone ever think that was a good hiding place?—and the face smiling at him from the driver's license photo was the same as the one he'd seen on Alexx's autopsy table.

He opened the book at random and read aloud the first line his eye fell on: "There is a passion for hunting something deeply implanted in the human breast."

Very true, he thought. *Even if that something is only a little time on a beach to read a good book and maybe go for a swim. And out there, in the water, you became the focus of someone else's hunt.*

He put the book back into the knapsack, turned and stared out over the water.

And that hunter, in turn, has now acquired some hunters of his own . . .

Evidence collected at a crime scene was often composed of more than a single element. The machine the crime lab most commonly used to separate and identify various components was the gas chromatograph/mass spectrometer, or GC/MS. Wolfe hoped it could transform the trace found under Gabrielle Cavanaugh's fingernail from a scrap of latex into a unique index of components.

First, he removed an even smaller piece from the fragment and dissolved it in a solvent, heating it at the same time. He used a syringe to inject the resulting fluid into a coiled glass tube attached to the GC/MS, where a burst of nitrogen propelled it from one end to the other, and the device identified each component of the fluid by the speeds at which it passed through the tube. The fluid was then bombarded with electrons from a heated cathode, which ionized it into electrically charged fragments. The fragments were accelerated and deflected into a circular path, where their position and intensity identified their mass and how much of the sample each made up.

That was only half the process, however. When he was done, he knew what the latex was made of, and in what proportion—what he didn't have was a match with a known product. For that, he turned to the Internet and a variety of databases.

He looked up when Delko entered. "Hey," he said.

"Hey," Delko answered. He went straight for the comparison microscope, set down the evidence box he was carrying and opened it up.

"What do you think Horatio wants to talk to us about?" Wolfe asked.

"The case, obviously," Delko said. He pulled out two large envelopes and carefully extracted Gabrielle Cavanaugh's bikini top from the first.

"You think he's got a break already?"

"Guess we'll find out when he gets here. I heard he found the vic's personal belongings in Oleta River State Park."

"Yeah, thanks to you. Good job finding that rope."

"Don't thank me yet," Delko said, pulling the rope itself from the other envelope. "So far, I haven't actually linked the rope to the DB. I'm hoping the tool marks on the ends of the bikini strap and the rope are the same."

"Good luck. I just ran the fragment from under the vic's fingernails through the GC/mass spec. Here's a question for you: What do rubber and rabbits have in common?"

"A significant carotene content," Delko said with a grin.

"Right," Wolfe admitted.

"Hey, you're talking to a scuba diver. I spend more time with rubber in my mouth than—"

"Don't say it, please," Wolfe said. "Anyway, I'm learning all kinds of things about rubber I never suspected. The plant *Hevia brasiliensis* comes from Brazil—hence the name—but it's almost extinct there now. Blight wiped out almost every plant in the early twentieth century."

"Yeah, ninety percent of the world's rubber comes from Southeast Asia now," Delko said. "It's one of the few places in the world with enough rainfall—rubber plants need around a hundred inches a year to do well. Right?"

"Right," Wolfe said. "Okay, then—can you tell me why rubber plants in plantations only grow to around eighty feet high?"

"Yes I can," Delko said, smiling. "Carbon. The plant needs it to grow, but it's also an essential component of rubber. Since only carbon dioxide from the atmosphere can supply carbon to the plant, carbon winds up being split between the two needs when the tree is in production, which restricts its growth."

"Well, that and the fact that the tapping process limits foliage to the top of the tree, which cuts its carbon dioxide intake . . . how do *you* know so much about this?"

"What, as opposed to you?" Delko asked innocently. "I guess it's just my years of CSI experience . . ."

"Sure," Wolfe said skeptically. "Anyway, only ten percent of natural rubber is turned into latex—"

"—Which consists of an aqueous suspension of cis-polyisoprene, a linear polymer of high molecular weight," Delko said. "The actual rubber content of the suspension is around thirty percent."

This time, Wolfe chose to ignore him. "—a substance whose biological purpose is still not entirely clear. Rubber trees are tapped every other day, producing a cupful of latex; to extract rubber from the emulsion they coagulate it with formic acid. Then it's processed in one of two ways: compacted into seventy pound blocks—"

"—Seventy-three, actually—"

"—or compressed into sheets and dried over a fire."

Wolfe stopped and looked at Delko. Delko stretched and yawned, then smiled at Wolfe.

"I'm not boring you, am I?" Wolfe asked.

"No, no, I just didn't get enough sleep last night. Out clubbing. You were saying?"

"A *smoky* fire," Wolfe said. "The smoke contains natural fungicides, and also gives the latex an amber color." He paused.

Delko paused, too. "Interesting," he finally said.

"So . . . depending on the grade, latex has different distinguishing characteristics. It's rated according to the Mooney scale and the Lovibond index, which measure viscosity and color respectively. I'm not sure where my sample falls according to those two, but I can tell you exactly how much carotene, ash and hydroxylamine hydrochloride it contains.

My next step is checking in with manufacturers and seeing which ones handle latex with these particular qualities. Unless you've got a better idea?"

"Me?" Delko pretended to look surprised. "Hey, I wouldn't know where to start. This is your baby—run with it."

Wolfe narrowed his eyes and smiled. "I've noticed that despite having to know a little about everything, CSIs still tend to have areas they're better in than others. Calleigh, for instance, and firearms."

"Some of us even have more than one," Delko said.

"Like you. You're a diver, but you've also written forensics articles on—what was it again?" It was Wolfe's turn to pretend, frowning and scratching his head. "Oh, yeah—tire tracks."

Delko's grin got bigger. "Busted."

"Which would mean you would know all about what tires are made of, too. Ergo, your extensive technical knowledge of rubber."

"Rubber, yes. Latex, not so much. You're blazing a new trail, there."

"Hopefully, one with fewer smartasses on it," Wolfe muttered, and Delko laughed.

"All right," Horatio said. "What do we have so far?"

His CSI team was gathered in the conference room. Calleigh and Wolfe were seated on one side, Delko and Frank Tripp on the other. It was a bit unusual for Frank to sit in; Horatio obviously had something serious on his mind. He stayed on his feet, at the front of the room.

Calleigh went first. "The Farallon shark dart isn't being made anymore, hasn't been for years. I've come up with a very short list of people that will admit to owning one, and I've talked to half of them. So far, nothing that even approaches a viable suspect."

"Keep going. Eric?"

"Looks like the same blade cut through the bikini strap and the end of that rope. Can't tell you much about it other than it was extremely sharp."

"The bikini strap was cut through on the back, right?" Horatio asked.

"Right," Delko said.

"But there were no cuts on the DB's back. The sexual assault suggests it was removed antemortem, either when the vic was swimming or drowning—which means our killer is either very stealthy, very good with a blade, or both. Mister Wolfe, what about the trace from under her fingernails?"

"Latex. It had talc on one side and the mass spec came back with trace amounts of silicone. I'm still working on finding the manufacturer."

"Uh—Horatio?" Tripp said. He had a gruff, blunt voice that matched his appearance and attitude exactly. "I hate to rain on your parade, but what exactly am I doing here? This is all hops and barley—won't make any sense to me till you've brewed it into beer. I mean, I appreciate being kept in the loop, but—"

"But this particular loop is somewhat outside your area of expertise? I know, Frank, but bear with me. I've got a very good reason for asking you to attend."

Horatio paused, one hand on a hip and the other rubbing his chin. "Okay. I talked to a dolphin researcher today, and she more or less confirmed my suspicions. It's highly unlikely that a dolphin killed Gabrielle Cavanaugh—in fact, it's highly unlikely a dolphin was involved at all. The glue found in the leg wound is one used by taxidermists, which means that while dolphin teeth made that wound, they weren't attached to a dolphin at the time.

"Taken one piece at a time, the evidence points to a rape that's being disguised as an animal attack. Considered as a sum, though, the answer is a lot more disturbing . . ."

Horatio held up a finger. "One. Although at least three weapons were present—the dart, the blade, the fake dolphin jaws—none was used in a lethal fashion. They were brought along as tools, which indicates a high degree of preparation. Two, the violent and sexual nature of the assault, culminating in the desecration of the body, suggests a great deal of rage. And three, the placement and condition of the body, which shows our killer put a lot of thought into exactly how his little scene would be interpreted."

"He really thought we'd believe a dolphin did this?" Wolfe asked.

"It's not as far-fetched as you might think," Horatio said. "The researcher I talked to even admitted it was a possibility, though a slim one."

"Why go to all that trouble to frame Flipper?" Tripp asked. "I mean, are we looking for someone who hates dolphins in particular, or just cute animals in general? What's next, planting a smoking gun in a basket of kittens?"

"I wish it were that innocuous, Frank," Horatio said. "But it's not dolphins this guy is trying to implicate, it's the Navy." He told them what Zhenko had told him, about the Navy's supposed swimmer nullification program.

"A deep-seated hatred of the military is often a result of direct experience," Horatio said. "Our guy is very probably ex-Navy himself. He's a careful planner, he's good with a blade, he's ruthless and he's getting a sexual charge from what he's doing. The intricate knot tied around the pipe suggests organization to the point of ritual . . . and I can see by your faces that you've all come to same conclusion I have."

Calleigh was the one to say it. "He's a serial."

"One who's been planning this kill for a long time," Horatio said. "Which means he's just getting started . . ."

"Hold on," Tripp said. "You really think more bodies are gonna turn up exploded from the inside out?"

"Not necessarily," Delko said. "Serials tend to refine their methods as they go along. If this was the guy's first kill, the next one might be different. But I bet one thing will stay the same."

"He likes the water," Wolfe said. "That's why the vic was drowned instead of cut up."

"That's right," Horatio said. "He dragged Gabrielle Cavanaugh underwater, clamped some sort of device to her leg and raped her as she drowned. Afterward, he dragged the body to that mangrove island and used the shark dart on it. This is a dangerous and sick man, my friends; he's gone to a lot of trouble to live out his twisted underwater fantasy, and he's not going to be satisfied with just doing it once. That's why I wanted you here, Frank—this investigation is going to expand, and we need to be ready."

"I'm on board, Horatio," Tripp said. "I'll talk to the Coast Guard, too—though it sounds more like we're gonna need a submarine."

"Which, despite Delko's best efforts, we do not have," Horatio said. "What we do have is our training, our experience and the evidence. Let's hope it's enough to catch this guy before he decides to go for another swim . . ."

4

MARGO QUIST LOVED THE ocean. She loved its brisk, salty smell; she loved the sound it made against the beach as she was drifting off to sleep; she loved its many moods, from the glassy stillness of a quiet lagoon to the symphonic booming of waves against the shore during a storm.

Most of all, she loved how it felt. The water off Miami was so warm and buoyant you could fall asleep in its embrace, rocked gently by the tide and lullabyed by the surf . . . if, that is, you could ignore the raucous cries of the gulls, the horns of the cruise ships and the occasional whining roar of a Jet Ski.

Still, all of that faded away—mostly—when your ears were underwater, so Margo preferred to float face-upward with her head tilted back. She was a large woman, as she herself would admit, but in an aquatic environment she might as well be in space; she weighed nothing at all, was as free of gravity as dandelion fluff on the wind.

But even fluff settles to earth eventually . . . and not, as Margo discovered, always gently.

Something touched her hip. She was swimming alone—a bad habit, she knew, but solitude was part of the experience—and it was enough to make her jerk upright with a gasp. Her first panicked thought was that it was a shark or stingray.

It wasn't, though.

It was a body.

"Found by a woman out swimming," Tripp said. He and Horatio stood together on the prow of a police boat; in the water, Delko adjusted a sling around the body and motioned the crew it was ready to be lifted aboard.

"Doesn't really fit the pattern you told me to look out for," Tripp said, "but I figured you'd want to be notified anyway."

"Good call," Horatio said. "We're not really that far from the location of the first DB."

"Still in Biscayne Bay, anyway—but the victim's male. No guts hanging out of his mouth, either."

Doctor Alexx Woods was waiting as the winch operator swung its load over and onto the deck. "Careful!" she snapped. "That's not a load of tuna you're carrying . . ."

Horatio helped her disconnect the winch rope from the sling, revealing the body of a man in his mid-to-late thirties wearing a pair of blue trunks and swimming goggles. His limbs were lean, his body hairy, with a belly distended by gas. He sported a short brown beard and a large bald spot on the top of his head.

"No shark dart used on this one," Alexx said. "Gunshot wound, under the right arm." She turned the body partly onto its side and examined the back. "No exit trauma, so the bullet must still be in there."

"No pockets in the trunks, so no ID," Horatio noted. "I do see a wedding ring, though."

"If we're lucky, his wife's filed a missing-person report," Tripp said.

"Unless," Horatio said, "her luck turns out to be as bad as her husband's . . ."

Serial killers, in Horatio's experience, often claimed to be something more than human. Because they preyed on people, they equated themselves with other animals who did so—wolves, bears, lions. This gave them a certain sense of grandeur, added a sheen of glamour to their cruelty and mayhem. They didn't view themselves as murderers; they were hunters, stalking their rightful prey.

So they thought. Horatio took great pleasure in explaining to the ones he caught exactly why they were wrong.

"Betrayal," he'd say. "That's the only way you can accomplish any of your goals. A wolf doesn't get a rabbit to trust him; a bear doesn't pretend friendship with a salmon. You use civilized preconceptions to get close to your victims, then slaughter them for your own pleasure. Not for food, not for survival. You aren't a hunter—you're a *disease*."

It was an accusation he could make in the great majority of serial-killer cases, and know he was right. Ted Bundy lured women into his vehicle by pretending to have a broken arm; Jeffrey Dahmer enticed men to his apartment with the promise of sex. Serials posed as policemen, as real-estate buyers, as friendly strangers offering a hitchhiker a lift— anything to get the potential victim into a zone of control. They preyed on assumptions as well as people, using the social contract of civilization as a weapon of deception.

Some of them, anyway. Serials came in different flavors: organized and disorganized, lust killers and visionaries, missionaries and hedonists. Some committed their crimes for sexual satisfaction, others out of sheer sadism. Some chose their targets carefully and stalked them for days, weeks, even months; others acted on impulse, killing when an opportunity presented itself. If the murder took place in a situation the killer controlled, the sequence of events was often made to last as long as possible, while a more public killing was usually quick and brutal.

But this killer didn't seduce his victim, drawing

her into an innocuous-looking trap; nor did he invade her home, turning what was once safe and familiar into a chamber of horrors. Instead, he yanked her into his own domain, a hostile realm where the victim couldn't even scream. In fact, it was the environment itself that had actually ended Gabrielle Cavanaugh's life . . . an environment the killer obviously felt completely comfortable in.

There was no deception here, no pretense of being harmless. It was the act of a predator, as ruthless and single-minded as a shark. Gabrielle Cavanaugh had been a target of opportunity, one that had the bad fortune of wandering into his hunting ground; Horatio suspected that any swimmer would have done. And unlike a true wild animal, this hunter wouldn't stick to the same area. He could roam up and down the entire East Coast if he wanted to . . .

Horatio sighed and rubbed his eyes with a thumb and forefinger. He was in the lab, going over Gabrielle Cavanaugh's possessions again in the hope they could tell him something. He picked up the diving mask and turned it over in his hands, looking at it from every angle. He could imagine her wide, terrified eyes behind the glass, trying to make her last breath last a few seconds longer as this terrifying stranger did horrible things to her . . .

"Hey, H," Wolfe said, walking through the door. "Anything new?"

"Just a very bad feeling," Horatio said. "How about you?"

"Still analyzing the data on that scrap of latex. So far I can tell you it's natural, not synthetic, and the silicone came from a polish."

"Okay . . . the talc on it probably means it was worn next to the skin. Have you tested for epithelials?"

"I did. Nothing."

Horatio put down the mask. "Not surprising. We were lucky we got any trace at all, considering the environment."

"Yeah. Processing an underwater crime scene—not a lot to go on."

"Well, we still have the body," Horatio said. "And a signature killer like this one will have a unique pathology." A signature killer was one that always left a distinctive pattern at the crime scene—no matter how hard he tried to disguise it, it was an essential element of the crime itself.

"Yeah, but his signature is the fact that he kills underwater. That's like saying his pattern is that he leaves no trace behind."

"But he does, Mister Wolfe, he does. He may kill underwater, but he doesn't live there. He breathes the same air you and I do . . . and sooner or later, he has to surface. When he's on dry land, he leaves just as much evidence of his presence as anyone else—and that's the presence we have to identify. The water may be his element, but this"—

Horatio said, indicating the lab with a sweep of his hand—"is ours. His victims may be random, but his methodology is not. And I assure you, even a crime scene scoured by the Atlantic leaves plenty of information behind."

Wolfe nodded. "Speaking of victims—is our new DB one of them?"

"Hard to say. Doesn't fit the pattern of the first one, but not too many people get shot while swimming, either. We'll know more after the autopsy—so far, we don't even have an ID . . ."

Alexx gazed down at the body on the autopsy table and shook her head. "Took such good care of yourself, and you wound up here anyway," she said sadly. "I'll bet you went swimming every day, didn't you? You've got the build for it. Nice healthy heart, good pair of lungs, lots of muscle tone . . . what a shame."

Horatio had heard her speak to the dead before—so often, in fact, that it no longer really registered in his mind as a quirk, just part of her routine. She sounded so matter-of-fact that he almost expected the corpse to answer.

And it would, in a way. It held all sorts of answers beneath its still, pale surface, and Alexx knew just how to ask the right questions.

"COD?" Horatio asked. CSI shorthand for "cause of death," it was the sort of jargon that got tossed around so frequently nobody really thought about it; today, though, Horatio was suddenly and absurdly aware that he'd just spelled the name of a fish.

"Gunshot wound to the left upper quadrant of the abdominal region. No stippling or GSR around the entrance. Bullet entered just below the tenth costal cartilage, penetrated the abdominopelvic cavity, nicked the top of the large intestine, then traveled through the liver, the diaphragm, the pericardium and the top of one lung. It lodged in the clavicle—and wait until you see the bullet."

She pulled out a small, clear plastic bag with what appeared to be a spike in it. "Four and a half inches long, thirteen point two grams in weight— I have no idea what caliber it would be, or even what would fire such a thing," Alexx said.

Horatio took the envelope from her and studied it intently. "I've never seen anything like it, either. Could it have come from a speargun, maybe?"

Alexx gave Horatio a look. "Do I *look* like Calleigh?"

Horatio smiled. "Point taken. Ms. Duquesne doesn't do autopsies, you don't do ballistics. How about the angle of entry?"

"Fifty-two degrees, traveling toward the head."

"And the bullet entered from the side. Which is a very awkward position to shoot someone from . . . unless they're swimming above you."

"Or below you," she pointed out. "He might have been shot from a boat."

"True. Do we have an ID yet?"

"I sent his prints to Delko, he's running them through AFIS."

"No hits on the vic's prints, H," Delko said. He was dressed in lab whites over his usual T-shirt, and held a bulky evidence envelope under one arm.

Horatio crossed his arms and said, "And yet, you seem strangely cheerful for a failure."

"That's because I didn't fail," Delko said. He reached into the envelope and pulled out a pair of swimming goggles. "Take a look at these. Notice anything unusual?"

Horatio, like Delko, was already wearing gloves and a lab coat. He took the goggles, held them up to the light. "I see," he murmured. "And with these on, so did our vic. Prescription lenses."

"Yeah, with a serial number and brand name inside. I tracked it down to a Miami optometrist and got a name: David Stonecutter. Nobody's reported him missing yet."

"Good work. Do we have a next of kin?"

"His wife. I've got a number and address, but haven't been able to reach her."

"Okay," Horatio said, handing the goggles back. "Here's what I want you to do. See if the Stonecutters own a vehicle and put out a BOLA for it." BOLA was copspeak for "be on the lookout for." "Ask that particular attention be paid to parking lots on or near any beach."

"Got it. What are you thinking, H?"

"I'm thinking, Eric," Horatio said, "that Mister Stonecutter didn't go swimming alone . . ."

A radio car found the Stonecutters' 2003 Toyota Echo parked in a lot just off Crandon Park Beach, on Key Biscayne. Six miles from Miami proper, Key Biscayne was a barrier island situated on the other side of Biscayne Bay, across from Coral Gables. Seven miles long and two miles wide, Key Biscayne was bordered on the south by Bill Baggs State Park and on the north by Crandon Park.

Horatio took the Rickenbacker Causeway to get there, arriving in the Hummer with Delko just after sunset. The last few grumbling stragglers were being cleared out by police officers closing the beach down.

"Big difference between the last site and this one," Delko observed as they got out of the vehicle.

"True," Horatio said. "The beach at Oleta River State Park is small and relatively isolated. Key Biscayne is five miles of prime tourist shoreline . . . but even so, I have a hunch."

The car was locked and had a ticket on its windshield. "Another twenty-four hours and it would have been towed," Delko said, shading his eyes with his hands and peering through the driver's-side window.

"Something tells me that's the least of their worries," Horatio said. "All right, we've got a lot of ground to cover. Calleigh and Wolfe should be here in a few minutes, and we're getting assistance from foot patrols, too. Grid it, flag it and search it. We're looking for anything that looks abandoned—a blanket, a picnic basket, a backpack. Search all the trash barrels, too—their stuff may have been found and thrown away."

Horatio talked to the employees of the concession, made sure nothing had turned up in the lost and found. None of the lifeguards had seen anything unusual, though they admitted the beach had been extremely busy during the day.

Horatio made his way back across the cooling tarmac of the parking lot to where his team was combing the beach. Calleigh was working the near edge, and glanced up as Horatio kept pace with her. "What's up, H?"

"Lake Sammamish," Horatio said.

"I'm sorry?"

"It's a vacation spot in Washington State. Fills up on summer weekends with people looking for a little relaxation and sunshine, just like this place."

"Sounds familiar, but I can't quite place it."

"Ted Bundy liked it for recreational purposes, too. Took a woman right out of a crowded parking lot, just like this one. He enjoyed doing it so much, he came back and did it again—a few hours later."

"You think this is our guy." It wasn't a question.

"I do. Even though the vic was male, even though he was shot instead of drowning, I just have this feeling."

"Well, if it's him, I hope he left something be-sides a corpse behind this time. I tracked down the rest of the Farallon shark dart owners, and they all had watertight alibis."

"That's all right. We keep looking, sooner or later something will turn up . . ."

It was Wolfe who found the wallet in the trash barrel. There were no credit cards or cash left, but a tattered membership card from the Miami Pub-lic Library verified it had belonged to Janice Stone-cutter. There was also a thermos half-full of coffee, a Stephen King paperback and a blue sweater.

"So their stuff was probably found by someone walking along the beach, maybe last night," Ho-ratio said. "He or she took what they wanted and threw out the rest."

"Doesn't tell us where the Stonecutters went into the water, though," Wolfe said.

"No, unfortunately it does not," Horatio replied. "But having no other point of reference, we'll de-clare this barrel the Point Last Seen. We draw a straight line from here to the shore, and start from there."

What he meant, of course, was that Delko start from there. The young CSI was suited up and in the water within minutes, though he had a fair bit of wading to do before the water was actually deep enough to swim in—there was an extensive sandbar just off the shore, which very slowly and gently sloped into deeper water.

Delko was familiar with all the local dive sites. It had long been a practice in Florida to purposefully place derelict ships, scrap metal, limestone boulders or other debris on the seabed—not as a way of dumping junk, but to create artificial reefs by giving coral something to grow on. This benefited both the ecology and the economy, providing a habitat for aquatic wildlife and an underwater attraction for scuba enthusiasts. The artificial reef off Key Biscayne was a popular dive site, boasting numerous vessels of different types. Some of them were boats that had been seized by the Coast Guard for drug smuggling; every time Delko swam through a hold filled with glittering fish, he couldn't help but wonder if at one time it had been stacked high with bundles of cocaine.

One of the most unusual crafts wasn't a boat at all, but a 727 called the *Spirit of Miami*, deliberately placed in 82 feet of water in 1993, supposedly with a time capsule hidden somewhere inside it. The artificial reef was located more than three nautical miles from the shores of Key Biscayne, but for a moment Delko thought that somehow he had gone too far and wound up there anyway—what he saw in front of him had to be a new addition.

A car rested on the bottom. Not just any car,

either; Delko knew cars, and this was a 1957 Chrysler 300C, with the kind of fins that made it look like it belonged underwater. He swam up and inspected it, shining a light in the windows.

A pale face wearing a diving mask stared back at him. The corpse of a young woman occupied the driver's seat, her clothing gone and her torso eviscerated. Delko had seen a DMV photo of Janice Stonecutter; he recognized her immediately.

Horatio had been right.

The car was too far from the shore to simply winch it out. They had to get a barge with a crane to haul it out of the water.

Calleigh and Horatio watched from the bow of the barge as Delko supervised in the water.

"How did it get way out here?" Calleigh asked, leaning against the railing. "Is it one of those Cuban conversions?" Nineteen-fifties-era cars, left behind from pre-Castro times, were sometimes turned into boats in Cuba and used to cross the eighty miles between their island nation and the Florida coast.

"Possibly," Horatio said. "If so, it certainly wound up in an odd place."

"And so did our vic. Why would he stick her behind the wheel?"

"To keep the body from being eaten, maybe. Some serials return to their kills and continue where they left off."

"Well, there's a cheery thought . . ."

Delko surfaced and gave the thumbs-up to the crane operator. The winch made a loud, clanking noise as it rotated, pulling its cargo from where it rested seventy feet below.

"Here's an even cheerier one," Horatio said. "Our merman has expanded his repertoire. He's going after couples, he's moving into high-traffic areas—and he's using a firearm."

"Yeah, I heard about that," Calleigh said. "Haven't seen it yet, though. Can't wait."

"Any thoughts?"

"Horatio, you know me better than that," Calleigh said with a mock frown. "Yes, I have some thoughts—but I don't want to say until I have the bullet in front of me. Evidence always outweighs supposition, right?"

"That it does," Horatio said. At that moment, the car broke the surface, gushing water from the wheel wells.

"And some evidence weighs a little more than others," Horatio observed.

"This bullet," Calleigh told Horatio, "is a *very* specialized beast. It was designed by Oleg Krachenko and Pytor Sazonov, who—along with Vladimir Simonov—bagged themselves a USSR State Prize in 1983 for it."

"It's Russian?" Horatio asked.

"You betcha," Calleigh said, holding the bullet

up with a pair of padded tweezers and admiring it. She and Horatio were in the gun lab, Calleigh perched on a stool beside her worktable and Horatio standing at her shoulder. "Specifically engineered to work in an aquatic environment. See, regular ammunition performs poorly underwater—it's not the ignition that's the problem, it's the path of the bullet. The rifling in a regular firearm imparts a spin to the bullet, stabilizing it in flight; that doesn't work so well traveling through a heavier medium. Kravchenko and Sazonov figured that they could get around the problem by imitating the darts fired by spearguns—and they were right. A cavitation bubble forms between the long axis of the bullet and the water, keeping it stable."

"So what kind of gun uses this for ammunition?"

"The *Spetsialnyj Podvodnyj Pistolet*, or SPP-1. A non-automatic, manually operated handgun with four barrels. Barrels are hinged to the frame, just like a break-open shotgun; double-action trigger unit with the striker on a rotating base. Holds four 40-millimeter rimmed bottlenecks, each holding a 203-grain steel bullet, firing at a muzzle velocity of eight hundred twenty feet per second. Accuracy and range depend on depth, getting worse the deeper you are: at sixteen feet deep, the effective range is about fifty-six feet, while at a sixty-six-foot depth it's only accurate to about thirty-six feet. Fire it out of the water, you're lucky if you can hit anything at all."

"Okay, suddenly we're in a James Bond movie," Horatio murmured. "This isn't the kind of thing you buy on the street."

"No, it was developed for combat divers," Calleigh said. "As a matter of fact, the Soviet Navy was so happy with the SPP-1 it developed an assault rifle version of the same thing."

"Which hopefully our killer doesn't have access to . . . The Russian angle is interesting, though."

"You thinking maybe a mob connection?"

"Red Mafiya? I suppose one of our Eastern Bloc friends might have smuggled something over . . . but that's not really the direction I was going." Horatio shook his head. "Never mind. It's probably just a coincidence. Anyway, excellent work. I have to go check on Wolfe and Delko, see how they're doing with that Chrysler."

"Okay, H. I'll see what I can do about tracking down any SPP-1s—they surface occasionally on eBay or through private gun collectors."

Horatio took the elevator down to the garage level, where Delko and Wolfe, both in coveralls, were processing the car they'd taken from the bottom of Biscayne Bay. It was in bad shape: Rust had eaten jagged strips around the wheel wells, the tires were flat, one fender was missing entirely. The entire room smelled of wet, rotting upholstery and seaweed.

"Gentlemen," Horatio said. "What can you tell me?"

"Well, for one thing," Delko said, "despite its overall appearance, it hadn't been down there that long. From the barnacles and the algal growth, I'd say a week, week and a half."

"And we can tell you how it got there, too," Wolfe said. He held up a thick, khaki-colored strap. "Delko found four of these under the car. Take a look at the ends."

Horatio did so. "Hmm. Not only charred but shredded. Blast damage."

"Right," Delko said. "We did a mass spec on fibers from the straps and found traces of Semtex. There was also transfer at different points along their length—rust and paint from the car, but also a different color and grade of paint closer to the ends. It's industrial, often used for machinery or—"

"Barrels," Horatio said. "I'm getting the picture. Our guy strapped a bunch of barrels to the car, towed it out into the bay—probably in the middle of the night—and used explosive charges to sever the straps. The car sinks, he leaves."

"What about the barrels?" Wolfe asked. "Wouldn't they sink, too?"

"Depends on how big a hole the charge made," Delko said. "If the guy knew what he was doing, the barrels would probably still float. He could collect them up afterward and tow them back."

"Yeah, but why bother?" Wolfe said. "I mean, he's gone to all this trouble to put a car on the bottom—why not just leave the barrels to sink or not?"

"Why indeed," Horatio said. "And the answer is *setting*. This is stage dressing, just like the tableau at the mangrove island—but this wasn't staged for us. This was for him . . . and he would no more leave barrels lying around his set than a fashion designer would clothe his models in cardboard boxes. He's trying to create a specific mood, a specific illusion, and this car is a big part of that."

"The car part I kinda get," Delko said, nodding. "Personally, I have extremely fond memories involving the backseat of a nineteen-eighty-nine Taurus—but it wasn't parked on the bottom of the Atlantic at the time."

"Maybe he's trying to re-create an important event in his life," Wolfe suggested. "Recapture part of his past."

"Recapture or maybe rewrite," Horatio said. "Putting the car underwater might be his attempt to impose control on a situation where he previously had none . . . and I'm guessing this specific make and model figures prominently. Eric, I'd like you to track down the last owner of this car, find out what he has to say. Then hit the archives—see if it, or a car like it, was involved in any major crime or accident in Florida."

"How far back you want me to go, H?"

"Well, I wouldn't go back any further than nineteen-fifty-seven, myself . . ."

Delko grinned and nodded. "Right."

"Mister Wolfe, keep working on the vehicle itself. I'm going to see what Alexx has to say about the DB . . ."

The body on the autopsy table was a grisly sight. The torso had been gutted, ripped open and torn apart. Cuts crisscrossed the arms and legs; only the face was untouched.

"If I didn't know better," Doctor Alexx Woods said quietly, "I'd say she was killed by an animal."

"She was," Horatio said. "Unfortunately, this particular breed walks upright . . . Cause of death?"

"Exsanguination. She bled to death, Horatio— and it probably took a long time. Twelve to fifteen hours, I'd say."

Horatio frowned. "Wait a minute. That would mean she was removed from the water, right?"

Alexx shook her head. "I'm afraid not. Her lungs showed patchy atelectasis—they were partially collapsed, which is one of the symptoms of pulmonary oxygen toxicity. Divers call it the Lorraine Smith effect; it's the result of breathing too rich a mix of oxygen over too long a period of time."

"So he kept her there . . . the cuts were done before death, not after?"

"The ones on her limbs, yes. The disemboweling was last—she was already dead by then. I found the same artificial bite mark on her calf as the last one, but she didn't drown. Take a look."

Horatio leaned in and examined the wound, then the other cuts on the leg. "Four parallel wounds, over and over," he said. "Like claw marks."

"Almost exactly like claw marks," Alexx agreed. "But I didn't find any organic material in the wounds themselves—and since claws grow in layers that are continually flaking off, it's normal to find bits of them embedded in wounds after an attack. I'd say this was done by something made out of metal that's approximating a claw."

"Like the jaws imitating a dolphin," Horatio murmured. "Was she raped?"

"More than once, I'd say. Genital bruising was much worse than the last one."

Horatio took a step back from the autopsy table. Put his hands on his hips. Didn't say anything for a moment, just studied the body with narrowed eyes.

"Horatio?" Alexx said.

"This is the last one, Alexx," Horatio said grimly. "I'm not going to let this guy drag another woman under the surface. He kept her alive as long as he possibly could, cutting her to pieces while she couldn't even scream . . ."

"It must have been like being in hell," Alexx said quietly.

"That's where this guy comes from," Horatio said. "And I'm going to make sure he goes back . . ."

5

WOLFE HAD A GREAT deal of admiration for his boss. It wasn't just that Horatio had a keen intellect and a ferocious dedication to his job—he was also calm and collected under pressure. Wolfe had never seen Horatio intimidated or at a loss for words, no matter how unusual or intense the situation.

But that wasn't the only reason he looked to Horatio for guidance. Horatio didn't hide from the maelstrom of powerful emotions that often swirled around a case; if anything, he felt the pain of the people involved more strongly than anyone. He stayed strong amid horror and despair and grief, and seemed to have an inexhaustible store of compassion.

Wolfe himself couldn't make the same claim. His interpersonal skills, while not entirely absent, weren't that sharp; he made remarks when he should have kept his mouth shut, he interrupted people in the middle of conversations, he was oblivious of certain social protocols . . . until something disastrous occurred.

He found this process deeply frustrating. Wolfe relied on science the way most people relied on oxygen, and the more factors he could quantify in any given event, the happier he was. Unfortunately, this equation meant he was happiest in the lab and unhappiest in a crowd; any large group of people just had too many variables. He had approached this problem in a methodical and reasoned way ever since he had become aware of it in his teens, by studying and analyzing the process of social interaction. He used to make long lists when he was younger, detailing everything from appropriate comments in specific social situations to subjects best to avoid. He eventually gave up the practice when he figured out an essential truth: Human beings were just too unpredictable.

In part, this was what led to his becoming a cop. The job of the police, as Wolfe saw it, was to impose order on chaos; they enforced the rules. Being a CSI was even better, because it meant you used science to enforce the rules—and natural laws were always more quantifiable than human ones.

Having Horatio for a boss had altered his point of view. He saw now that it was possible to balance the two, though the precise mechanism of this still eluded him. In the meantime, he studied Horatio's methods carefully, and emulated him whenever possible.

Which included dressing like him.

Like many geeks, Wolfe didn't put that much thought into what he wore. When he first started working as a CSI, he favored sweater vests and long-sleeved shirts. That had gradually shifted to suit jackets over T-shirts, and finally to the sort of open-collar shirts and blazers that Horatio favored. Wolfe didn't quite have the designer-label thing down yet, but he was working on it.

As he scrolled through a depressingly long list of sex offenders, Wolfe found himself thinking about appearances and how unreliable they were. Some of the criminals on the list looked exactly how you would expect a rapist or pedophile to look; others looked as harmless as a kindergarten teacher. You just couldn't tell.

Monsters, Wolfe thought. *If they just had horns growing out of their foreheads or something, our job would be a lot easier.*

Of course, he'd had similar thoughts about women with boyfriends, desk sergeants having a bad day, small children next to him on a plane who were about to throw up . . . in fact, it would be nice if people in general came with some sort of identifying label.

He clicked on a name, calling up the history of David Posterly. The guy was pudgy, had watery-looking eyes, a big nose and a receding hairline. Looked like he worked in a bank.

His priors included seventeen cases of sexual assault, nine of them on minors. Apparently he used to drive an ice-cream truck.

Wolfe shook his head. Could you even call someone like that human, or had he handed in his resignation from the species? And if you met the guy, talked to him, how would he come across?

Probably a lot better than I do.

"Hey, Ryan," Calleigh said, walking into the computer lab. "What's up? You look kind of gloomy."

He sighed. "It's nothing. It's just this case— makes me wonder about the things some people are capable of."

She sat down at another monitor and started tapping keys. "Yeah, I know what you mean. The whole underwater rape thing is really creepy . . . I'd even think twice about using a swimming pool right now."

"Well, you might not be that far off. I've found a couple of cases of sexual assault that happened at public pools. Indecent exposure and improper touching, mainly—no actual rape."

"You think that's where our guy got his start?"

"I don't know. He had to start somewhere . . . What are you working on?"

"The claw marks from the third vic. The spacing doesn't match any known animal claw, but that fits with Horatio's theory they're artificial. The wound pattern indicates they have a slight hook on the end, though—just like real claws."

"This guy does his homework."

"So do we, Ryan. So do we . . ."

*   *   *

Delko had waded through a ton of archive material. He was now familiar with every gas-station robbery, vehicular accident and case of theft that involved a 1957 Chrysler 300C—in Florida, anyway. He'd sifted through it all, trying to find something that might have sparked the career of a psychopath—a rape that took place in the backseat, a crippling auto crash, a hit-and-run or some other crime. Most of it was petty stuff, though; minor fender-benders, cars being reported stolen.

The problem, he thought as he looked over yet another report, *is trying to figure out what's actually important.* A joyride by a couple of teenagers might seem like an insignificant event, but what if it led to one of the teenagers being cruelly beaten by an abusive parent? For that matter, what if the event triggered by the car was never reported as a crime?

He sighed, got up and stretched. So far, nothing had jumped out at him. He supposed that any of the incidents he'd reviewed could lead to something horrific, but if so, that horror was down a path he couldn't see.

His cell phone rang. "CSI Delko. Yes, Miss Pershall, thanks for getting back to me. I understand you sold a car a few weeks ago, a 1957 Chrysler? That's right, the 300C. I was wondering if I could ask you a few questions about it, in regard to an ongoing investigation . . . In person would be better. Sure, I can come down. What's the address?

Uh-huh. Uh-huh . . . Okay, I'll be there in about an hour. Thank you."

He hung up. Maybe he'd have better luck with the previous owner of the car itself.

"Horatio! Hold up a minute!" Lieutenant Frank Tripp jogged up just as Horatio was about to get into his Hummer.

"What's up, Frank?"

"Just wanted to touch base. Any luck on the bullet?"

"Calleigh found a possible source for the gun— I'm on my way there right now. Gun dealer in Miami Beach, specializes in unusual stuff."

Frank nodded. "Yeah, I guess it was only a matter of time."

Horatio slipped his sunglasses on. "How so, Frank?"

"New World Order, Horatio. Before the wall came down, you'd hardly ever hear a conversation in Russian—nowadays, you're as likely to hear it as Spanish. Wasn't bad enough we had to worry about the Cosa Nostra and the Colombians—now we have ex-KGB lookin' to make a buck, too."

Horatio paused before replying. "Just because the weapon's Russian doesn't mean the shooter is, Frank."

Tripp scowled. "That's not what I mean. I don't have anything against Russians, Horatio—it's all the stuff that's coming over here with 'em. Did you hear that for a while the Red Army couldn't afford to pay the soldiers they had guarding nuclear silos? Out in the middle of nowhere, sitting on a bunch of warheads they could peddle on the black market for ten million dollars in hard currency apiece, and these poor slobs don't even get a paycheck? That's a recipe for disaster no matter what country you're talking about."

"Very true," Horatio said. "I suppose we should consider ourselves lucky that all we're dealing with is a single gun. What worries me more is the training he has to use it."

"You think he could be some kind of professional assassin? Soviet black ops, maybe?"

Horatio opened the door of the Hummer. "Anything's possible, Frank. But our guy has already tried to shift blame toward the Navy—this might be another red herring. I'm betting he has *some* kind of military background, though."

"Yeah," Tripp said, "but which military?"

Horatio got into his vehicle. "More importantly," he said, "what weapons does he have that he *hasn't* used yet?"

The previous owner of the '57 Chrysler lived southwest of Miami, out past Medley on a property that could charitably be described as rural. An A-frame house that seemed perilously close to becoming a D-minus slouched over a yard overgrown with brambles and weeds; kudzu snaked its way through a variety of old machinery that ranged from broken-spoked wheelchairs to the rusting chassis of tractors and pickups. Chickens scrambled out of the way of Delko's Hummer as he pulled up, and a brindle-colored pit bull on the front porch raised its slablike head, studied him indifferently and decided to go back to sleep.

Delko got out of his car and walked up the front steps. The dog watched him out of the corner of one eye and yawned, displaying jaws Delko was sure could be used to crush bricks.

He knocked on the front door. There was an ancient air conditioner the size of a public mailbox mounted in the front window to his left; the loud, wheezing rumble it made gave the impression the entire house was about to taxi down a runway.

He knocked again, louder. No response. "Hello?" he called out. "Miss Pershall?" He wondered if he had the right address.

"Yeah?"

He turned around. The woman stood at the foot of the steps he'd just climbed; she must have come from around the side of the house. She was dressed in a pair of big, black army boots, a flowered hat, and her underwear.

"Uh, hi," Delko said. The woman didn't seem embarrassed or surprised; her body was sinewy and tanned, with an intricate tattoo of a bird outlined in flames across her torso, the wings upraised so they framed her breasts like fiery parentheses enclosing a double zero. Her bra was black and lacy, and she wore a pair of white men's boxers instead of panties. Delko guessed her age at mid-thirties; her hair was cropped short under the hat, and very black.

"You must be the cop," she said. Her voice had the rough throatiness of a longtime smoker—he recognized it from their phone conversation. "I'm Bonnie Pershall."

If it doesn't bother her, I'm not gonna let it bother me, he thought. "Thanks for agreeing to talk to me," he said.

"No sweat," she said.

He realized she was older than he'd first thought; despite her excellent physique, the wrinkles around her eyes and mouth gave her away. Mid-forties, maybe.

"You mind if we talk in the back?" she said. "I'm right in the middle of something."

"Sure," he said. He followed her around the corner of the house and into the backyard, which turned out to be in better shape than the front. The grass was mowed, there was a table with a white shade umbrella and matching chairs on a little patio of red brick—and then there was the bike.

Delko whistled. "Old Indian, right?" The motorcycle was parked on a blue tarp, with a variety of chromed socket wrenches and other tools scattered around.

"Nineteen-fifty-three Chief. Eighty-cubic-inch engine, telescoping front forks. Last year the heavyweight was produced before the company took a nosedive."

"Nice," he said. "You a mechanic?"

"Guess you could call it that," Bonnie Pershall said. She walked over to the table, bent over and fished a can of Coors out of the cooler beneath it. The view, Delko had to admit, was just as impressive from behind as the front—she had a pair of angel wings tattooed on her back, just as large and detailed as the ones on her front.

"Like to tinker with engines, get paid for it sometimes," Pershall said, straightening up and popping the can open with one hand. "Was just tuning the critter up." Her voice was casual.

"Well, I won't take up too much of your time. I just need to know about the person that bought the '57 Chrysler from you."

"Sure. It was kind of strange, to tell you the truth. The guy phoned me up—don't know how he got my number, either—and said he'd noticed I had an old Chrysler in my front yard. Asked what I'd take for it, but not if it was in running condition, anything like that. Just wanted to know if the glass was all intact, which it was."

"Doesn't sound that strange," Delko said. He'd taken out a pad and paper and was making notes.

"Oh, that wasn't the strange part. We agreed on a price, and he asked if cash was okay. I said fine with me. The next day, I find the full amount stuffed in an envelope in my mailbox—

no note, nothing. I get a phone call while I'm counting it, and it's him. Says he came by while I wasn't here, decided to leave the money so I wouldn't sell it to anybody else. Now, that old junker sat out there for most of my marriage and all of my divorce—which is to say a good ten years—and it's never been exactly a hot-ticket item."

"Yeah, that's pretty weird," Delko admitted.

"It gets weirder. See, we try to make arrangements for him to come by and get it, and he keeps suggesting a time then remembering something he had to do instead, until we finally arrive at something that works for both of us. Well, I get home one night—I work in this bar over in Hialeah—and the car's gone. Thinking back on it, I realize the whole back-and-forth time thing is him trying to figure out when I *won't* be home."

"So you never actually met him."

"Nope. I suppose I could have kept the cash and reported the car stolen, but he probably figured I wouldn't bother. And guess what? He figured right. I was just glad to have it gone."

Delko nodded and wrote a few things down. "I don't suppose you still have the envelope the money came in?"

"Sorry—I threw it out. No point in keeping it, you know?"

"Not for you, anyway. I'd sure like to get my hands on it."

She gave him an amused look, looked as if she was about to say something and then changed her mind. Delko heard it anyway: *Anything else you'd like to get your hands on?*

"Well," Delko said, trying to keep his smile from turning into a grin, "is there anything else you can think of?"

This time she actually laughed out loud. "Yeah," she said, meeting his eyes. "Couple things."

"Which would be?"

"First off—is this guy dangerous?"

It wasn't the question he'd expected, but he had to admit it was probably the right one to ask. "I can't say too much about an ongoing investigation," he answered carefully. "But if you deal with him again, be extremely careful. I don't think that's going to happen, though—I think he's already gotten what he wants from you. He also went to a lot of trouble to not leave any traces, so it wouldn't make any sense for him to come back."

"Okay, second question: If I was worried about my safety, would the police department send someone over to hold my hand?"

He did his best to keep his grin under control. "The Miami PD always has the interest of the public in mind. If you have any . . . *concerns*, I'd be happy to discuss them with you."

"Oh, good," she said, raising the can of beer to her lips without taking her eyes off him. "Because I'm feeling a little *concerned*, right now . . ."

*   *   *

Miami, as Horatio well knew, was a city of extremes. One of those extremes was age; it sometimes seemed as if the only residents were those in their twenties and senior citizens. Horatio was used to this effect . . . but occasionally he ran across an example that surprised even him.

The proprietor of Max's Military Curios looked like he could have served in the Civil War. He stood around five feet tall, with a hunched back that gave him a build like a question mark. His bald head was speckled with liver spots, his ears and nose were enormous, and the wattles of loose, wrinkled flesh that dangled under his chin almost obscured his Adam's apple. He was wearing a tropical shirt loud enough to kill someone with a hangover and yelling into a cell phone when Horatio entered his shop.

". . . No, no, no! I don't care who owned it, I got so many of those flintlocks I could storm the Bastille! You tell him that's my final offer, and if he doesn't take it, good luck finding another schmuck with too much money and no sense."

Horatio glanced around. The shop projected the same odd dichotomy many antique stores did, when folksy art met filthy rich; on one hand it was striving for down-home, authentic and old, while on the other it was catering to those with high-end sensibilities and designer budgets. Usually, that meant a ten-thousand-dollar lighting system carefully arranged to display an armoire or wardrobe probably built by someone a century ago—in Max's place, the same lighting was used to show off a glass case full of World War II pistols. Japanese swords mounted on racks of dark, laquered wood covered one wall, while another held rifles that ranged from muskets to Winchesters.

The glass-topped counter Max—at least, Horatio assumed it was the man himself—stood behind held row after row of medals and military insignia from a wide variety of countries and regimes, including a few that were unexpected. He was studying them when Max finally finished his cell phone conversation and said, "So? Anything catch your eye?"

"You have quite an assortment," Horatio said.

Max shuffled over to where Horatio stood and glanced down. "I know what you're thinking," he said, tapping the glass with one wrinkled finger. The case beneath held Iron Crosses, SS patches and medals embossed with swastikas. "What's an old Jew like me doing selling stuff like this, hmm? What right do I have? Shouldn't I throw this stuff out with the trash, or burn it or something?"

He didn't wait for Horatio's reply. "I'll tell you what right. My sister, both my brothers, my parents—*that's* what right. They died in the camps, every one of them, and the Nazis took everything they owned, right down to their fillings. I got out in thirty-seven, went to find my fortune, and I never saw them again. The bastards took all that from me, I figure it's all right to get a little money back."

"Not much compensation," Horatio said.

"So? You get compensation from the Black Plague, from a horde of locusts? If you got insurance, maybe, but most of the time they don't cover you worth bupkiss. Acts of God, they're called—acts of the Devil, more like—but what they mean is some things are too big to take personal. Most people, they don't see the Holocaust like that, they think it was like everybody in the country turned into Hannibal Lecter, but that's not true. It was like a factory, like suddenly everybody's job was to kill Jews. That sounds crazy, but that's what it was like. All of a sudden we weren't human, like we all turned into firewood overnight. And who cares about firewood?"

There was no good reply. Horatio didn't even try to answer the question, just gazed at the man levelly and waited for him to continue.

"Anyway," Max said, "anything I make from that crap, I give to the Jewish Defense League, so maybe it does a little good in the end. But I don't tell them where it comes from, because who needs the grief?"

"That's commendable," Horatio said. He showed Max his badge. "But actually, I'm more interested in items with a Russian origin than German."

"Soviet? That, I have plenty of. Too much, to tell you the truth. Since the wall came down, it's been like an avalanche, all the Red Army stuff. I could open a separate store if I wanted, which I don't. One is plenty enough aggravation."

"I understand a certain specialized firearm passed through your hands—a pistol designed to work underwater, used by the Soviet Navy."

Max frowned. "An SPP-1, you mean? I hope so, because I've never even seen one of the semi-autos. The pistol, though, I sold one once. About six, seven months ago, I think."

"To whom?"

"Just a second. I'll check my records." He shuffled off to the end of the counter. Horatio half-expected him to start rummaging around in a dusty old filing cabinet, but instead he pulled aside a black velvet curtain to reveal a desktop computer in a small niche. Max tapped a few keys in quick succession, and muttered something under his breath.

"I'm sorry, I didn't quite get that," Horatio said.

"Nothing, nothing, I'm just cursing Bill Gates and all his descendants . . . this thing is so slow I could catch cold and die while I'm waiting. Ah, there we go. I sold it to a man named Avery Barlow, seven months ago. All the proper forms filled out, no problems."

"Well, there is one problem, Max," Horatio said. "See, we have no record of that gun—a colleague of mine tracked you down via a posting on eBay. As a matter of fact, there are no registered owners of an SPP-1 underwater pistol in the state of Florida."

"Ah. Well, you know, with items of a certain provenance, the paperwork doesn't always line up with the real thing. What I'm trying to say is, I couldn't find a form for an underwater pistol, so I fudged it a little."

Horatio shook his head. "Would you like to explain to me, please, exactly what that means?"

"I filed it as a Makarov. Hey, it's still a Russian gun."

"I'm going to need a printout of the transaction, Max."

"Sure, sure, happy to help. It's not like I was trying to get away with anything, you know—I mean, it was a legal sale, his background check was fine."

"Then let's hope," Horatio said, "that everything else about Mister Barlow checks out as well."

Back in the nineteen-twenties, when George Merrick was building the Mediterranean fantasy of a city he named Coral Gables, the raw material needed for his plazas, fountains and esplanades was excavated from a nearby limestone quarry. And as the streets and buildings grew, so did the excavation in the ground, an ugly, rocky pit with no apparent use.

And now, mused Wolfe, *it's a rocky pit on the National Register of Historic Places. Funny what adding a little water will do . . .*

Of course, "a little water" wasn't really accurate—825,000 gallons of artesian spring-fed H_2O was. Not to mention the palm-tree-shaded island in the middle, the three-story observation towers, the Spanish-styled porticos and loggia. The Venetian Pool, as it was now called, even boasted coral rock caves and two waterfalls.

But Wolfe wasn't there to admire carefully crafted beauty. The subject he had come to discuss was considerably less appealing, and he hoped he could do so without stepping on any toes.

He met with the manager, a man named Anthony Osella, at the wrought-iron gate that led inside. Osella unlocked the gate and let him in; the pool wasn't open for another hour or so.

He followed Osella, a slender man dressed in a white linen suit, to a shaded table at poolside. He'd been doing some paperwork, it seemed—a coffee mug emblazoned with the logo of the pool anchored a stack of forms against the warm breeze.

Osella sat and motioned Wolfe to do the same. The manager had a narrow face, with a hooked nose and an arrow-sharp black goatee. His eyes were hidden behind mirrored sunglasses against the sunlight glaring off the blue-green water, but his smile was open and friendly.

"Thank you for seeing me," Wolfe said. He pulled out his palmtop and a little plastic stylus to take notes.

"Not at all. I appreciate you coming here during

off-hours—this is a sensitive subject, and I would prefer not to alarm anyone."

"I understand," Wolfe said, then hesitated. "So, this—incident. I've read the police report, but I'd like to hear your take on it."

Osella nodded, his face losing its smile. "It was last March. We get many, many visitors—a hundred thousand a year. We don't allow alcohol, but it's inevitable that we encounter troublemakers now and then. The lifeguards know how to handle that, it's not a problem. But this . . . well, it's not the same."

"No, I guess not."

"We have many different areas—the waterfall, the lap pool, the island and the caves. We're very thorough when it comes to safety."

"I'm sure you are," Wolfe said patiently, though he really wished Osella would get to the point.

"But we can't supervise everywhere all the time. And what this man was doing . . . well, it's hard to prove."

"And what *was* he doing, exactly?"

"According to the woman who complained, he was just . . . watching. He wore a pair of swimming goggles, and he would wait at the far end of the cave until a young woman entered. Going from the brightness outside, it takes a moment for your eyes to adjust; I'm sure many of the women never noticed him at all. Anyway, he would then hold his breath and submerge. The water is waist deep, so it's enough to completely hide you if you crouch."

"And then he'd just sit there?"

"Yes. But this gave him a very good view, you understand, from a very close range. I don't know how long he was doing it before we noticed, either—though one of our cashiers said he had been coming in for weeks."

"But he never went any further than that."

"No. He never touched any of the women, never even talked to them." Osella picked up his mug of coffee and cradled it between both hands. "I asked him to leave, naturally."

"And did he?"

"Oh, yes. He was a short man but very well built, and I was worried he might give me some trouble—but such was not the case. He simply nodded and left without a word of argument."

"Sounds like he almost expected to get caught."

"Perhaps so. In addition to the swimming goggles, he wore a thick belt around his waist, with heavy pouches sewn onto it. I recognized it as a weight belt, the kind scuba divers use."

"To reduce buoyancy during dives," Wolfe said. "Or let you sit on the bottom of a swimming pool and play I Spy."

"I would imagine so, yes." Had Osella winced, ever so slightly?

"Can you tell me what he looked like?"

"He was white, about five-eight, quite muscular,

in his late thirties or early forties. His hair was a reddish blond color, cut very short. Clean-shaven. His face . . . well, there wasn't anything unusual about it, no scars or anything. I couldn't really see his eyes, so I don't know what color they were."

"Any scars or tattoos?"

Osella frowned, considering. "Not that I remember, no. I recall his bathing suit was a dull sort of green—I wanted to fix it in my mind in case he came back."

"Wedding ring or jewelry?"

"I don't think so, no."

Wolfe was scribbling notes on the surface of his PDA. "All right . . . do you think you could come down to the station later and look at some mug shots? There's a good chance he's been arrested before, and it would really help if you could ID him."

Osella nodded. "Of course. Has this man . . . done something?"

"It's too soon to say—it's just a lead we're following up. But I can tell you this is part of an ongoing investigation and we're taking it very seriously."

Osella said he'd come by that afternoon; Wolfe thanked him and stood up. *Well*, Wolfe thought, *that* didn't go too badly . . .

"If this man comes back, I will of course notify you immediately," Osella said. "If I had thought he was dangerous, I would have insisted he stay here until the police arrived."

"It would have been hard to prove any criminal intent," Wolfe said. "Technically, he didn't break the law."

"I suppose not," Osella admitted. "Still . . ."

"Yeah, I know," Wolfe said. "Creepy. Lurking in the cave like some kind of underwater troll, crouched on the bottom with his eyes only inches away from some strange woman's . . ."

Wolfe stopped when he saw the look on Osella's face. He mumbled another goodbye, quickly turned around and left.

Damn. And I was doing so well . . .

"A Makarov?" Calleigh exclaimed. "That's not even—" She grabbed the printout from Horatio's hand and frowned down at it. "An IJ-70-18H? That's got a double-stack ten-round magazine—it's not even *close* to the SPP-1! No wonder I couldn't track it down . . ."

"But you did," Horatio said. "Despite somebody else's shoddy bookkeeping. And now we have an address."

"I suppose," Calleigh muttered. "Have we picked this guy up yet?"

"Not yet, but I was about to do that very thing . . . care to join me?"

Calleigh immediately brightened. "Why, Horatio—you do know how to make a girl feel special . . ."

Avery Barlow lived in an impersonal, mirror-windowed apartment building on Collins Avenue, along the hotel and condo strip north of twenty-first that locals called Miami Modern, or MiMo. Horatio and Calleigh walked in the front door alongside a blond woman struggling with several bags of groceries and a stroller. Horatio held the door for her, receiving a grateful "Thank you!" Calleigh smiled at the baby in the stroller and got a wide-eyed look of bafflement in return.

The elevator took them up to the fifteenth floor. Barlow's door was at the very end, right where the hallway ended with a floor-to-ceiling window that looked out over Biscayne Bay. Horatio glanced at the sparkling expanse of blue-green water, slashed with the white teeth of sailboats, and wondered how much the view cost.

He rapped on the door, Calleigh standing just out of view to his right.

"Yes?" The voice was surly and suspicious; the door remained shut.

Horatio held his badge up to the eyehole. "Miami-Dade Police, Mister Barlow. We'd like to ask you a few questions."

The door opened. A short, well-built man stood there, dressed in sweatpants and sandals, a blue towel draped around his neck. A few flecks of shaving cream dotted his scalp; apparently he'd just finished shaving his head.

"What's this about?" he snapped.

"A gun you purchased from Max's Military Curios," Horatio said. "Specifically, a Russian-made SPP-1 pistol."

He looked at them blankly. *"What* pistol?"

"An SPP-1, a weapon specifically designed to work underwater," Calleigh said.

The man frowned. "I don't own anything like that," he said. "You must have made a mistake." He started to shut the door.

Horatio slapped his hand against the wood, stopping it dead. "The one making a mistake is you, Mister Barlow. I have your name on a gun purchase application form, and that's enough for me to get a warrant. Do you want to talk to me now, or after I've searched every square inch of your residence?"

The man stared back at him levelly. "Look, I told you—I don't own a gun like that, and there isn't a piece of paper anywhere that says so. So good luck with that warrant thing—you'll need it."

He slammed the door shut.

"Charming," Calleigh said.

Horatio nodded thoughtfully. "Not to mention suspicious . . ."

6

"IN HER *underwear*," Wolfe said skeptically.

"Hand to God," Delko said, grinning.

They were back in the CSI garage, reexamining the Chrysler. Bonnie Pershall, after talking to Delko for a while, had remembered some old photos of the car she still had and dug them out. Wolfe and Delko were comparing the pictures to the vehicle, seeing if the killer had made any modifications.

"Great," Wolfe said. "You get the hot, semi-naked woman and I get to embarrass myself to a pool manager."

"Luck of the draw," Delko said. "Anyway, all we did was talk—mainly about engines. You know, gearhead stuff."

"Sure. Of course."

"Yeah, she's got this whole rant about the interface between human and machine getting narrower and narrower all the time . . . when she rides her bike, she says it feels like an extension of her. Wanted to know how I felt about that."

"Yeah? What'd you say?"

Delko laughed. "I told her I felt the same way sometimes, on really long dives. You use a rebreather, you can stay down for days . . ."

Most scuba gear was "open circuit," which meant that when the diver breathed out, everything he exhaled was expelled into the surrounding water. On average, a human being consumed only about one-quarter the oxygen he breathed in; the rest was exhaled, along with carbon dioxide and nitrogen.

A rebreather recovered exhaled oxygen, letting it be used again, as well as filtering and absorbing the poisonous CO_2 in a canister of soda lime. By supplementing the recycled air with new oxygen, a rebreather rig greatly extended the time a diver could stay submerged.

"After a while," Delko said, "you start feeling like it's where you live all the time. Like the gear that's letting you breathe are actually your lungs."

"Huh," Wolfe said. "Lately I've been trying to be less technology oriented—now I find out everybody else is headed in the opposite direction."

"Maybe you'll intersect somewhere in the middle . . . Anyway, I'm not seeing a lot of difference between these photos and the car itself. If he changed anything, I can't tell."

"Let me take a look." Wolfe took the photos and studied them. "Hmmm . . . Well, there's one obvious discrepancy."

"What's that?"

"The car smells a lot worse."

Horatio heard her before he saw her. He didn't know much Russian, but he knew cursing when he heard it.

". . . *Ya tebial dostal! Ti durak!* Where is he? Let me in to see him or I'll drive this damn thing over your feet!"

Horatio walked up to the reception desk, where a furious Nicole Zhenko was berating anyone within earshot. Her Levo wheelchair was in full upright position; she was actually a few inches taller than the sergeant she was yelling at, a harried-looking man with a paper cup of coffee in one hand.

"Doctor Zhenko?" Horatio said. "What seems to be the problem?"

"The problem?" she spat, spinning around with an electric whir. "This! *This* is the problem!" She had a newspaper in one hand, and she threw it at him as hard as she could.

Horatio let it bounce off his chest, then calmly leaned down and picked it up off the floor. He looked at one side, then the other before he saw the article that had her so angry. He frowned.

"What in *chyertu* do you think you're doing—"

He held up one finger for silence as he quickly scanned the article. Amazingly, it worked; she waited a full three or four seconds until he looked up again.

"You can't say such things! You—"

"Doctor Zhenko, this is the first I've heard of this. Let me assure you, I'm not happy about it either— but I don't think standing here and shouting at each other is going to produce a lot of hard data."

"Ha! There *is* no hard data, only lies and innuendo!"

"So it would seem," Horatio said patiently.

She already had a lungful of air ready for another outburst, but now she paused and studied him suspiciously. "You really didn't know about this?"

"Rather than stand here and debate my innocence," Horatio said, "why don't we step into my office and I'll prove it?"

She gave him a grudging nod. Horatio turned and walked up the hall to his office; he could hear her chair whirring along behind him.

Once they were both inside, he leaned against his desk and reread the article more carefully.

"Well?" she said acidly. "Where is your proof?"

"First of all," he said carefully, "what possible reason could I have to claim that a dolphin murdered a swimmer?"

"I don't know! It's ridiculous!"

"Yes. It is. That was the conclusion I and my

team came to almost immediately, and we've been pursuing other avenues since then."

"That's not what the paper says."

"What the paper says is incomplete and highly speculative. If I was going to leak a story like this to the press, don't you think I'd at least give them some facts to back up such a bizarre theory?"

"It would be moronic not to."

"Exactly. This story makes us look like half-baked amateurs on a wild-goose chase. Does that sound like something I'd want to see in print?"

She glared at him. "I don't know. You have a reason, maybe, for wanting to look like a fool. But I don't care about that—what I care about is suddenly half of Miami thinks dolphins are going to try to have them for dinner."

"I would have thought you'd approve of that. 'Fear breeds respect'—isn't that what your friends in the Animal Liberation Alliance say?" Horatio's voice was still calm, but his eyes were intent.

She paused before replying, and now her tone was more guarded than hostile. "Ah. I see. You've been doing some research on me, like a good little policeman."

"Good research produces good results . . . unless, of course, those results were obtained unethically."

She gave him a hard, tight smile. "And you want to debate ethics with me? Sorry, I don't have the time. But don't make the mistake of thinking

my ethics are the same as the ALA—I parted ways
with those idiots some time ago."

"But not before you were arrested."

"It was a demonstration against the use of dragnets. You know how much destruction those
things cause? It's like running a threshing machine
over the bottom and throwing away anything you
don't like."

Horatio eyed her coolly. "So you decided to respond with a little destruction of your own."

"Sinking those boats wasn't my idea—that was
all Anatoly. After that, I was done with them, the
whole group. You can't fight crazy with crazy."

"That would be Anatoly Kazimir, the founder
and leader of the group, correct? He has quite the
record, too: destruction of private property, illegal
possession of explosives, resisting arrest. Somehow,
though, he's managed to avoid jail time."

She snorted. "So far, you mean. Sooner or later
he'll do something incredibly stupid and idealistic,
and then all the lawyers in the ACLU won't be
able to get him out."

"But you wouldn't do such a thing."

"I'm a scientist, not a revolutionary."

"And I'm a police officer—one who knows better than to spread wild rumors to the press."

She looked at him through narrowed eyes, then
shrugged. "So okay, we both know who we are.
But if this story didn't come from you, then who?"

"That's a very good question," Horatio admitted,

folding his arms. "The article quotes an anonymous source. I'm guessing the tip may have come from the killer himself."

"I think I see. A—how do you say—framing job."

"It's beginning to look that way, yes . . ."

She hit the joystick on the arm of her chair and rolled right up to Horatio, wheels stopping just short of his shoes.

"All right, all right, I believe you," she said. "You're too smart to do something this stupid. I guess."

"That almost sounded like an apology."

Her smile looked more rueful than apologetic. "It's the best I can do. Where I come from, there are two kinds of police: corrupt and smart, or honest and dumb. Mainly I know the first kind—the other doesn't live long enough to make friends."

"Sometimes Miami can be the same way . . . but so far, I've managed to survive."

She sighed. "This is terrible. The damn article is still there, and now I don't have anyone to yell at."

"I could issue a formal denial, but that'll sound like we're trying to cover something up."

"So then what?"

"A news story is like a fire—the more air you give it, the bigger it gets. Without fuel, it dies on its own."

"Just ignore it?" She considered this, then abruptly spun around and headed back toward the door. She paused at the doorway and glanced backward. "I suppose. But if any rednecked yahoo shoots a bottlenose, I'm going to beat them to death with a frozen fish."

"You know," Horatio observed, "for someone still getting used to a new ride, you're pretty nimble in that thing."

"I'm a fast learner," she said, and whirred away.

Horatio smiled. "So am I, Doctor Zhenko. So am I . . ."

"Bad news, Horatio," Calleigh said. "Avery Barlow reported his so-called Makarov stolen a few days after he bought it."

"So we can't even ask him to produce the gun the paperwork says he owns," Horatio said.

He and Calleigh were in his office, Horatio behind the desk and Calleigh sitting in front of it. Horatio took a long, meditative sip of his coffee.

"Plus," Calleigh said, "we don't even know if his gun is the one we're after. I mean, the SPP-1 isn't common, but there's more than one out there."

"If we can't go at him from that angle, we'll try something else. If he's our guy, he's probably in the system in one way or another—military record, prior criminal involvement, probably a scuba license as well. Let's find out what we can and go from there."

"I'm on it," Calleigh said, rising from her chair. "Shake the tree, see what falls out, right?"

"You shake the tree," Horatio said, "and I'll round up some chainsaws . . ."

Wolfe passed Calleigh going out, nodded a brief hello and said to Horatio, "H? Got a minute?"

"Certainly, Mister Wolfe. What's up?"

"Talked to the manager of the Venetian Pool. He's coming in later today to look at some mug shots, see if he can identify a suspect that was spying on women underwater. I was just wondering . . ."

"Yes?"

"Well, when I was talking to him earlier, I think I . . . made an inappropriate comment. Not," he added hastily, "anything offensive, just—well, not quite professional, I guess."

"And?"

"Well, I was thinking maybe it would be better if someone else interviewed him. Calleigh and Delko are both busy, so . . ."

"So you want to know if I'll do it?"

"Could you?"

Horatio smiled. "I could . . . but I won't. Dealing with the public is part of the job, Mister Wolfe; even when you feel you have both feet firmly planted in your mouth, you carry on. Right?"

"Right, H," Wolfe admitted.

"Anyway, I have a dental appointment this afternoon."

"Oh? You have a tooth giving you trouble?"

"A whole set of them, Mister Wolfe . . ."

*   *   *

The scenes in *Psycho* that Horatio always found the most disturbing weren't the ones featuring a shower; they were the ones where a smiling Norman Bates did his best to be helpful to the clientele of his motel while the dead, glassy eyes of the animals he'd stuffed stared blindly in the background.

The shop was called Mt. Trophy Taxidermy. It was a storefront in Liberty City, arguably the worst section of Miami. Rusting iron bars on the front window caged a snarling stuffed grizzly, while an eagle with spread wings and outstretched talons appeared to be swooping down from a painted blue-sky backdrop.

Horatio stepped inside, the tinkle of a door-mounted bell announcing his entrance. The shop wasn't large, but every square inch of it was crammed with dead animals in various poses: wolverines flashed fangs at bobcats, squirrels posed alertly on driftwood, mountain goats stood shoulder to shoulder with bighorn sheep. Aquatic specimens that ranged from rapier-nosed marlins to barracuda adorned the walls; falcons and hawks hung suspended from the ceiling by nigh-invisible monofilament. The air was hot and thick and dusty, the only sound a siren dopplering into the distance like the wail of something being hunted.

Horatio looked around the menagerie of the dead slowly. There was no counter, only a card table with an ancient cash register on it.

"Hello?" he called out.

No answer. A raven gazed at him balefully from a varnished tree stump, looking as if it were just waiting for a chance to croak, "Nevermore."

Horatio walked over to the cash register, peered around for signs of anything that wasn't long deceased. There was a door in the back wall with a sign on it that read, FOR SERVICE, PLEASE STATE THE NATURE OF YOUR BUSINESS LOUDLY AND CLEARLY INTO THE VULTURE.

Sure enough, there was a turkey vulture on a shelf next to the register, its beak open in a silent cry. Horatio looked closer and saw the glint of a tiny lens in the back of its mouth.

He pulled out his badge and showed it to the bird. "Lieutenant Horatio Caine," he said. "I'd like to talk to someone about dolphin teeth."

The vulture didn't reply. Horatio waited.

There was a loud click as the door unlocked. It swung slowly open, to reveal a wide, bespectacled woman in her sixties, her grey hair up in a grandmotherly bun. She wore a stained plastic butcher's apron over a plaid shirt and jeans, and held a cordless drill in one hand.

"Well, I always knew this day would come," she sighed. "Take me away, officer. I did it. I snuffed them all."

"Uh—"

"No, wait—*stuffed*, that's what I meant. I *stuffed* them all." She smiled brightly. "Sorry, I just always wanted to say that. You have no idea how long you have to wait for a straight line, sometimes."

"In a place like this," Horatio said, "I imagine it could be a while."

She pointed her drill at him and said, "No. Idea. Don't worry, it isn't loaded. I'm Hattie Klezminster. What's this about dolphin teeth?"

The woman's not so much Norman Bates as Kathy Bates, Horatio thought. "Ms. Klezminster—"

"Hattie, please!"

"—we're conducting an investigation where a set of artificial dolphin jaws have been used in a homicide. Several people recommended you as the expert to talk to."

"Ha! I guess I do have something of a reputation in the field. I gotta tell you, though, that story about me stuffing and mounting John Wayne is strictly an urban legend. Well, the stuffing part, anyway." She beamed at him. "Well, if we're going to talk shop, that's where we should do it. C'mon in the back."

He followed her through the door. On the other side was a workshop, easily three or four times the size of the showroom. It was brightly lit by wall sconces shaped like torches, and the walls had been painted to resemble the sort of large, grey, rough-hewn stones you'd find in the basement of a castle. Those walls were adorned with trappings appropriate to a dungeon as well: skulls that ranged from the long, thin snout of a crocodile to the thick-horned mass of a bison. Furry pelts hung from a standing rack in thick, bristling rows.

The illusion was spoiled—or at least warped—by the corner stocked with power tools, including a bandsaw. Tables lined three of the walls, most of them holding animal carcasses in various states of reconstruction. Hattie went straight to a cabinet beside the bandsaw and opened it up.

"Jack Daniels is my preferred poison when talking to policemen," she stated, putting down the drill and pulling out a bottle and a glass. "You want some?"

"No, thank you."

"Didn't think so. Hell, I was just being polite." She poured herself a shot, then put the bottle back and closed the cabinet.

"Lucky you're not a reporter, or I would have had to pull out the absinthe," she said. "And the last plumber that showed up is still in rehab." She took a ladylike sip of her glass.

Horatio glanced around the room with a bemused smile on his face. "This is quite the place . . . but I have to say, your security seems a little lax for the neighborhood."

"Don't worry about me, I've got everyone in a six-block radius spooked. 'The Pet Cemetery Lady,' they all call me. And the last crackhead that decided he wanted a red-tailed hawk for a souvenir got a *big* surprise." She chuckled. "I don't keep any money in the register, but try to take one of my exhibits and the door locks, a ten-thousand-watt strobe goes off and a loop of Godzilla roaring plays at the decibel level of a jet engine. Wanna see? I've got the last three on tape."

"That's okay . . ." Horatio rubbed the back of his head. "About the dolphin teeth—"

"Right, right. What kind? Atlantic Spotted, White-sided, White-bellied, Long-beaked Common—"

"Bottlenose."

"Ah, *Tursiops truncatus*. Did you know that the 'bottle' referred to in their name is specifically an old-fashioned gin bottle? Maybe the Jack was the wrong choice . . . Dorsal fin is dark and curved back. Round melon—that's the forehead—pointed flippers, dark cape. Upper jaw has between forty and fifty-two teeth, lower between thirty-six and forty-eight. Teeth themselves are sharp, conical and around a centimeter in diameter. They use 'em, too, and not just on fish—dolphins can get downright vicious when they're competing with each other during mating season. That's how researchers tell them apart."

"By their behavior?"

"By their scars. You ever take a close look at a dolphin hide? They've got more gouges, nicks and scratches than a thirty-year-old Volvo in a bad neighborhood."

Horatio nodded. "And how difficult would it be to fake teeth like that?"

She took another drink, grinning at him over the rim of the glass. "Let me show you something and ask *you* a question, first," she said. She walked back out to the showroom, motioning for him to follow.

"There," she said, pointing to a sailfish mounted on the wall. The trophy was a good six feet in length; the needle-like nose and immense dorsal fin arched over its back gave the impression of an oversize punk-rock mosquito with an iridescent blue mohawk. "Tell me—what percentage of that fish do you think is artificial?"

Horatio studied it carefully. "Eighty-five percent?" he said.

She laughed. "Well, you did better'n most. Try one hundred."

"So it's not really a fish at all."

"Nope. It's what's called a re-creation—kind of the tofu of taxidermy. Fiberglass-reinforced polyester resin, with a painted skin. Lasts forever, and no actual fish has to die. Popular with the catch-and-release crowd."

"I see. What about constructing a working model?"

"You mean something that could actually bite someone? Well, anything's possible. Lemme show you something else."

They went back into the workshop. Hattie went over to a tall wooden cabinet, fished in her pocket for a key, and unlocked it. She threw open the double doors that ran down its length with a flourish; a row of spotlights mounted inside came on automatically.

"Well?" she asked with a mischievous look in her eye. "What do you think?"

"I think," Horatio said, "that you enjoy people's reactions almost as much as you enjoy creating your art."

The creatures displayed in the cabinet had never crawled, swum or shambled in any country on the planet. They had lurched, instead, straight from someone's bad dream into reality.

A monkey's wizened body supported the head of a pig. A human fetus with horns, a forked tail and reptillian eyes floated in a jar of greenish fluid. A two-headed calico cat—one head spitting in rage, the other cocked to the side quizically—appeared to have a winged scorpion trapped under one paw. A chihuahua with octopoidal tentacles instead of limbs used them to hold a variety of bones—some of which looked disturbingly human.

"Art, huh?" Hattie said. "Thanks. Some of the responses I get aren't as kind."

She was smiling, but there was a glint in her eye that didn't seem to have been there before; she didn't seem like a slightly eccentric grandmother anymore, but something else entirely. Horatio had a sudden urge to put his hand on his gun.

He stepped closer, bent down and examined the pieces critically. "Nice attention to detail," he said.

"I assume these are a combination of animal and artifact?"

"Yep. I haven't started messing around with animatronics yet, I'm looking into it. I just wanted to show you how far you can go with a little imagination and technical skill."

"Pretty far, I'd say," Horatio murmured. "Are these sorts of pieces common in your trade?"

"Oh, every mounter has a jackalope or a three-headed squirrel in a closet somewhere, but it's not really a big part of the business. Most people that really like this stuff wind up building Japanese monster model kits or going into special effects. I'm kind of an odd bird—I like working with actual animal parts, but I keep coming up with ways to improve on Mother Nature." She laughed and took another drink. "Well, maybe *improve* isn't quite the right word."

"Uh-huh. So working dolphin jaws aren't implausible at all . . ."

"Hell, no. Give me the time and the budget, I could probably make you a working dolphin. Of course, mine would probably have bat wings and a lion's mane."

"How many taxidermists do you know of locally that might have the skill or inclination to build a set of operating bottlenose jaws?"

She took another swig, polishing off her drink. "Let's see . . . I'd have to go over an NTA list, but I could probably come up with a half dozen names, easy. 'Dermists do more fish mounts than anything else, so there's lots of work in Florida."

Horatio pulled out a business card and handed it to her. "I'd appreciate it if you could get me that list as soon as possible."

"Sure," she said cheerfully, glancing at the card and then slipping it into a pocket. "Business is kinda *dead* right now, anyway . . ."

7

"STATISTICALLY," WOLFE SAID, "most rapes are committed by men between twenty-five and forty-four years old."

He and Delko were having lunch at Auntie Bellum's, an old-style diner not far from the Miami-Dade crime lab. Wolfe gesticulated with his grilled cheese sandwich to emphasize his point, while Delko took a tentative sip at his steaming hot *café con leche*. Three thimble-sized *tacitas* of Cuban coffee with heads of white, sugary foam were lined up in front of him like shot glasses of beer.

"Yeah, and the ratio of black rapists to white is approximately fifty/fifty—the same as the proportion of rapists that know their victims to the ones that don't," Delko said. "Which means, statistically, that those numbers are basically useless. There's a slight tendency for the rapist's victims to skew toward his own race, but not enough to be much help."

"Well, maybe not in any obvious way," Wolfe said. "But it helps give us an overall picture." He took a bite of his sandwich.

"Remember what Mark Twain said," Delko advised. "'There are three kinds of lies: lies, damned lies, and statistics.' The so-called typical rapist, according to the stats, is a twenty-year-old male from a low socioeconomic group with priors for acquisitive crimes like robbery—at least according to law-enforcement data. But other sources say the number of rapists that know their victims is closer to eighty percent—that the extra thirty percent is never reported."

"But that's unreliable data," Wolfe countered. "It's just conjecture."

"Conjecture by people with experience," Delko said. "The eighty-percent figure comes from people working in rape crisis centers."

"That's not exactly an objective source."

"Rape isn't exactly an objective subject."

"No, but *we're* supposed to be objective." Wolfe shook his head. "I don't know. It seems to me that being murdered is worse than being raped, but the last time I expressed that opinion a woman almost punched my lights out."

Delko put down his coffee cup and tossed back one of the Cuban shots. "Big surprise. Do you *ever* date?"

"Actually, this was *on* a date."

Delko grinned. "Yeah, I imagine *that* went over

well . . . Look, our job as CSIs is to collect information and process data, but that doesn't mean we're machines. Objectivity is one thing, being disconnected from humanity is another. You have to remember *why* we do what we do." Delko glanced around, then pointed a finger at two teenage girls in another booth. "See those girls? Complete strangers to us, right? We'll probably never meet, never exchange a word between us—but if we do our job the way we're supposed to, we make their lives safer. You can't quantify that, can't measure it—but sometimes, after a long day at work, it can make getting to sleep a little easier."

Wolfe stared at him. Took a bite of his grilled cheese sandwich, chewed it thoughtfully, swallowed. "So what you're saying," he said at last, "is that it's okay to think about teenage girls before you go to sleep."

"Are you *sure* your date didn't punch you out?" Delko downed another shot of *café cubano*.

Wolfe frowned. "You know, caffeine isn't actually a stimulant."

"I agree. It's more like the stuff of life itself."

"Seriously. All caffeine does is block the receptor sites for adenosine, which helps regulate neurotransmitter production. It doesn't even do that perfectly—if it did, it would be a depressant."

"I'd *still* seriously consider decking anyone who stood between me and the first cup of the day."

"Yeah, well, I wouldn't advise drinking any

more than you've got right there. Studies have shown that after four cups of strong coffee, it starts interfering with phosphodiesterase. It'll actually make you less alert, not more."

"Maybe in a lesser man. I've been drinking this stuff for so long my tolerance isn't normal."

"So you're an addict."

Delko sighed extravagantly. "I can't deny it. In my defense, Your Honor, I plead an upbringing of Coke, Pepsi and Mountain Dew."

"Laugh if you want, but it's still a drug. A hard-core coffeehound like yourself probably needs ten to fifteen times more caffeine than when you started. Take it away, and you'll get withdrawal symptoms: headaches, fatigue, depression, increased muscle tension, lethargy—even vomiting."

"Ten to fifteen times?" Delko shrugged. "That I can live with. A long-term heroin addict can need *ten thousand times* his starting dose—if I start downing that much coffee, you have my permission to perform an intervention."

"Well, you won't be hard to locate. I'll just look for the guy with a bladder the size of a Volkswagen."

"Yeah, and the attention span of a hummingbird. Be nice if our perp was that easy to spot . . . You said you have someone coming in to look at mug shots?"

"In about an hour. Witnessed a peeping Tom-type at a public pool—figure it fits our guy's profile."

"Something tells me that when we catch him, our guy is gonna turn out to be one of a kind."

"Maybe. More than twenty percent of rapes involve more than one perpetrator. And don't scuba divers always use a buddy system?"

Delko stopped with his last coffee shot halfway to his lips. "You know, I never thought of that. I mean, it's such a . . . *unique* crime in the first place, it never occurred to me there might be more than one guy involved. Have you mentioned this to H?"

"Not yet. It just came to me while we were talking, actually. You think I'm right?"

"Don't know. But maybe we should revisit some of the evidence and see if it fits."

"You know what this means, don't you?"

"What?"

"Statistics aren't so bad after all . . ."

Horatio spent much of the day talking to taxidermists, working off the list Hattie Klezminster had faxed him. Most of them dealt with fish, a few worked in special effects, but none of them had created a working dolphin-jaw re-creation.

The most interesting man he talked to was a Mexican named Felipe Segredo. Felipe was semi-retired, but he still did the occasional high-end piece; he was well known in Guadalajara, he said, where he had established his reputation in the eighties by doing custom work for drug kingpins.

"It's not what you think," he assured Horatio. "I

mean, it wasn't like I was hollowing out water buffaloes so they could be stuffed with bags of cocaine. No, it was all about prestige. Someone saw one of my pieces, a lion I did for a department store display, and he demanded to buy it on the spot. A few days later, I get a call from someone who claims he's a friend of the first man, and he wants something bigger—a Bengal tiger. The next thing you know, I'm making full-size Indian elephant mounts with a built-in wet bar."

Horatio had asked him how he knew what his clients did for a living, and Felipe had laughed. "You know, when you show up to install a piece at a house the size of a shopping mall, and five guys with machine guns pat you down before you go inside, it's not too hard to figure out. And of course, they always paid in cash."

But those days, Felipe said, were long gone. These days, he did more re-creations than mounting actual dead animals, and his customers tended more toward sport fishermen than drug runners. "Most of those guys are probably dead or in prison by now," he said cheerfully. "But me, I'm still around. The grim reaper doesn't bother with me, and you know why? Professional courtesy."

Felipe had laughed again.

Horatio had only smiled.

Calleigh Dusquesne didn't know what to do.

She could tell you the make and model of every

gun that had ever passed through her hands. She could list every major manufacturer of firearms in the world and most of the minor ones. She could make a bullet do everything but sit up and talk.

But photocopiers were her nemesis.

She glared at the implacable machine in front of her. It wasn't that she had any trouble understanding how it worked—or was supposed to work, anyway—because that was perfectly straightforward. And even if it wasn't, Calleigh got along just fine with all sorts of technology; she could send a fax or upload a file as easily as she could fieldstrip and reassemble an AR-15 rifle, which is to say without much thought at all.

But photocopiers *hated* her.

She knew it wasn't rational. She knew it made no sense at all. Nonetheless, she had witnessed a copy machine calmly print and collate fifty copies of a three-hundred-word document with nary a problem, then choke to death in front of her when she tried to run off a single page. She had long since stopped trying to understand the phenomenon, and now just tried to avoid it.

"One. Copy," she hissed at the stubborn thing. "That's all I need, and then I'll leave you alone. Mess with me, and I swear I'll introduce you to the business end of a SIG-Sauer P-220."

"Ahem," Horatio said.

She spun around. "Ah, hi there, Horatio," she said. "Been there long?"

"Well, I wasn't here for the start of the conflict, but I did arrive in time for the death threats . . ."

She colored. "I know it's stupid," she said. "But unless I threaten it, the darn thing doesn't take me *seriously*."

"That," Horatio said, "would be a serious mistake on its part—or parts, as the case may be."

"Thank you. Anyway, I think I may have something on Avery Barlow." She handed him the sheet of paper in her hand. "Seems Mister Barlow not only collects a variety of unusual weapons, he sells them as well. He's got his own online business, which deals in all sorts of things: knives, swords, blowguns, you name it. All of which is legal—at least in Florida."

"But?"

"But some of the things he sells are prohibited weapons in other states. New York, for instance, bans the sale of martial arts weapons like throwing stars and nunchuks—both of which he offers on his site. But I figure NY is too big a market and too close to ignore, so he's probably shipping stuff there anyway."

"Which would only help us if we were in New York."

Calleigh smiled. "True. What *does* help us is a friend of mine named Danny Fortrenzo. He's a cop in Queens I met at a conference two years ago, heavily into Ninjitsu—you know, the martial art that Ninjas are supposed to use? Anyway, he col-

lects the kind of stuff that Barlow sells, so I gave
him a call. He did some checking around for me
and sure enough, found a couple of people who
claimed they'd bought prohibited weapons from
Barlow's site—including ballistic knives."

Horatio smiled back. "Which are just as illegal
in Florida as New York. Do we have anything more
than hearsay to back it up?"

"That's what I was photocopying. See, authen-
tication is important to collectors, so Barlow pro-
vides documentation wherever possible. What
you're holding is a form Danny faxed me stating
that this particular ballistic knife was once owned
by the son of Bruce Lee."

"Your friend got it to you awfully quick," Horatio observed.

"Well, I didn't ask him who actually purchased
the knife . . . but the form proves Barlow was in
possession of an illegal weapon. Who has it now
is a matter for New York."

"Leaving the person who sold it squarely in our
purview," Horatio said. "Good work. This should
be enough for a warrant to look at his current
stock—and I'm betting Mister Barlow has more
than one thing under his roof that he
shouldn't . . ."

Horatio was still waiting on the warrant when
Wolfe showed up in his office. "H, think I got
something," he said. "Manager of the Venetian

Pool just IDed the guy that was ogling women underwater. Ezekial Redfield, one prior for sexual assault, one for breaking and entering."

Horatio was already up and moving. "We have an address?" he said as he strode into the hall, Wolfe close on his heels.

"Yeah. North Miami. Spitting distance from Biscayne Bay."

"Then let's go get him . . ."

Delko went over the car again, inch by inch. As he did, he tried to imagine the sequence of events that would have taken place if there were two attackers instead of one.

Okay. Do they both attack her at once, or does each one have a specific job to do?

The rusted, dented hulk of the car seemed like the empty shell of some dead mollusk or crab, and the reek it gave off reinforced the impression. He knelt on the front seat and ran his hands along the underside of the dash.

The attack was planned in advance, by a person or persons familiar with diving. They would have split up the responsibilities, thought of different scenarios in advance. There were a lot of variables in diving, and Delko knew the mindset an experienced diver developed: calculate everything you could beforehand, to make sure there *was* an afterward.

*   *   *

The house in the middle of the block was like a rotten tooth in a friendly smile. The houses on either side weren't large or expensive, but they were neatly maintained; red tile roofs were kept in good repair, green lawns were mowed and watered. Ezekial Redfield's residence, though, was sagging, dirty, and in bad need of a coat of paint. The weed-filled front yard was bounded by a wooden fence with many slats missing and no gate. Dirty, stained curtains were visible through the windows that faced the street, and the moss growing on the roof was thicker than the shingles.

"Stay sharp," Horatio told Wolfe as they stepped onto the porch. He rapped on the peeling surface of the wooden door, waited a moment, then did it again. No answer.

Then they both heard it.

"Is that—splashing?" Wolfe asked.

So one stays on the bottom with the extra tank. The other goes hunting. They pick a spot with enough traffic to insure a victim comes along sooner or later.

Nothing under the dash. Delko hunkered down, shone a flashlight under the seats.

No, that doesn't work. Makes more sense if they hunt together—they can clamp on and drag a victim down quicker. Plus they have to get the regulator on her somehow while she's thrashing around, panicked and on the verge of drowning.

Nothing under the seats, either—just like the last time he looked. He got out, thought for a second, then climbed into the backseat.

So they somehow get the regulator in her mouth. Get her calmed down enough to understand the situation. How do they communicate with her?

Scuba divers often used dive tablets and underwater writing implements; the rapists must have, too.

Horatio pounded on the door. "Miami-Dade police!" he shouted. "Open the door, *now*!"

Wolfe drew his gun a second after Horatio did. Horatio tried the door, found it was unlocked. He pushed it open slowly with one hand.

With the door open, the splashing was louder, almost frenzied. Horatio entered, moving quickly but cautiously, his Glock held rock steady in front of him with his finger on the trigger. There was a foyer of sorts, with a table overflowing with old newspapers and junkmail taking up most of it. The splashing was coming from a room to the left, off a short corridor.

Horatio motioned for Wolfe to stay where he was, then crept down the hall. Now that he was inside, he could hear another noise, underneath the first: a low, throbbing hum.

The rest of the scenario was brutally simple. They would have taken turns, the one not with the vic-

tim either standing guard or returning to a dive
boat. They would have waited until near the end
before they started cutting her, to avoid unnece-
sary attention from sharks—

*Wait. She would have been bleeding from the dolphin-
jaw device all along. Why use something that will attract
sharks when you have two sets of hands to subdue her
from the very start?*

He frowned. It just wouldn't quite add up . . .

The smell in the back of the car was somehow
worse than up front. Delko wondered where
they'd kept the air tanks, the front or the back—
they'd want them close by to make any adjust-
ments. Probably the front, leaving the roomier rear
half of the vehicle free.

Free to commit unspeakable atrocities.

The anger in the pit of his belly surprised Delko.
He had dealt with horrible crimes before, but this
one was different—and he knew why. Diving had
always been an activity he associated with a certain kind of serenity, a certain kind of peace. Even
when recovering a string of bodies tied to an an-
chor, he could maintain a certain distance from
the horror. That came partly from professionalism,
but also from the sense of control he got from diving; under the water, you had to be the master of
your environment or the environment would kill
you.

Now that feeling of control had been tainted,
corrupted. The killer or killers had perverted it into

a tool for inflicting pain and death. He felt like a sculptor who'd just found someone murdered with a chisel.

The best word for the sight that greeted Horatio as he whipped around the corner, gun aimed ahead of him, was *bizarre*.

The only furniture in the room was an immense fishtank, with a capacity of several hundred gallons at least. Belly-high, it stood on a bare wooden floor with a short ladder—the kind used for kid's bunk beds—propped against it. Illumination was provided by several green spotlights on the far side of the room, shining through the tank and silhouetting what was inside.

The pulsing hum came from an air compressor beside the tank. Two thick, black hoses led from the compressor into the water, providing oxygen to the tank's occupants: a naked man and woman. The splashing came from the woman's legs, which stuck out of the water and were moving vigorously.

Horatio moved forward, took out his badge and rapped on the glass, which prompted an immediate response: they stopped what they were doing and stared at him, startled eyes wide behind the glass of the full-face scuba masks they wore. They disentangled and surfaced, the man pulling his mask off first.

"What the *hell* are you doing in my house?" he

exclaimed angrily. The woman kept her mask on, giving Horatio the feeling he was being studied by some kind of undersea alien.

"Interrupting a bout of synchronized swimming, apparently," Horatio said. "You *must* be Ezekial Redfield . . ."

8

EZEKIAL REDFIELD WAS as described: short, powerfully built, with barely a millimeter of red-blond stubble covering the top of his head. He'd dressed in baggy white shorts, a Miami Dolphins sports jersey and white sneakers to come down to the station, and Horatio was still trying to decide if the shirt was Redfield's attempt to be clever. He stared at Horatio with pale blue eyes and a scowl, slouched in his chair on the other side of the table like a recalcitrant high-school student.

Horatio stared back, then glanced down at the rap sheet in front of him. "Mister Redfield. It appears you have a certain affinity for water sports."

Redfield smiled. It was an unpleasant expression, exposing crooked, nicotine-stained teeth. "Water sports? Nah. That's like golden showers and stuff, I'm not into that. I'm an aquaphile."

"Right . . . and your 'aquaphilia' extends to sexual assault, does it?"

"Weren't you paying attention, cop? Wasn't no assault involved—she was *into* it, man. Got some mermaid in her, for sure."

"I was referring," Horatio said, "to some of your past activities."

"Hey, that was all a mistake, awright? Just a misunderstanding."

"The young lady who filed charges against you felt otherwise."

"Yeah, well, she *dropped* those charges, so no harm done."

"I'm afraid I don't agree, Mister Redfield. And the conviction for breaking and entering—an aquarium supply shop?—tells me this little quirk of yours is more than just a hobby. I'd say it's closer to an obsession."

Redfield studied him through half-closed eyes. "I don't expect someone like you to understand."

"So make me."

"You wanna know? Okay, I'll tell you. There's no big secret—it's not like I was molested by a fish or something. I just like water. I like floating, I like the way sound is all echoey and muffled. I like the feeling of something warm and wet touching every inch of my skin. It turns me on. Is that so bad?"

"No," Horatio said. "It's not. But sexually assaulting a lifeguard while trying to drown her is."

"Hey, you really *don't* understand. I wasn't trying to drown her, I was the one *drowning*."

"According to the report, you pretended to have trouble swimming, tried to drag her under the water when she came to your aid."

"It's common for drowning victims to panic and push their rescuer under the water."

Horatio noted that Redfield didn't actually deny that he'd done so. "Is it also common for them to feign unconsciousness and then grope their rescuer as she's performing mouth-to-mouth?"

"I *was* unconscious. I didn't know what I was doing."

"You know, Ezekial, that almost sounds reasonable . . . except, of course, it was the third time you'd tried it."

Redfield grinned and shrugged. "Guess I'm just not a very strong swimmer."

"Yet you have a scuba-diving license."

"Hell, anyone can swim with fins and an airtank."

"Is that so. You do any diving in Biscayne Bay recently? Say off Oleta River State Park or Key Biscayne?"

"Maybe. I dive a lot, all over the place."

Horatio nodded. "But only kill people in a few of them."

Redfield's mouth opened, but no sound came out.

Horatio put his forearms on the table and leaned

forward. "Here's what's happening. Right now, my team is going over your place with a very fine-tooth comb. They have a warrant to confiscate your computer, your scuba equipment and anything with a cutting edge. They're going to process it all, and I think they're going to find evidence that you killed Gabrielle Cavanaugh, David Stonecutter and Janice Stonecutter."

Redfield finally found his voice. "What? That's—that's ridiculous! I'm not a killer! I'm—I'm the opposite!"

His response was odd enough to make Horatio hesitate. "What, exactly, is *that* supposed to mean?"

And now Redfield looked more than scared—he looked embarrassed, too. "Look, being an aquaphile isn't just about being turned on by H_2O. A bunch of us, we also have fantasies about drowning. But it's a *passive* thing, all right? That's what I was going for with those lifeguards—I wasn't trying to hurt any of them, I swear to God. I just . . ." He stopped, looking miserable. His next words came out as a hoarse whisper. "I just wanted to have someone beautiful hold me underwater."

Horatio studied him. "If you're innocent," he said, "then you won't mind providing a sample of your DNA, will you?"

"No. No, of course not."

Horatio had a kit with him. He opened it, then

pulled out a pair of gloves and pulled them on in preparation for taking the swab.

"Uh, just be really careful with those," Redfield said nervously.

"Don't worry, I've done this before," Horatio said. He stood up and came around the table.

Redfield held up a hand. "No, I mean the gloves—keep 'em away from me, unless you want to deal with someone going into anaphylactic shock. I'm really, really allergic to latex."

Horatio stopped.

"Is that so?" he asked mildly.

"Tough break," Calleigh said. "He really was allergic, huh?"

"According to his medical records," Horatio said. He and Calleigh were in his Hummer, on the way to serving Avery Barlow with a search warrant.

"Yeah, latex is one of those things people can have really severe reactions to, like peanuts or shellfish," Calleigh said. "Latex itself is a very weird substance. Nobody really knows the reasons some plants produce it—some scientists think it's a defense against predation or wounding; others say that rubber and other hydrocarbon compounds are carbon traps that maintain the balance between atmospheric CO_2 and planetary biomass. There's even a theory that the isoprene emissions latex-producing species give off are Mother Nature's antidote for ozone."

"In that case, Mother Nature doesn't seem to be too crazy about Ezekial Redfield. About one percent of natural liquid latex is made up of proteins, and those proteins can trigger three types of immune response: irritation, delayed hypersensitivity and immediate hypersensitivity. Guess which one our boy has."

"I'm gonna go with door number three."

"Bingo. The latex allergens bind to the receptors on mast cells, causing a massive release of histamine—which leads to hives, itching eyes, swelling of lips and tongue, breathlessness, dizziness, abdominal pain, nausea, hypotension, shock . . . and death." Horatio shook his head. "He's so sensitive he started to breathe funny as soon as I opened my kit."

"Probably from the cornstarch on your gloves," Calleigh said. "Most medical products use ammoniated latex; the curing process involves heating them to a hundred-and-thirty C for thirty minutes, which can cause proteins in the latex—including new ones that form during vulcanization—to leach into the powder they coat the inside of the gloves with."

"Well, there's no way he could stand to have the stuff next to his skin," Horatio said. "Still, his allergy doesn't entirely eliminate him as a suspect. Wolfe has a theory that there may have been more than one attacker, in which case the latex sample we found might have come from the other one. He's checking out Redfield's alibi right now."

They pulled up in front of Barlow's apartment building and got out. Frank Tripp was already there, warrant in hand.

"Horatio. Calleigh," he said with a nod. "Ready when you are."

This time when Avery Barlow opened his door, Horatio didn't bother being polite. He just held up the warrant and said, "Step outside, Mister Barlow. We're going to do a little inventory of your merchandise."

Barlow took the warrant and stepped into the hallway. "Knock yourselves out," he said.

Calleigh and Horatio entered. The place was spacious, decorated in an Asian theme: hanging red silk lanterns, white rice-paper screens, low-slung couches upholstered in dragon-print satin. Horatio examined a set of Japanese swords on the wall, and wondered if they'd been bought from Max.

"A *tachi* and *nodachi*," Calleigh said. "The *tachi* is slightly longer and more curved than a traditional *wakizashi*, for cavalry use; the *nodachi* has the extended handle because it's worn slung over the swordsman's back. Depending on the smith, the steel used could have as many as sixty-five thousand folds."

"Yes," Horatio said. "And an owner with a lot less integrity. Let's see what he has in the other rooms . . ."

That Barlow operated his business out of his

apartment was obvious when they looked in the
guest bedroom. It was stacked, top to bottom, with
weaponry: machetes, crossbows, battleaxes, everything from medieval swords and fencing foils to
knives and batons and body armor.

"I don't see any firearms," Calleigh said. "Though
I do see a suspicious indentation in the carpet right
next to this door."

"As if something heavy had recently been
moved . . . it seems our previous visit made Mister Barlow a little nervous. He's relocated that por-
tion of his stock we might find questionable—but
that doesn't mean there isn't anything left to find.
Let's go to work."

What Delko was looking for was a message.

The question, he thought, *is whether Janice Stonecutter was left alone long enough to leave one.*

He was still in the garage, studying the car. If
there were two attackers, she probably wasn't;
they would have taken turns, and tried to wring
every last second of sadistic pleasure out of her
captivity.

But if there was only one, chances were good
that he would have left her to return to the surface sometime during that twelve to fifteen hours.
She would have had to be restrained of course, to
keep her from taking her own life as well as trying to escape. But how?

He remembered the white rope he'd found,

tethered to the mock submarine. Maybe she'd been tied up with more of that, in such a way that she couldn't move. Still, the captor's intentions put certain sheerly mechanical factors of positioning into play—factors he'd rather not think about, but which had to be considered.

Her hands would have certainly been restrained. Even if they weren't, what would she have to write with, or on? To scratch a message in metal required a tool she wouldn't have. He checked the upholstery carefully, but it was leather and too tough to mark easily.

Which left . . .

Delko pulled out his cell phone and called Alexx.

"Mister Barlow," Horatio said. "I'm so happy you finally decided to cooperate with us."

"Yeah, you're a real model citizen," Frank Tripp said.

On the other side of the interview table, Avery Barlow responded to their sarcasm with a look that suggested both disdain and boredom. "I just want to get this cleared up so I can get back to running a business, right?" he said. He was even dressed like a businessman, in a three-piece pale green silk suit so finely tailored it made Horatio feel underdressed. Barlow's shaved head shone like it was freshly waxed—which, Horatio supposed, it probably was. He'd nicked himself over one ear, too.

"Yes, the vital and life-affirming work of a weapons dealer," Horatio said. "You may have hidden some of your stock from us, Mister Barlow, but your days of selling illegal weapons are over. We're going to be keeping a very close eye on you from now on, and I understand you'll shortly be getting a visit from the Queens DA's office."

Barlow shook his head. "Then I guess I'll have to be careful, won't I?"

"You can do more than that. Give us the information we're looking for, maybe we can persuade our friends from NYC to go easy on you. Local jurisdiction counts for a lot."

Barlow smiled. "This would be about the SPP-1, right? The underwater pistol you're looking for?"

"That's correct."

Barlow sighed. "Suppose I have some information on its present whereabouts. If I give you said information, can you assure me that I won't be charged with filing a false police report?"

"If," Tripp growled, "said information is accurate, I don't see a problem."

"Then I think I can help you," Barlow said smoothly. "I have the gun."

Horatio studied him carefully before he responded. "And you're willing to turn it over to us?"

"Sure. It's not like I committed a crime with it . . ."

* * *

Alexx pulled the body drawer open. "Janice Stone-cutter," she told Delko. "Did my best to sew her back together, but she was pretty cut up." She pulled back the sheet covering the corpse.

Delko nodded. "Yeah. No offense, Alexx, but I think there might be something you missed. Something everybody missed."

The raised eyebrows on Alexx's face told him she wasn't exactly pleased with his assessment. "And what, exactly, are you looking for?"

"The last words of a dead woman," Delko murmured. "Except it may not be in words, as such." He ran the illuminated magnifier he held slowly over the DB's torso, carefully examining the stitches that covered it. There were so many they resembled a patchwork quilt made of flesh.

"See, I remembered that Janice had long fingernails. We didn't find anything under them, but that doesn't mean she didn't use them. Thing is, I don't think she used them on her attacker—I think she might have used them on *herself.*"

"You mean cutting a message into her own *skin*?"

"Yeah. It would have been the only tool she had, and the only surface she could use. Depending on how she was bound, there would have been a limited number of places on her own body she could reach. If it was anyplace but on the torso, I'm sure you would have found it."

"Hmph," Alexx said, only slightly mollified. "So you think it was on her belly?"

"You tell me," Delko said. He held the magnifier still, motioned her to bend over and look. She did.

When she straightened up, she looked mortified. "Eric, I'm sorry. I don't know *how* I could have—"

"Hey, I missed it first, remember?" Delko said. "Let's not play the blame game. The question now is, what was she trying to tell us?"

"Depends on what that symbol represents." The scratch that Delko had found was shaped like an X with a vertical line through it; unless you were specifically looking for it, it simply disappeared into the crisscross of wounds.

"Oh, I know what it represents," Delko said grimly. "What I don't know is what it *means* . . ."

"Good news or bad news first?" Calleigh asked. She and Horatio were in the ballistics lab and she'd finished examining Barlow's pistol.

"I'll take the bad," Horatio said.

"This isn't the gun used to kill David Stonecutter," Calleigh said. "Actually, I don't think this gun has been fired in a while. And while it's possible Avery Barlow simply gave us the wrong gun, there's no proof he owns more than one."

"All right—but if the gun isn't our murder weapon, why report it stolen?"

"Maybe he just saw an opportunity to take advantage of some shoddy paperwork. The gun drops off the books, he can sell it and not report the income."

"That's a possibility. And the good news?"

"While he was in a cooperative mood, I asked Mister Barlow about Farallon shark darts. Seeing as how they aren't illegal, he was willing to give me some information about one or two that have passed through his hands."

"You have addresses?"

She pulled a list out of the pocket of her lab coat with a smile. "I do."

"Well then," Horatio said, "perhaps Mister Barlow will turn out to be a civic-minded citizen after all . . ."

Horatio wasn't really surprised when the investigation ground to a halt.

It had nothing to do with the diligence of his team, or even a lack of evidence. It was simply that a number of leads had all turned into dead ends simultaneously, which to an outside observer would look like there was no place left to go.

Horatio knew different.

Ezekial Redfield had been visiting an aquarium in Georgia when the Stonecutters were killed, though his whereabouts during Gabrielle Cavanaugh's death were less provable; home watching *The Little Mermaid II* on DVD was hardly a rock-solid alibi, but Horatio thought it was probably the truth.

Avery Barlow claimed to do most of his business from his home, and had been online during the times Gabrielle Cavanaugh had gone missing and Janice Stonecutter had been tortured. His computer records seemed to confirm it.

Of the three Farallon shark darts Barlow had bought and sold, two had been shipped out of the country, one to Europe and one to South America. The last one had been sold to a surly, seventeen-year-old punk rocker in Little Haiti, who reluctantly handed it over after Horatio had a brief and extremely polite talk with him. The kid had cut the shaft down to a short handle and wrapped it in black electrical tape, turning it into a shiv. Calleigh was examining it to make sure, but she'd taken one look at how the full CO_2 canister was securely bonded to the frame with rust and said it had probably never been used.

And then Delko had shown him what he'd found.

Horatio studied a photo of the mark on Janice Stonecutter's stomach and said, "You're right. It's much shallower and more jagged than the other cuts."

"Yeah," Delko said. "You recognize it?"

"I do," Horatio said. "It's a letter in the Cyrillic alphabet, though I couldn't tell you which one."

"Zheh," Delko said. "As in 'Zhivago'."

"And also," Horatio said grimly, "Doctor Nicole Zhenko."

That's what happens when a case seems to be jammed up, Horatio thought. *You just have to poke at the right piece, and suddenly everything starts moving again . . .*

Calleigh liked order. She liked her guns cleaned and oiled and neatly stored, her boxes of ammunition sorted and clearly marked, her paper targets filed in the correct drawer. When she wasn't busy on a case, she devoted a set amount of time every week for maintenance of her workspace, making sure everything was in its proper place.

When she *was* on a case her priorities were entirely different—but she still tried to keep things orderly. She was doing a little straightening up when Wolfe walked in and asked her if she had a minute.

"Sure, Ryan," she said, slipping a file folder into a drawer and closing it. "What's up?"

"Got two different things on the go and I was wondering if you could take one of them on."

"Do I get to pick which one?"

He hesitated, then said, "Actually, I was kind of hoping—"

She sighed. "Let me guess. One involves fieldwork and the other the lab?"

"Well, yeah—"

"I'll take the lab work."

He smiled. "Good. That's what I was going to ask you to do."

She looked at him suspiciously. "Wait a minute, that was too easy. Either you're going out to interview suspects in a strip club or the lab work involves something extremely disgusting."

"Nope. Actually, I have to go out to Verdant Springs to talk to this woman about a possible sexual assault."

"And the lab work?"

"Testing commercial latex samples against the scrap we found under Gabrielle Cavanaugh's fingernails."

She shook her head. "Okay, I don't get it. You're passing up actual, genuine science in favor of conducting an emotionally volatile interview with a stranger? What gives?"

Wolfe shrugged. "Just taking Horatio's advice. Dealing with the public is part of the job, right?"

"Absolutely. A suggestion, though?"

"What's that?"

"Try not to mention the aliens and their ice-cream ray. I find it makes people look at you funny . . ."

Horatio didn't spend much time in his office, but he was there now. He sat behind his desk with the lights off, the only light leaking from the cracks between the blinds. He steepled his hands in front of his face, stared at nothing in particular and thought.

Like many cops, Horatio believed in knowing as

many of the answers as possible before starting to ask questions. The research he'd initially done on Doctor Zhenko was mainly to establish her scientific credentials; neither her activist background nor the loss of her legs had been mentioned in the articles he found. It hadn't been until after their first meeting that he'd gone a little deeper—partly out of curiosity, partly out of instinct—and brought some of the darker details of her past to the surface.

Her legs had been taken by a tiger shark, while she was on a dive off the Great Barrier Reef in Australia. Double above-the-knee amputations hadn't been enough to get her to give up the water, though it had changed her priorities. After the attack she'd gotten involved in the Animal Liberation Alliance, a militant animal rights group whose tactics bordered on ecoterrorism—a border they apparently crossed two years ago when several of their members were arrested during a demonstration on a fishing dock. Somebody had planted explosive charges on the bottom of seven fishing trawlers, somebody with experience in both scuba diving and underwater demolitions.

Doctor Nicole Zhenko had the former but not— as far as Horatio could determine—the latter. But the killer Horatio was hunting didn't necessarily have a military background; he just hated the Navy.

He . . . or she. Doctor Zhenko's disapproval of

how the Navy treated dolphins was obvious. And so far, despite the rapes, there was no definitive evidence that the killer was male. Doctor Zhenko had already demonstrated she was proficient with one kind of prosthesis—why not another?

Rape, Horatio knew, was less about sexual release than it was about violence and control. While there were few female serial killers, they did exist. And one of the things that often pushed a serial killer over the edge from fantasy to murder was a traumatic event—losing a job, a spouse, a parent.

A limb?

He could hear indistinct voices beyond his door, cops and office workers discussing cases, making small talk, the occasional burst of laughter. Underneath it, the omnipresent hum of the building's air-conditioning. The cool, muffled dimness was almost like being underwater . . .

9

HORATIO PARKED THE HUMMER and got out. He
paused on the sidewalk and slipped on his shades,
the heat coming off the cracked cement making
him feel like he was standing on a griddle. He
stared at the building in front of him for a moment, trying to get a sense of the place.

The headquarters for the Animal Liberation Alliance was in a secondhand thrift store, a cracked
and peeling yellow wooden door beside a dirty
plate-glass window with the words *ALA Charity
Rummage and Goods* painted on it in fading green.
On the other side of the glass were a few items: a
wicker basket full of golf clubs, some Key West
T-shirts, a tray of sunglasses and a few stuffed animals—the plush kind as opposed to deceased and
mounted. Horatio pulled the door open and went
in.

The interior was hot, the air heavy and dead.

Dust motes moved sluggishly through the air, too tired to dance. The room was long and narrow, crowded with racks of clothes and open cardboard boxes on the floor overflowing with used gimme caps and cheap scarves. It wore the reek of old polyester like a bug repellent for youth.

A glass display case doubled as a counter, holding a cash register on top and a bored-looking man behind it. The case itself held an assortment of watches, rings and bracelets, none of which looked as if they were worth the glass protecting them. The man was in his forties, with a long, sallow face, wispy brown hair framing a freckled pate, and a large, thin-lipped mouth. He wore a faded orange T-shirt, tan shorts and nylon sandals, and was the only person in the shop.

There was a stack of photocopied sheets next to the cash register. Horatio picked one up and studied it. It was a rant against animal exploitation, featuring grainy, black-and-white slaughterhouse pictures and details of the alleged practices of the cattle, poultry and fur industries. It ended with a plea for donations and a box office number to send them to.

"We don't carry any animal products whatsoever," the clerk said. "No leather, no fur, not even wool."

"Commendable," Horatio said. He pulled aside his jacket, revealing the badge clipped to his belt. "And you are?"

"Malcolm. Torrence," the man said, his tone shifting to something colder and more formal. "Is there a problem?"

"Well, that depends, Malcolm. I'm looking for an associate of yours—Anatoly Kazimir. Is he around?"

Torrence gave a dry little grunt of laughter. "No. No, he's not. He hasn't been around for a while, and he's not going to be around for a while yet."

"And what," Horatio said, "is that supposed to mean?"

"It means he's not here."

Horatio smiled. It wasn't a happy smile, but Malcolm seemed unfazed. "I gathered that, Malcolm. Seeing as how his absence leaves something of a hole in my social calendar, maybe you can take his place."

Malcolm looked at him with eyes as flat as painted glass.

"What I had in mind," Horatio continued, "was a nice long game of twenty questions, with a different set of rules. See, I get to ask as many questions as I can think of . . . and if you give me the wrong answers, there's a penalty."

Horatio's smile got a little wider. "Now, I would *rather* play this game with Mister Kazimir. But if he's unavailable, I suppose you'll have to do . . ."

Malcolm gave another grunt of laughter. "Okay. Sure. But I got something to say before I tell you where he is."

"Go ahead."

"You guys are all the same. Big guns in leather holsters. Scratch a cop and you'll find a cowboy underneath, all swagger and yee-haw and let's-go-shoot something. You all think you're at the top of the food chain—well, you're *not*."

Horatio eyed him coolly, but said nothing.

"You want to know what is?" Malcolm continued. "*Worms*. The worms eat us all, my friend. Even you."

"Well, I hope they like barbecue," Horatio said, "because I'm seriously considering cremation. Now—where is Anatoly Kazimir?"

And Malcolm told him.

"Good job spotting Janice Stonecutter's message," Calleigh said. She was in the lab, getting Wolfe's latex samples ready for testing.

"Thanks," Delko said, slipping on his lab coat. "I don't think Alexx is very happy with me, though."

"Oh, she's just angry with herself. Sometimes we focus so much on esoteric details that a more obvious piece of information gets lost. It's happened to all of us—I think she just takes it a little more personally."

"Well, I hope she doesn't take it out on me. She gave me a look in the break room that could freeze vodka . . . What are you working on?"

"Trying to figure out exactly where the scrap of latex we found under Gabrielle Cavanaugh's fingernail came from."

"Yeah? I thought Wolfe was working on that."

"He's following up a lead on a sexual-assault victim. Did you know that opium is a latex?"

Delko came over and peered at the samples she had laid out. "Yeah, they make cuts in the seed pod and collect what bleeds out," he said. "Similar to what they do to rubber trees. Why? You think our killer is a junkie, too?"

"No, I'm just spouting trivia," she said cheerfully. "In school, my favorite sport was show-and-tell."

"Mine was recess," Delko said with a grin. "That's when you could talk to girls without getting in trouble. Well, much trouble, anyway."

"*Anyway,*" Calleigh replied archly, "there are a number of different ways to shape latex. We don't have to worry about foam rubber, thread or adhesives, which leaves three possibilities. The first is dipping, which is pretty self-explanatory: a template made of porcelain or glass is dipped into a coagulant of calcium nitrate, then into a bath of prevulcanized latex, after which it's dried and vulcanized. That's how gloves, balloons and condoms are produced."

"Think they ever get them mixed up?"

"Let's hope not. The next time I'm gloving up I don't want to be suddenly confronted by something featuring ribbing and a reservoir tip . . . The second method is called casting. When done on a small scale it's used to make molds, which can then reproduce objects composed of materials capable of setting at low temperatures, like plaster. That comes in handy in all sorts of ways: mass-producing toys, archaeology, even theatrical makeup."

"And when it's done on a large scale?"

"Then they extrude sheets that can be used for industrial purposes, like backing concrete—or garment-making."

"What's the third method?"

"Liquid latex. It self-vulcanizes at room temperature, and the main solvent is good old H-2-O. A typical formulation is around thirty-four percent natural latex sap, sixty-five percent water, and point three percent ammonia—the ammonia's added to keep the mix at a high pH level and to stop spoilage. Takes five to ten minutes to dry to the touch, an hour to dry fully, and around four hours to cure. It'll bond permanently to just about anything porous enough to absorb it."

"Okay. How about color?"

"Latex is naturally translucent, but you can add dyes to get whatever you want. Take a look for yourself." She gestured to the comparison microscope and the slide she'd just put in.

Delko took a look. "Dark blue but shiny," he said. "And so's the sample you just added. Looks like a match to me."

"I think so, too," she said. "It's a commercial grade called Supatex Pearlsheen. Very distinctive.

I'm going to see if I can get a list of their distributors and follow up on that. What are you working on?"

"H wants me to dig up some background on a group called the Animal Liberation Alliance—apparently they have some sort of Russian connection."

"That's what you get for being multilingual."

Delko grinned and said, "Well, you know what they say: *Zi detka, eto mnye do huya.*"

Calleigh raised her eyebrows. "I may not know what that means," she said, "but somehow, I don't think I *want* to . . ."

The desk nurse in charge of the HMU of the South Miami Hospital was a small, elderly black woman, with a puff of silver hair on her head like dandelion fluff. Horatio identified himself, told her who he was there to see and followed her down the hall to a door emblazoned with a large sign banning the use of any open flame.

Inside was a bright yellow metal cylinder the size of a Cadillac, with a rectangular bank of controls attached to the side. A round hatch at one end with a thick-spoked metal wheel in the center presumably provided entry, and a curving Plexiglas window beside the controls provided a view of the interior—though it was mostly blocked at the moment by a television on a rolling stand, the screen facing inward. A soap opera oozed midafternoon melodrama through the harsh smell of medical disinfectant.

Horatio walked up and rolled the TV out of the way. The hyperbaric chamber's occupant, a burly man with a scruffy black beard, looked at him with surprised annoyance. Horatio suppressed the urge to rap on the glass and ask for a driver's license and registration.

"Hello, Mister Kazimir," Horatio said. He showed him his badge. "I'm Lieutenant Horatio Caine. I'd like to ask you a few questions."

The man shrugged. He wore a pair of white cotton pajamas and lay on a hospital bed with the back inclined, on top of the sheets. When he spoke, his voice was high and squeaky as a consequence of the increased pressure of the chamber, as well as carrying a heavy Russian accent; it made Horatio feel as if he were talking to a character from an old *Rocky and Bullwinkle* cartoon.

"Why not?" the man squeaked. "It's not like I have much better to do."

"I understand you had a diving accident?"

"Not accident. Stupidity. Too many things, all at once."

"I'm sorry, I don't understand. What things?"

Kazimir scratched the underside of his chin. "You dive?"

"Not myself, no."

"Many things to consider when diving. Many tables, many charts: depth, time underwater, rate of ascent, gas mix. That part, I do okay. But also you must think about yourself—how you feel. How tired you are, how much sleep you have. That part, I don't do so good."

"What happened, exactly?"

"Was diving the Tenneco Towers. You know about them? Oil platforms, three of them, towed from the Gulf of Mexico by barge and sunk in 1985. Beautiful site—orange cup coral all over girders. When they open at night, look like flowers on fire. Hundreds kinds fish—barracuda, amberjack, bull sharks. Deepest tower is a hundred ninety feet—a technical dive. I've done it before, but this time, I wasn't feeling so good. Thought it was flu, maybe some bad food. Turns out, was just bad thinking."

"And you wound up with decompression sickness." The bends, as it was usually called, was caused by nitrogen bubbles leaving the tissues of the body too quickly. For every 33 feet a diver descended, the pressure went up another 11.6 pounds per square inch. The more the pressure increased, the more nitrogen dissolved into the bloodstream, the muscles, the organs. Horatio had heard Delko compare it to the carbon dioxide in a bottle of pop: when the bottle was sealed, the CO_2 was invisible, dissolved in solution; when you popped the cap, the pressure was released and the gas bubbled to the surface as carbonation.

"A diver comes up too fast," Delko told him, "it's

like shaking the bottle first. Your whole body tries to fizz—and while that might sound like it would tickle, it doesn't."

Kazimir shook his head, then winced. "My own fault. Well, that and the damn Navy tables. But any diver should know better than to trust them."

"Oh? You feel the Navy is partially to blame?"

Kazimir rubbed his temples with a thumb and forefinger. "This *nee da dyeloni* headache is killing me," he grumbled. "You know the worst part of the bends? It makes your brain *oblom*. I know this one diver, only symptom he got was he became a complete *pidaras*. Got fired, his wife left him, people think he went crazy. Then they got him into a chamber like this and he started making sense again."

"I hope you're not suffering from any neurological symptoms."

"Me? No, I was a *pidaras* before I got in here." Kazimir chuckled, an eerie, tinny sound. "But you never can tell. My memory has been acting funny ever since I arrive."

The man was smiling openly, but Horatio knew an excuse when he heard one. "I'll try not to tax it, then," he said. "How long have you been here?"

"In the hospital, almost a week. I only have to stay in the chamber for a few hours every day, but I can't dive for at least two months. No plane travel, either."

Horatio nodded. There was no way Kazimir

could have been responsible for either of the attacks, but that didn't mean he wasn't involved. "And what about your activities in the ALA? Are they going to suffer as a result?"

Kazimir's smile grew broader. "Ah, some truth at last. You know what, Mister Lieutenant? This whole accident, it's finished me. I can go on no more. I think I will just stay here, safe in my little metal shell, and become a hermit crab. No more being angry with all the bad people in the world." Despite the mockery in his words, the high-pitched squeak they were delivered in robbed them of their weight. Horatio found himself fighting down a smile and sternly reminded himself of why he had come to talk to this man.

"You know, Mister Kazimir, I find that hard to believe. You have a long and colorful history when it comes to animal rights—actually, some would say you care more for animals than you do for people."

"Is that supposed to be insult? Animals are always true to their nature. People? Pfah. I would rather deal with something wild than something from 'civilization' any day."

Horatio had the brief but powerful feeling he was arguing with a militant Mickey Mouse. "Wild animals don't use high explosives to make a point, Mister Kazimir."

"I'm not interested in making points, Mister Lieutenant. What I want is change. *Real* change.

And you don't do that by waving petitions or signs with clever slogans on them."

"I know a few civil-rights activists who would disagree with you—but that's not really relevant at the moment. The important thing to remember, Anatoly, is this: *I* disagree with you."

Kazimir made a dismissive gesture and looked away. Horatio slammed his open hand against the Plexiglas, the impact loud enough to draw Kazimir's gaze back in startled reflex. Horatio leaned down, met his eyes and held them.

"I'm not going to debate ethics with you, Anatoly. I don't like bombs, and I like the people who use them even less. Make another mistake like the one you made with the fishing boats, and I *will* come after you."

The look Kazimir gave him was more bemused than intimidated. "The boats were a long time ago. Why are you really here?"

"I came to give you a present," Horatio said. He pulled a piece of paper from his inside breast pocket, unfolded it and held it flat against the window. "A warrant for the ALA's membership list. See, despite your disdain for due process, it really can be quite an effective tool for us civilized types . . ."

The woman Wolfe needed to talk to didn't live in Miami proper, but down the coast near a little town called Verdant Springs. None of the department Hummers was available, so he signed a midsize sedan out of the motor pool and fought his way up the highway against a seemingly endless tide of slow-moving RVs and four-by-fours towing bass boats. The air-conditioning in the car didn't work properly; it would pump hot, moist air in, but that was it. Driving with both front windows open was only marginally better.

By the time he got there, he was hot and sweaty and had been smacked in the forehead at least twice by kamikaze bugs. The cool, wet blue of the Atlantic beside the road taunted him the entire time, and he finally pulled into a roadside gas station, bought a plastic bottle of iced tea the size of a bucket and drank half of it.

The woman's name was Eileen Bartstow, and she lived on the outskirts of town. Her yard was small and neat, her house a double-wide trailer with a wooden skirt around the base and a set of concrete steps leading to the front door. The trailer itself was painted sunshine yellow and eggshell white, with rose-patterned curtains in the window. He pressed the doorbell and heard the first few bars of "Raindrops Keep Falling on My Head" chime inside.

The door opened. The woman standing there was in her thirties, with blond hair pulled back in a bun. She wore a sundress of pale pink, flip-flops and a suspicious squint on her face. "Yes?"

"Mrs. Bartstow? I'm CSI Wolfe of the Miami-Dade crime lab," he said.

"It's Miss. May I see some ID, please?"

He pulled out his identification and showed it to her. She studied it gravely, then nodded. "Come in."

She led him into a small dining room/kitchen just inside the front door, and pulled out a wooden chair for him to sit in. "Would you like some coffee?" she asked.

"No, I'm fine." He sat, opened the dossier he'd brought with him and pulled out a pen.

She poured herself a mug from the coffeemaker, added cream and sugar, then sat down across from him. The kitchen was clean and tidy, with the sort of fake-wood paneling that used to be popular in the seventies. The table was reddish wood-grain Formica and matched the countertops.

"Now," she said, "I understand you want to talk to me about the monster."

Wolfe nodded. "Yes. The monster," he said seriously.

"Well, I'm glad *somebody* is finally doing a follow-up. This thing could have *killed* someone by now."

"I apologize for the slowness of the department," Wolfe said. "Ordinary police officers don't always have the training to handle the more . . . *esoteric* cases."

"But you do?"

"I have a background in science, ma'am."

That seemed to reassure her. "Well, good. I

guess you'd probably like to go over what happened again—that's what you do, right? Review the case?"

"That's a good place to start, yes."

She took a long sip of her coffee. "Okay. Well. It was three months ago. I was with some friends, and we were having a barbecue at Poker Cove, on the beach."

Wolfe consulted his notes. "That would be Glen Fairgrove, Jake Landry, Elke Cummins and Fern Kwan, correct?"

"Yes. It was a warm day, so some of us decided to go swimming. We had brought our suits along, just in case. Fern and Glen went in, and Elke and Jake stayed on the beach. Fern and Glen were horsing around, splashing each other and so on, so I thought I'd swim out a little farther, by myself. I'm a good swimmer, you know."

"I'm sure you are."

"I was probably about fifty yards out when it happened. That's right about where the water starts to get really deep; it drops off quite steeply . . ." She paused, her face suddenly troubled.

"And then?" Wolfe prompted.

"Something grabbed me," she said. "A hand— no, a *claw*. Around my ankle. It had a very strong grip. It dragged me under the water."

"Did you get a good look at the—thing?"

"Yes. Everyone says that I must be confused, that you can't see clearly underwater—well, I want you to take a look at something. Just a second, I'll be right back." She got up abruptly and left the room, returning a moment later with something in her hand. She tossed it down on the table in front of Wolfe. "There," she said defiantly. "See anything wrong with those?"

They were a pair of swimming goggles. Wolfe picked them up, examined them critically, noted that the lenses weren't tinted or scratched and that the seal seemed intact.

"No, ma'am," he said.

"That's what I was wearing when that thing dragged me under. They didn't get knocked off. It was a bright, sunny day, and the water was as clear as—well, as clear as my vision."

"And what did you see?"

His eyes met hers, and suddenly Wolfe could see the anger in them, not just at her attacker but at all the people she'd dealt with since, all the ones who'd thought she was exaggerating or imagining things or even outright lying.

"I saw a monster," she said flatly. "It had shiny, dark-blue skin, like some sort of fish. It had a big, spiny fin on top of its head, fins on its arms and legs and feet, and long, curving talons on its hands. Its head was . . . well, it had big, bulging eyes and a mouth full of razor-sharp teeth. It had a rounded back, sort of like a whale."

Wolfe considered his next words carefully before replying. "Did any of your friends see it?"

"No. I was too far away. If I hadn't just taken a deep breath and had the presence of mind to hold it, I probably would have drowned—or worse." Her voice was steady, but both hands were wrapped around her mug of coffee so tightly the knuckles were turning white.

"What happened next?"

"It reached up—it was below me, pulling me down—and raked me with one claw. Tore my bathing suit and gave me four long gashes on my stomach."

"Were they serious? The file doesn't mention a hospital report—"

"They weren't that bad, really. No stitches, and you can't even tell where they were, now. But they were bleeding pretty good at the time."

"Okay. And then?"

"I kicked it. In the head, as hard as I could. It let go, and I swam for the surface. I don't know how far down we were—it couldn't have been that far, there was still plenty of light—but it seemed to take forever to get back. Like it had pulled me down for miles, and I'd already taken the last breath I was ever going to take . . ."

She trailed off, then gave her head a little shake and flashed a brief, embarrassed smile. "I'm sorry, that sounds melodramatic. I just keep replaying it in my head, and every rerun makes it seem a little bit worse and a little less real at the same time. Like a nightmare you can't stop obsessing over."

"It's all right. You need a minute? We can take a break."

"No, no, I'm fine." She took another long drink of coffee, and it seemed to steady her. "When I got to the surface, I took a big gulp of air and let it out a second later as a scream. All I could think was, I had to let the others know what was happening. It wasn't even that I thought they could help—I just knew I had to *warn* them, so they could get away. Like it was a grizzly bear or something. Isn't that strange?"

"I think it's very selfless," Wolfe said.

"I suppose. Anyway, my second thought was that I didn't have any chance of getting away— you don't try to outswim a shark, right? So even though I was terrified, I took another deep breath and dove under again."

Wolfe blinked. "How did it react?"

"I surprised it, I think. I sort of went over backward, and then got turned around to face it. It was just sort of . . . hovering there, and watching me. You know, like a fish will do? It even sort of turned its head from side to side, like it was looking at me with one eye and then the other. I— you'll probably laugh, but I put up my fists. You know, like you do before a fight? I don't know what I hoped to accomplish."

"You were operating on basic animal instinct," Wolfe said. "Fight-or-flight. I think you made the right choice—like you said, you can't outswim a shark. But you can convince it you're more trouble than dinner is worth."

"I don't think I did, though. Both Fern and Glen heard my scream and came torpedoing over, and I think I just made it hesitate long enough for it to notice them approaching. It—well, it looked at me for a second, and then it turned and swam away. By the time my friends got there it had vanished."

Wolfe looked down at his papers, thumbed through them and pulled out several sheets from the middle. "I see that Miss Kwan gave a statement but Mister Fairgrove declined."

"Fern believed me. Glen didn't," she said coldly. "At least, not enough to put his reputation on the line. Thought he'd be labeled some kind of nutjob if he put his name on anything official."

"Uh—right. Miss Bartstow, I hate to bring this up, but there's part of your statement we haven't discussed yet."

She sighed in exasperation. "I know, I know." She gave him a long, intent look. "Go ahead and say it."

"Uh—you say it was . . . anatomically correct?"

She frowned, as if that wasn't what she expected him to say. "That's right. I got a really good look when we were facing each other, and it was *aroused.*"

"That's why you filed it as a sexual assault?"

"Yes. I don't know what excited it—ripping off

half my suit, dragging me under, maybe even the blood in the water—but when I saw the condition it was in, I knew what it wanted."

Wolfe cleared his throat. "And was it—normal?"

"Human, you mean? In shape and size, yes. But it was the same shiny blue the rest of the creature was, and there was no hair. If it had testicles, I couldn't see them."

Wolfe nodded. He studied Eileen Bartstow for a moment, weighing not only her words, but his sense of her as a person. She seemed a little old-fashioned, a little reserved, but not eccentric or unbalanced. She didn't seem like the type that craved attention, or would even be comfortable with it. She did, however, seem familiar.

As a beat cop, Wolfe had dealt with cases of sexual assault before. He'd seen victims display many reactions: rage and shock, fear and disbelief, self-imposed guilt and shame. But there was a strange sort of mix he'd seen more often than anything, a sort of angry embarrassment, and that was the emotion he felt from Eileen Bartstow. That, and weary resignation—she didn't really expect him to believe her.

But he did.

"Miss Bartstow, there's a saying that skeptics of fringe science like to use: extraordinary claims demand extraordinary proof. I've always thought that statement was misleading—whether or not a claim is 'extraordinary' is purely subjective, while proof is always objective. Regardless of what is being claimed, evidence is evidence."

She eyed him warily, and he quickly said, "Anyway, what I'm trying to say is, I believe you're telling the truth—but what I believe, or don't believe, is ultimately meaningless. What matters is the evidence. No matter how extraordinary your claim might sound, if that's what happened then the evidence will back you up—and so will I."

"Except I don't have any."

"Maybe you do. Do you still have the bathing suit he tore?"

She thought for a second, then said, "Yes, I think I do. I was going to throw it away, but—just a moment." She got up again and left the kitchen.

When she came back, Wolfe had a large evidence envelope ready on the table, and he'd slipped on a pair of gloves as well. He took the bathing suit from her, held it up and examined it briefly. It looked not so much torn as cut; cut by several very sharp, parallel blades. He slipped it into the envelope and closed it.

"I'll run some tests," he said.

Now she was the one studying him. "I know how this all sounds," she said. "And if it had just been something I'd seen, I probably wouldn't even have mentioned it to my friends, let alone filed a police report. But this thing *attacked* me—and if it attacked me, it'll attack others. If someone died because I was afraid to come forward—and not even because I was afraid of being attacked again, just afraid of looking like I was crazy—then I wouldn't be able to live with myself."

"You did the right thing," Wolfe said. "Everybody's afraid of looking like a fool. But you're absolutely right; if speaking up means you might save a life, you just have to take that risk . . ."

10

"ALL RIGHT, PEOPLE," Horatio said. He stood at the head of the conference table, his team seated around it. "Let's see what we have so far. Eric?"

"The Animal Liberation Alliance has been operating since nineteen ninety," Delko said. "Formed by Anatoly Kazimir, a Soviet ex-pat who managed to get out of Russia in the early eighties. Hooked up with Greenpeace for a while, but his views were too radical and he left before they could turf him. There's a rumor he provided intel to the French in retaliation."

"You mean when the *Rainbow Warrior* was sunk?" Calleigh asked. "Doesn't seem like something an environmentalist would get involved in, no matter how extreme his views."

"Kazimir is hard-core," Delko said. "Not a lot of background available on him, but supposedly he was KGB, as well as being a trained combat diver.

According to the people I talked to, he doesn't just love animals—he hates people."

"Well, that would dovetail with my impression of him," Horatio said. "Any indication he might have a history of sexual assault?"

"Not in this country," Delko said. "Maybe back in Russia, but there's no way to know."

"What about the organization itself?" Horatio asked.

"Not large. About a dozen members, all told: a few Russians, a few Americans, the rest European. All handpicked by Kazimir. You want to join the ALA you need an invitation, not to mention a fairly impressive résumé—and I'm not talking about a degree in environmental science. Most of them have some sort of military background."

Horatio nodded thoughtfully. "May I see those, please?" Delko handed him a file folder, and he flipped through it quickly. "So our Mister Kazimir has built his own private mercenary squad, the better to take on the evil forces of humankind . . . and even though Anatoly himself can't be our merman, there's a very good chance one of his recruits is. Well done, Eric. Calleigh, what do you have?"

Calleigh cleared her throat, then said, "The latex sample we retrieved from the first vic's fingernails is a specific type called Supatex Pearlsheen. It's used primarily in the clothing industry."

"Like jackets and boots?" Wolfe asked. "That could be a pretty big field."

"Not so much," Calleigh said. "Actually, this particular color and grade of latex is sold mainly to a very small niche market. There's only one retail outlet in Miami that carries it, and I plan to pay them a visit later today."

Delko was already grinning, but Wolfe didn't get it. "What sort of niche market?" he asked.

"Fetishwear," Calleigh said. "You were right about the boots, but not that many people wear thigh-high lace-ups with six-inch heels. Or latex bodysuits, corsets or thongs, for that matter."

"Depends on who you know," Delko said.

"Or how much you'll admit to," Calleigh replied. "Either way, it looks like our killer may have a latex fetish, so I thought I'd check out the scene."

"There's a scene?" Wolfe asked.

"More like an *ob*scene," Delko said. "Don't forget to hit that club on Lincoln Road."

"Oh?" Horatio said. "Something you'd like to share with us, Eric?"

Delko held up his hands in defense. "Oh, no," he said. "The only time I put on anything like that is when I'm going underwater. You have any idea how *hot* latex is?"

"No, Eric, I don't," Calleigh said sweetly. "How hot *is* it, exactly?"

Delko laughed. "All I'm gonna say is, in Miami the humidity alone would kill you. And the only reason I know about that club is every Friday night there's enough people wearing PVC lined up outside to restock a condom factory."

"Well, I'm going straight to the source," Calleigh said. "It's called the Sintight Boutique—apparently they do custom work as well."

"Good," Horatio said. "Mister Wolfe—I understand you took a little trip up the coast?"

Wolfe shifted in his seat, leaning forward and putting his elbows on the table. "That's right. I talked to a woman about a sexual assault that took place three months ago. Nobody took it seriously at the time because of the details, but I think it could be our merman."

"And those details would be?" Horatio said.

Wolfe hesitated, then said, "She claims she was attacked by a monster." He gave them a brief rundown of what Eileen Bartstow had told him. By the time he had finished, both Delko and Calleigh had odd looks on their faces and Horatio was frowning.

"Look, I know it sounds strange," Wolfe said. "But it could be our guy in some sort of costume. Latex is used in masks and makeup, right?"

"That's a definite possibility," Horatio said. "But that's not the problem. You said this attack took place just outside of Verdant Springs?"

"That's right."

"And the monster had long claws, a humped back and a spiky fin on the top of his head?"

"Well, yes," Wolfe said, puzzled. "How did you know?"

"Doctor Creepoid's Friday Night Fright-fest," Calleigh said regretfully.

"Yeah, that's where I saw it, too," Delko said. "Boy, he really used to show some stinkers, didn't he?"

"What are you talking about?" Wolfe said.

"What they're talking about," Horatio said wryly, "is Verdant Springs' claim to fame. A B-movie called *Creature From the Deep* was filmed there in the fifties."

"They're about to celebrate their fiftieth anniversary, actually," Delko said. "They're having a whole festival—T-shirts, wide-screen showings of the movie, all the trappings. And the monster you described is a dead ringer for the star of the show."

"I'm surprised you're not familiar with the movie," Calleigh said. "Didn't science and science fiction go hand-in-hand in your youth?"

Wolfe frowned. "Actually, my parents didn't let me watch horror movies as a kid. After the whole robot thing, they . . . never mind."

"Didn't the woman mention any of this?" Calleigh asked.

"No," Wolfe admitted. "I guess she thought it would make the whole thing sound like a publicity stunt."

"Well, it certainly has all the trappings," Horatio said. "But that doesn't mean it isn't significant. Mister Wolfe, you were the one that talked to her. What's your professional opinion of her story?"

Horatio's eyes were on Wolfe, and the young CSI was suddenly aware that so were everybody else's. He paused, swallowed, then said, "She's telling the truth. That's what my gut says."

"All right then," Horatio said. "Follow up on it. If our merman made his first appearance three months ago at Verdant Springs, he may have some connection to the cinematic version."

"I also have some actual physical evidence," Wolfe said. He told them about the bathing suit.

"Easy to fake," Delko pointed out.

"Even so," Horatio said, "let's compare it to the other claw marks we have and see what we get."

Horatio leaned against the front of the table, toward his team. "All right. What we have so far is a killer with an underwater fixation, a taste for latex and a grudge against the military. Mister Wolfe, you're following up on the Verdant Springs case. Calleigh, keep going on the latex source. Delko, you and I are going to go through the ALA membership list one by one and take a long, hard look at every one of them."

Horatio straightened up, put his hands on his hips. "Remember, this guy is intelligent, highly organized and sadistic. He's not going to stop until someone *makes* him stop—and that, ladies and gentlemen, is precisely what we are going to do . . ."

The woman's name was Ingrid Ernst. She was in her thirties, with a bristly crew cut of dark hair, a wiry physique and a pinched-looking face. She faced Horatio across the interview table, radiating a cold, fixed hatred that contradicted her willingness to come in and talk. Horatio suspected that she lived for confrontations, and he was currently doing his best to deny her the satisfaction.

"Ms. Ernst," he said, putting as much ease and friendliness into his voice as he could. "Thank you for coming in and talking with us."

"Better than being dragged down here in handcuffs," she said frostily. Her German accent, while slight, sharpened the edge of her words. Her arms were crossed in front of her, her hands gripping her forearms like she wished they were pistols.

"Oh, we only do that for criminals," he said. "I don't think you qualify, myself—civil disobedience is hardly in the same class as thieves and murderers, is it?"

"Of course not," she snapped. "But my activities are political in nature, which means I am used to being harassed by those in authority—"

"Well, I'm not going to do that," he interrupted gently. "Actually, this isn't about the ALA *per se*."

"What do you mean? What are you talking about?" she demanded.

"I'm talking about someone who takes things a little too far, Ms. Ernst. Someone with a great deal of anger at the human race. Someone who feels more at home underwater than on dry land, so much so that it's become an obsession. Do you know anyone like that, Ms. Ernst?"

Abruptly her manner changed. She laughed, then leaned back. "I am German. I know all about obsession. You must be more exact."

"Very well. I'm referring to an unhealthy obsession—one which expresses itself through acts of violence. Specifically, murder and rape."

The cynical smirk on her face shifted to something a little more wary. "Murder and rape? You must be desperate, to question a woman about such things."

"Women have been known to participate in all sorts of unsavory practices," Horatio said. "But your gender isn't as important to me as your background. You managed to get yourself kicked out of PETA for your activities, which isn't easy."

"Throwing paint at fur-wearing socialites is for naïve children," she said. "It really doesn't have the impact of a dead cow in your living room."

"Especially when the residents have been gone for two weeks in July," Horatio said. "But again, that's not why you're here. I understand your anger at a certain segment of society . . . but I don't think that anger extends to innocent young women."

A folder lay on the table in front of Horatio. He opened it, took out two photos and slid them over. She looked at them without flinching, but Horatio noted a subtle widening of her eyes, a slight intake of breath.

"The person I'm looking for is responsible for the deaths of both of these women," Horatio said. "He has an erotic fixation on being underwater, a hatred of the military—especially the Navy's Marine Mammal Program—and a sexual attraction to latex. I have good reason to believe he may be connected to your group. If you have anything you'd like to share with me, I promise it will be kept in the strictest confidence."

"You think one of the Alliance is responsible? For *this*?"

"I know how strong your convictions are, Ms. Ernst, and I believe all the members of your group have the same devotion to your cause. But all of you are still human beings . . . and you, more than anyone, are aware of the cruelty human beings are capable of."

She was silent for a moment, mulling over his words, before she replied. "I suppose. But it's also true you can never really know what is in another's heart . . . and if one of my comrades has this sort of darkness inside, he hides it well. But perhaps I am not the best person to ask."

"And why would that be?"

"Because my sexual preference is for women, and I have made that clear. I maintain a certain distance from the men in my group, and the women—mostly—maintain a certain distance from me. And to respond to your next question, I have no lovers from within the group at the present time."

"Oh? How about former members?"

"There have been one or two."

"Would they include Doctor Nicole Zhenko?"

"I don't see how that is relevant."

"Perhaps not. I'm just interested in talking to people who know Doctor Zhenko well."

"Hah! A very short list. Zhenko keeps to herself, always has. I think she quit the group not so much for politics as because none of us could breathe underwater."

"That's an odd statement," Horatio said. "Care to explain it?"

"Most people, they would be a little unsure of the ocean after it took half their limbs—Zhenko, she was back swimming before the bandages came off. You see those fancy new legs of hers? Can't walk worth a damn in them, but she doesn't care. As long as she can swim, she's happy."

"I see. So Doctor Zhenko had no problem with your methods?"

"She wanted change, same as all of us. As for methods . . ." She shrugged. "She's Russian, she's a scientist. 'Less theory, more practice,' she always used to say."

"The pragmatic approach," Horatio said. "I'm not unfamiliar with it, myself."

"If your purpose is truly to stop the person who did *this*," she said, indicating the photographs, "then we are not enemies. I joined the ALA to put a stop to suffering and misery; I am not blind to the pain of others." She gave him a wry smile. "Even the ones on two legs."

"Then do me the favor of keeping your eyes open," Horatio said. "I'm not asking you to spy on your fellow members—just be alert. I don't want anyone else to die, Ms. Ernst."

"In that, Lieutenant Caine," she said, "we are in agreement."

The one-piece bathing suit on the light table showed three long parallel cuts across the waist. Wolfe measured the distance between two of the cuts, then realized he wasn't getting accurate data; the material wasn't stretched to the proper degree. He rummaged through the lab's collection of mannequins until he found a female torso of approximately the right dimensions, and dressed it in the suit.

The distance between the cuts varied slightly, but if the claws were mounted on fingers that was to be expected. He looked at the cloth itself next, studying it on a microscopic level and noting that the cuts appeared to have been made by an extremely sharp blade.

The spacing of the slashes was consistent with the wounds on Janice Stonecutter's body.

Horatio studied the man across the interview table carefully before speaking. "Mister Torrence," he said. "We meet again."

Malcolm Torrence stared at him with undisguised disdain. "The only reason I'm here," he said, "is because Anatoly asked me to."

"Just following orders?" Horatio said. "Well, that's odd. According to your records, your time in the Navy wasn't quite so cooperative."

"I don't have a problem with following orders. It just depends on who's giving them."

"I see. How do you do with questions?"

"Ask away."

"Let's start with your whereabouts for the last few days . . ."

Torrence's alibi wasn't nearly as airtight as Kazimir's; he claimed to have been by himself during the times both Cavanaugh and the Stonecutters were murdered, though he offered to produce movie tickets to verify what he'd been doing. "I like to go to matinees by myself," he said. "Double features, if I can find them."

"Seems like a waste of a sunny day to me," Horatio said.

Torrence snorted. "That's why I go in the afternoon, to get away from the sun. Too bright and too hot. Give me a nice, dark theater with air-conditioning any time."

"Uh-huh. I'll need to see those tickets, Mister Torrence. And isn't it lucky you held on to them . . ."

Horatio smiled. Torrence didn't smile back.

*　　　*　　　*

Delko checked his notes carefully before speaking. "Mister Fiodr Cherzynsky . . . am I pronouncing that right?"

"*Da,*" the man said. He smiled at Delko pleasantly as he sat down, then settled in with his elbows on the table. "Glad to be of service."

"We appreciate you coming in. How long have you been associated with the ALA?"

The man rubbed his chin as he thought about the question. He was in his late forties, with a bony, scarecrow-like physique. He had deepset eyes, a prominent nose and a high widow's peak of jet black hair. "I've been working with them full-time since ninety-nine or so," he said. His English was perfect, with only a trace of a Russian accent.

"In what capacity?"

"Public relations."

"Sounds like a tough job."

Fiodr shrugged. "Challenging, certainly. But I believe in what they are doing, so for me it is a labor of love."

"Even when they break the law?"

"Sometimes laws need to be broken. After all, it used to be legal to own slaves."

Delko knew he shouldn't let himself be drawn into a political argument, but he couldn't resist. "You think comparing slavery to animal rights is a fair comparison?"

"No, not really. We didn't slaughter slaves for food."

Delko bit back a reply. "So, you send out press releases, give interviews, things like that?"

Fiodr nodded. "It's my job to present our case to the world," he said. "Until I came along, Anatoly didn't much care how people saw his organization. I've been doing my best to try to change that."

"Having any success?"

Fiodr smiled. "Our Website gets a few thousand hits a month. People are tired of talking; they want action."

"Careful what you wish for," Delko said. "No more talking means you're out of a job."

"Oh, I'll get by," Fiodr said, with just a touch of amusement in his voice.

Yeah, I'll bet you will, Delko thought. In his experience PR flacks were like remoras; they could always find another big fish to attach themselves to. "I need to know where you were on the following days . . ."

After the interviews were over, Horatio and Delko met in the break room to compare notes. Delko wolfed down a bagel while Horatio poured himself a coffee. "Well, what do you think?" Horatio asked.

Delko chewed and swallowed before answering. "Let's see. Most of the members I talked to had solid alibis. I have to do some verification, but the only one that seemed sketchy was Cherzynsky.

Said he was camping the whole time, all by himself."

Horatio pulled up a seat across from Delko, blew on the mug of coffee to cool it off. "Yeah, I ran into something similar with a guy named Malcolm Torrence. Says he was at the movies, but we both know how easy it is to buy a ticket and then slip out an exit."

"Right, just make sure it's a movie you've already seen so you don't get tripped up later . . . I don't suppose any of the movies he saw were about underwater monsters on a rampage, were they?"

"No, just a few run-of-the-mill comedies and action flicks." Horatio took a sip of his coffee, then winced.

"You all right, H?"

Horatio massaged his temple with a forefinger. "Yeah, fine. Talking to fanatics always gives me a headache."

"I know what you mean. They seem like reasonable, intelligent people up until a certain point, then suddenly they get this look in their eyes." Delko shook his head. "After that, you can't talk to them. Well, you *can*, but . . ."

"It becomes less a conversation than a diatribe," Horatio said. "Objectivity is not these people's strong suit."

"Hey, I'm all for animal rights, too," Delko said. "I don't approve of leg-hold traps or dragnets or clubbing baby seals—but I wouldn't use a *bomb* to express my point of view."

"Well, the ALA hasn't killed anyone yet," Horatio pointed out. "Not that we know of. The question is, which—if any—of their members has decided to take that last, fatal step . . ."

"Yeah. And is he gonna do it again."

"No, Eric," Horatio said quietly. He took a long, slow sip of coffee. "We already know the answer to that one. What we don't know is where, when . . . or *who*."

11

WOLFE REALIZED THAT if he'd actually driven into the town of Verdant Springs instead of just stopping at Eileen Bartstow's place on the outskirts, he would have had a very different reaction to her story. The giant, inflatable fish-man hovering over the local car dealership, for instance, was undeniably familiar.

Nor was that the only place the Sea Creature appeared. His bulging eyes stared out from posters on walls and pennants hung from lampposts; a row of finny plush toys goggled at Wolfe from the window of a drugstore.

"Sonofa—*fish*," he muttered.

He parked his car, got out and read a poster. It advertised the *Creature From the Deep* Seafest, starting next week. Not only was the local theater showing the film around the clock, but special screenings of a 3-D version were scheduled, followed by the film's actors appearing in person. The theater was listed as the headquarters for the festival itself; Wolfe noted the address and got back in his car.

Verdant Springs wasn't large, a few thousand people at most. It boasted a main street with a scattering of restaurants, a midsize supermarket, a few bookstores and bars and one motel. Wolfe understood why the place would want to capitalize on its brief moment in the spotlight; anything that brought a few people in to spend money on food, booze or entertainment would be welcome, maybe even desperately needed. He just wished he hadn't been the one elected to look like an idiot in the process.

He found the theater easily, an old-fashioned brick building with a big, Broadway-style marquee out front proclaiming COMING SOON! CREATURE FROM THE DEEP SEAFEST! with the dates below it. A fullsize, detailed cardboard cutout of the monster menaced patrons just inside the front door.

He parked and walked up to the box office window. There was no one inside, but a woman in a red-and-white striped shirt was visible through the glass of the front door, vacuuming the lobby's faded red carpet Wolfe rapped on the glass until she looked up, then held his badge against the window.

She shut off the vacuum, came over and unlocked the door. "Yes?"

"I'd like to speak to whoever's in charge of the festival," Wolfe said.

The woman, a young Latina with braces on her teeth, gave him a metallic smile and said, "Sure, that's Mister Delfino. I'll tell him you're here." She hurried away, leaving Wolfe alone with the life-size cutout for company.

He studied it curiously. It had a large, froggy mouth, gaping open to reveal rows of needle-like teeth, bulging black eyes, and frond-like gills jutting from its neck; a spiny fin arched over the top of its head like a mohawk, and other fins flared from its forearms, its calves, and down its back. Its feet and hands were webbed, with long talons extending from both fingers and toes. Overlapping, segmented scales covered the chest and stomach.

"Impressive, isn't he?" a voice said behind him. Wolfe turned to see a balding, rotund man in brown corduroy pants and a blue cardigan approaching. He put out his hand as he walked up and Wolfe shook it.

"I'm Leroy Delfino," the man said. He had a wide, smiling face, with a mouth nearly as big as the monster's. "And this, of course, is the Sea Creature—or Gilly, as we like to call him."

"Ryan Wolfe, with the Miami-Dade crime lab," Wolfe said. "I was wondering if I could talk to you for a few moments about—well, about Gilly, I guess."

Delfino laughed. "Well, I'm pretty busy getting

ready for the festival, but I can always take some time to talk about *him*. Come on back to my office."

He led Wolfe through the lobby, up a red-carpeted flight of stairs and into a small room beside the projectionist's booth. There was just enough space inside for a small desk, two chairs, a water cooler and a filing cabinet. Vintage posters in glass-fronted cases on the walls promised gory, lurid violence from a host of famous monsters ranging from Godzilla to the Wolf Man.

Delfino wedged himself into a chair behind the desk with practiced ease, then filled a ceramic mug shaped like the Sea Creature's head from the water cooler and asked if Wolfe wanted a drink, too. Wolfe declined and took the other chair.

"So, what would be your interest in our famous amphibian?" Delfino asked, clasping pudgy fingers around his mug.

"It's not so much him, as the people he hangs around with," Wolfe said. "People like Eileen Bartstow."

He watched Delfino closely for his reaction. The man blinked, then sighed. "Hoo-boy," he said. "That's . . . unfortunate."

"How so?" Wolfe asked neutrally.

"Look, Miss Bartstow has no connection with the festival," Delfino said emphatically. "I've heard the story, and I'm disgusted with the whole thing."

"Really? I would have thought you'd jump at the chance for some free publicity."

Delfino shook his head. "That's probably what she thought, too. Or maybe the guy who staged the so-called attack thought so. I don't know. All I can tell you is that it was a dumb idea."

"And whose idea was it?"

"I don't know. Honestly. I mean, it doesn't even really make sense, does it? Making crop circles after someone says they've seen a UFO, planting fake footprints in Bigfoot country—that I can understand. But this is a *movie* we're talking about. Nobody's ever claimed the Sea Creature was real."

"Eileen Bartstow does."

"But her version isn't even *accurate*. She says it had *genitalia*, for God's sake. That's—well, it's just *wrong*."

Wolfe sensed the sort of outrage that only a dedicated fan who's had the conceptual integrity of a valued icon violated could muster. "Well, maybe someone's trying to launch a twenty-first-century version."

"You know, I gave that some thought myself," Delfino said. He gulped back some water, apparently oblivious of the irony of what he was drinking from. "There's rumors of a remake every couple of years, and this is the kind of stunt a studio might pull. But all of my showbiz contacts swear nobody's working on anything like it—and besides, where's all the press? It didn't even make the local paper, if you can believe that. Everybody's reaction has been—well, sort of embarrassed, I guess. It's one thing to be known for a cheesy science-fiction movie; thinking you *live* in that movie is another."

Wolfe had to admit Delfino made sense. The point of a publicity stunt was publicity, and nobody seemed to be paying much attention to what had happened to Eileen Bartstow.

"Can you think of another reason for her to claim what she did?" Wolfe asked.

"She's not crazy, if that's what you mean. Little town like this, everybody knows everyone's business, and Eileen's always been as normal as the next person."

"Would she stand to gain anything by making this kind of claim?"

Delfino shrugged. "She doesn't own a local business, so tourism doesn't matter to her. As far as I know she hasn't tried to sell her story to anyone, though I guess she could have some kind of private deal going with somebody. If so, she's been awfully quiet about it."

Wolfe frowned. Eileen Bartstow hadn't struck him as the type to seek publicity—and she hadn't. "If she wasn't the one who staged it, who do you think did?"

Delfino smiled ruefully and poked a thumb at his chest. "I gotta say, I'd be your number-one suspect. I organize the annual festival, I own all sorts of memorabilia, I can recite the whole movie from memory—'Good Lord! It's some sort of fishman!'—but if I was guilty, I'd have done a lot better job. I'd be talking it up online, giving interviews, trying to get CNN down here, whatever I could do. And *my* Gilly wouldn't be sporting a big old boner."

"Or attacking women with razor-sharp claws?"

Delfino looked troubled. "It really tried to hurt her, huh?"

"So she says. Actually, it has some of the signs of a stunt gone wrong. Something that may have started one way, and turned out another. Is that what happened?"

Delfino met his eyes. "Look, I swear to you—I don't know what went on that night in Poker Cove. I don't know if anything actually happened or not. All I know for sure is that I wasn't involved."

"Let's say I believe you," Wolfe said. "You don't seem to think Miss Bartstow has any reason to lie; if you're innocent, who does that leave?"

Delfino thought for a moment. "Well, normally I'd say this sounds like a high-school or college prank, but I don't know. What's the point in a prank if you don't take credit for it? And staging the whole thing underwater seems a bit elaborate, too—after all, he's an amphibian; it would have been a lot easier to do the whole thing on the beach."

Unless it wasn't staged, Wolfe thought. *Unless Eileen Bartstow just happened to be in the wrong place at the wrong time . . . and our merman decided to take advantage of the situation.*

"Who else in town shares your interest in, uh, Gilly?" Wolfe asked.

"Well, a lot of the merchants have a vested interest—souvenir shops sell T-shirts, keyrings, things like that, the local diner even features a Gillburger—but nobody else here is really into it the way I am. For that, you'd have to go to Miami and look up the fan club."

"Then I guess that's what I'll have to do . . ."

Delfino gave him the president's name and contact information. Wolfe thanked him for his help and got up to go.

"Just a second," Delfino said, opening a drawer and rummaging around. "Ah, here we go." He pulled out a plastic action figure of the Sea Creature, around eight inches tall and made of translucent green plastic. He handed it to Wolfe. "Here, take this with you."

"I can't really accept a gift," Wolfe said.

"Don't think of it as a gift," Delfino said with a grin. "More like a visual reference of your suspect."

Wolfe went downstairs, got into his car and hung the figure from his rear-view mirror. "Okay, Junior," he said to its goggle-eyed countenance. "Let's go find your big brother . . ."

Wolfe found him in North Miami an hour later, in the section of a specialty DVD store marked SCI-FI

CLASSICS. Ten minutes after that Wolfe was in a coffeeshop with a tall glass of ice water beside him, slipping the disc into the DVD drive of his laptop, headphones snugged into his ears. The murmur of conversation around him faded into the background as the ominous, pounding orchestral theme swelled up like the rising tide.

Creature From the Deep had been shot in black-and-white, which somehow added something instead of being a deficiency; a sense of foreboding, of menace, or maybe just the historical gravity of something from another era. Like many monster movies, its plot was simple: Mankind had disturbed the ecological balance of the Sea Creature's natural habitat, and it had risen from its watery home to wreak vengeance as a result. Wolfe suffered through the slow opening, the pontificating of the "scientists" as they fed the audience the exposition needed to set up the premise, the introduction of the standard love interest and comic relief.

But once the film entered the Sea Creature's domain, everything changed.

The movie had been made at Verdant Springs largely because of the springs the town was named after; they gave a crystal clarity to the water that made the environment, even without color, come alive on the screen. The monochrome aspect made it seem even more alien, as if the bright-hued coral and fish had somehow been dragged under the moon of a distant planet . . .

*   *   *

Horatio studied his reflection as he waited. A green moray eel on the other side of the glass swam up and eyed him, razor-toothed mouth opening and closing as it worked water over its gills.

"Hey, pal," Horatio said. "What's the word on the street? Ran into any psychopaths lately?"

It had no answers for him. Horatio hoped he'd have better luck with his contact.

Meeting at the Miami Seaquarium hadn't been Horatio's idea, but Emilio Augustino had always had a peculiar sense of humor. Horatio suspected it was a direct result of belonging to the international intelligence community; Emilio claimed to be Cuban, but his Russian was impeccable—as was his German, his Polish and his Czech. Rumors swirled around him: he was ex-KGB, he was a CIA mole, he was a disgraced former confidante of Castro himself. Whatever he was, he was able to obtain information from Cuban sources unavailable to Horatio himself . . . and he owed Horatio a favor.

He arrived promptly a few minutes later, a tall, dark-haired man in bright yellow trousers and a loose-fitting white linen shirt, a black zippered case held under one arm. He gave Horatio a dazzling smile and shook his hand. "Mister Caine—a pleasure, as always."

"Good to see you, too, Emilio," Horatio said. "I hope this wasn't too much trouble."

Emilio shrugged. "Trouble? That would imply work, which you know I studiously avoid. No, by the strangest series of coincidences, the information you requested just fell into my lap. I was drinking coffee at the time and barely avoided being scalded." He shook his head and looked mournful. "But then, you have always had far better luck than I. It's what comes, I suppose, from having an entire career built on the misfortunes of others." It wasn't clear if he was referring to Horatio or himself—but then, Emilio wore ambiguity the way some men wore hats.

"My deepest condolences," Horatio said with a smile. "I hope this near-tragedy won't affect the quality of the information."

"Oh, I think not. The source, while somewhat elusive, is always very reliable." He unzipped the black case and pulled out a thin sheaf of papers. "I will not, of course, inquire as to why you need this particular piece of information."

"And I, of course, will not ask where you got it," Horatio said, taking the papers. "I'd thank you for your assistance, but—"

"—but, since I did nothing of any consequence, your thanks would be meaningless," Emilio finished. His smile got even broader. "Really, this entire exchange has had no significance whatsoever."

"It's almost as if we aren't actually here," Horatio said. "In fact, I can feel my memory of this non-event eroding even as we speak."

"Then perhaps we should say our farewells. Or we will find ourselves so forgetful we wind up two strangers with nothing to share but an awkward silence."

"Embarrassing. Especially in front of the fish."

"Yes, the fish. Goodbye, Mister Caine."

"Farewell, Emilio."

The man turned and strode away. Horatio sank onto a bench and started looking through the files. "Well, well," he murmured to himself after a moment. "Isn't that interesting . . ."

The movie surprised Wolfe more than once.

The Sea Creature itself, he had to admit, was a truly memorable monster. It seemed utterly alien and completely at home in its environment at the same time, as true denizens of the very deepest parts of the ocean often did. Much of the film took place underwater, and both the photography and the choreography were so skillfully executed it sometimes felt more like a documentary than a movie.

And it was actually scary.

Not in the cat-jumping-out-of-the-closet way most modern horror flicks employed, but in a slow, creeping sense of something terrible just out of sight. The Sea Creature's long, clawed hand reaching out slowly from a roiling black cloud of squid ink; its scaly, piranha-mouthed visage barely visible behind a waterfall.

Perhaps creepiest of all were the nude scenes of the female lead. Carefully shot from below as she swam in a moonlit cove, only her silhouette was visible—and then the Sea Creature appeared. It swam with her, mimicking her every motion, in an eerie aquatic ballet that was undeniably as sexual as it was menacing. The scene ended without him actually touching her, but his longing to do so was apparent.

Until that point, the monster had only been shown in the water. In the next scene he surfaced and—obviously driven by desire—lurched his way onto dry land, only to fall, clutching his chest as he struggled to breathe. The gills on his neck flared open, water pulsed sluggishly out, and then they shut once more as he lay unmoving.

A moment passed. The gills abruptly opened once more, but no water issued forth—only air, in a sibilant hiss. They shut, then opened again, establishing a rhythm. The monster climbed to his feet, adjusting to his new environment . . . then lurched off on unfamiliar legs in search of his new obsession.

"Forget it, buddy," Wolfe muttered. "She's swimming in a different gene pool, just for starters . . ."

When he realized who the first people to encounter the monster would be, Wolfe almost groaned out loud. *Why do they even call it Lovers' Lane?* he thought. *It's always the first place the killer heads for—they should just rename it Homicide Alley.*

The young couple parked underneath the trees, oblivious of their impending doom, traded witty, pre-sexual-revolution banter. The camera provided the monster's point-of-view as he approached.

Wolfe's eyes widened. His finger jabbed out and hit a key, pausing the image.

The tight, knotted feeling in the pit of his stomach, the one that had been there ever since he'd learned he was chasing a fictional monster, disappeared; it was replaced by the anticipatory feeling he got whenever a case was about to break wide open . . .

The file Emilio Augustino had obtained for Horatio was a translated version of the Soviet military record of Doctor Nicole Zhenko.

She'd emigrated to America right after the wall fell; before that, she'd been a combat diver with a degree in marine biology. According to the file she was also experienced in demolitions, intelligence-gathering and working with "animal-assisted weapons programs."

So, assuming the Soviet program was paralleling the Navy's, she knows a lot more about dolphin soldiers than she claims . . . and her background in intelligence raises even more questions.

The more Horatio found out about Nicole Zhenko, the less he understood her true agenda. Was she a dolphin researcher with a military past,

a disgruntled former animal-rights activist, or a Soviet saboteur trying to undermine the Navy?

He stared at the glass wall of the large tank in
front of him. The Main Reef Aquarium held
750,000 gallons of water, teeming with tropical
aquatic life: cobia, grouper, loggerhead turtles.
Green-hued marble columns on the bottom gave
the impression the fish were swimming through
the remains of some ancient, sunken city.

Horatio wondered, as he sometimes did during
an investigation, if the killer had sat in this very
spot, looking at the very same scene. Wondered,
and tried to imagine what had gone through his
mind at the time.

His mind—or hers.

By the time the movie's credits rolled, Wolfe knew
several important things he hadn't before. The first
and foremost of these was that Eileen Bartstow
hadn't been lying . . . but she hadn't exactly told
him the whole truth, either.

He decided to ask her why.

She opened the door before the doorbell had
gotten through the first four bars of "Raindrops
Keep Falling on My Head," dressed in a worn blue
terry-cloth robe and slippers.

"Mister Wolfe," she said hesitantly. "I was just—
come in, please."

He did, but this time he didn't take the seat she
offered. "This won't take long," he said. "I just

wanted you to know I've been following up on your case."

"And?" she said, resignation in her voice.

"There's a few things you didn't mention in your report."

She stared at him for a second, and then an angry, knowing look came over her face. "Oh, *I* get it. The joke's so much funnier if you set it up, first. Deliver the punchline with a straight face."

"What?"

"Okay, let me have it," she said. "You gonna tell me you're having trouble getting a search warrant for Davy Jones's locker? Or maybe you tried fingerprinting the suspect but you couldn't find any waterproof ink? Go ahead, I've heard them all."

He frowned. Then he pulled out his badge and held it out to her. She looked at it suspiciously, but didn't move.

"Go ahead," Wolfe said. "Please."

She sighed and took the badge from him.

"Take a close look," Wolfe said. "You think that's a fake? A novelty?"

She peered at it, hefted it in her hand. "No," she said grudgingly. "I suppose not."

"Posing as a police officer is a serious offense," Wolfe said. "I'm a real cop, and I take my job seriously. I didn't come here as part of some elaborate gag—actually, I came here to find out if *you* were trying to pull one on *me*."

She gave him back his badge. "Giving a false

statement to the police is a serious offense, too—believe me, I've had that pointed out to me enough times already. All right, so we're both serious."

"Then *why* didn't you mention the fact that your attacker bears an amazing resemblance to the movie monster this town is famous for?"

She narrowed her eyes. "You mean the one everyone's *heard* of? The one whose face is plastered all over *town*?"

"That would be the one, yes."

"You know," she said, "I wondered the exact same thing about *you*. At first I thought you were actually taking me seriously . . . but after I thought about it, I realized you must have been just humoring me. Like you were afraid I'd freak out if you suggested my attacker wasn't real. Either that, or you'd been living in a cave all your life and really didn't recognize what I was describing . . ."

Wolfe felt his face redden. "Just because there are a few gaps in my cultural knowledge doesn't mean I live in a *cave*," he said.

She studied him for a moment, then smiled. "You're kidding," she said. "You really didn't *know*?"

"Not at the time," he said. "Blame it on my overprotective parents and *Reader's Digest*."

"Excuse me?"

"Never mind," he said, grinning and shaking his head. "Let's just say that I did some research since the last time I talked to you, and my cultural database has been upgraded to at least the middle of the twentieth century."

She laughed. "Okay, let's. Does this mean you *were* taking me seriously, and now you're not?"

"No," Wolfe said. "It means I always took you seriously—and when I get back to Miami, I'm not going to be the only one . . ."

Horatio wandered around the Seaquarium for a while. He wasn't really paying attention to his surroundings; he needed to process what he'd just learned, and once he was back at the lab there would be other things demanding his attention. Here, he could lose himself in the cool dimness of the indoor exhibits, the anonymous crowds of tourists and schoolchildren.

Eventually, though, he found himself outside, on one of the bridges that led to the children's playground. He leaned against the railing and looked down, into the algae-skinned water of the concrete moat. Built in 1955, it was one of the Seaquarium's first attractions: the Shark Channel. Jack and nurse sharks, some of them weighing up to two hundred pounds, swam lazily down the length of their circular habitat. They would show a lot more energy at feeding time, Horatio knew, when the Seaquarium staff would throw chunks of raw meat into the water, inciting the sort of frenzy most people never got to see in person. You had to catch Shark Week on the Discovery Channel for that sort of mayhem, or browse the DVD store for a copy of *Jaws.*

Or, Horatio thought, watching small children run and scream and play on the jungle gym while inhuman predators glided through the water a few yards away, *you could always decide to stage a production of your own . . .*

12

SOUTH BEACH, CALLEIGH FOUND, was a lot like a playground for adults with attention deficit disorder; no matter how bright and shiny the toys were, you had to continually add new ones so no one got bored. Clubs and restaurants—especially on Ocean Drive and Collins Avenue—seemed to be in a perpetual state of change, remodeling or upgrading or shifting ownership, everyone competing with everyone else to have the newest, the hippest, the most up-to-the-second hotspot in Miami.

Despite the continual turnover though, there were still certain generalities that were slower to change, particular businesses that tended to clump together. Bars that catered to gay clientele were often found on the same block; restaurants that specialized in one kind of cuisine were usually not too far from something similar.

Washington Avenue ran parallel to the beachfront of Ocean Drive, two blocks west of it. It featured many high-end nightclubs, eateries and hotels, but not all of it was glamorous; the stretch Calleigh was paying a visit to had a decided preference for adult bookstores, strip clubs and triple-X video outlets.

The Sintight Boutique was located in the middle of the block, between a gentlemen's club and a parking garage. Its storefront was red brick, the sign done in pink neon over a heavy wooden door with an ornate brass handle and no window. She pulled it open and went inside.

The interior of the shop was long and narrow, opening up at the far end into a wider space. A glass counter ran the length of the wall to the right, while various kinds of merchandise covered the wall on the left from floor to ceiling. Track lighting in various colors provided focused illumination, islands of brightness punctuating the shadowy recesses of the high ceiling.

The man behind the counter was perched on a high wooden stool, reading a book. He was in his twenties and wore leather pants and a black silk shirt. His hair was short, brown and neat, and he had a small, Mephisto-like mustache and goatee. Twin silver cones jutted from just below his lower lip at either edge of the goatee, looking like chromed horns on the head of a tiny, hairy devil.

He looked up when she entered, but didn't say anything, just studied her with a neutral expression.

She met his eyes and smiled, and he smiled back. "Hi," he said. His voice was deep and just slightly amused, as if her arrival was the punchline to an elaborate joke he was about to explain to her.

"Hello," she said, then hesitated, feeling strangely off-balance. "I'm Calleigh Dusquesne, with the Miami-Dade crime lab. I spoke to the owner, a Ms. Keller?"

"Yes, Cynthia mentioned you'd be in. She isn't here right now," the man said. "Had a fashion emergency with a client."

"Oh. Well, when will she be—"

"It's okay," he said, putting down his book. "Cynthia told me what you were after. I can answer your questions." He got off the stool, but didn't come any closer. "If that's all right?"

"I hope so," Calleigh said. "I need to know a few things that you just can't find in a textbook. When I tried the Internet, I ran into the opposite problem; there's too much information, and most of it goes into the wrong sort of detail. I need an actual, experienced human being to talk to."

"I believe I meet those qualifications," he said. "I'm Archer. May I see your badge?"

"Of course," she said. She unclipped it from her belt, then stepped forward so he could get a better look. He studied it intently without touching it, but somehow the entire transaction felt more personal than it usually did.

He looked up and met her eyes **again**. His were

dark brown, almost black, with long lashes. "Thank you," he said. "I've seen quite a few fakes."

"Well, I can assure you mine is quite genuine," she said. It came out slightly defensive, and she told herself silently to get a grip. It was important to maintain the upper hand in an interview, or you'd never learn anything the interviewee didn't want you to know.

"I can tell," he said. "It's much more impressive than the ones we sell."

"You—sell badges?"

"Not real ones, obviously. Strictly for role-play."

"I see." It wasn't really relevant to the investigation, but she couldn't resist asking: "Do you get many of those?"

"People who dress up as police officers? Sure. But we sell more of the female version than the male." He placed a hand flat on the countertop, then vaulted over to her side, moving with the easy grace of an athlete.

"Excuse me," he said, reaching past her to a clothesrack against the wall. He pulled out an outfit on a hanger and held it up for her to see: It consisted of a short black skirt, fishnet stockings, a blue uniform shirt with a badge clipped to the pocket, a pair of mirrored sunglasses and a dark blue patrolman's hat.

"Oh yes, standard issue at the Academy," Calleigh said. "You had to bring your own high heels, though."

He smiled. "Accessories are always the expensive part. You could spend more on a good set of handcuffs than the entire outfit."

"I have my own, thanks," Calleigh said. "Although I'm sure you carry a fine selection." She felt ridiculous as soon as she'd said it, but he didn't seem to notice.

"So—why are you here?" he asked her politely.

She blinked. "Rubber," she said. She immediately wished she'd put it another way, but that was how it had come out and now the word just sort of hung there in the air, like a big inflated condom.

"What would you like to know?" he asked, his voice as neutral as if she'd asked him a question about taxes. *Well, of course he's matter-of-fact,* she thought. *This is where he works—he gets questioned by people every day. He's probably had inquiries a lot stranger than anything I have to offer.* "Actually, it's more specific than that. I need to know about latex, in an end-user kind of way."

His eyebrows went up, ever so slightly. "End-user?"

"Not prophylactics," she said. "That's not the sort of latex, or end . . . I mean, end-user, that's just sort of a technical term . . . what I *want* is kinkier. Oh, damn."

She stopped. Took a deep breath. "Look, can I start over?"

He smiled again, showing very straight, white

teeth with pointed canines. "Please. I can't wait to hear what you'll say next."

She exhaled slowly. "Okay. I'm researching a case where the evidence is pointing to someone with a sexual preference for latex. As in fetishwear. As in Supatex Pearlsheen blue, which is a grade of latex that you carry and no one else in Miami does."

"I see. Come with me."

He turned and strode toward the rear of the shop. Calleigh stared after him for a second, then forced her eyes higher and followed.

The back of the store widened into a much larger room, one with racks of clothing lining the walls, full-length mirrors with ornate, gilded frames, and several mannequins on a central raised platform. Two female mannequins, one in a schoolgirl's uniform and the other dressed in a nurse's outfit of shiny white PVC, flanked a male dummy dressed in leather chaps and vest. All of them stared blankly down at a long, low table with a fourth figure spread-eagled on it, wrists and ankles lashed to restraints at the four corners. A gas mask obscured the mannequin's face, its body dressed in a bright red head-to-toe latex suit that included a hood, gloves and boots. It took Calleigh a second to realize that the dummy was also trapped under a thin sheet of transparent plastic that fit snugly to its every curve.

"Looks like you forgot to take the shrink-wrap off that one," Calleigh said.

"It's called a vacuum bed," Archer said. "You use a pump to remove all the air inside, sealing the person up nice and tight."

"And the gas mask is so they don't suffocate."

"Right. Or if you're into breath control, you can use it to regulate how much oxygen your playmate is getting."

"Call me old-fashioned, but I don't consider air an optional accessory . . ."

"It's not for everyone," Archer said. "A lot of people are just into the scene for the fashion. We carry a lot of latex and PVC." He indicated the wall on his right, where shiny, predominantly black clothing filled two long racks, one stacked above the other. "Red is our second biggest seller, then white. There's a few pieces in pink, purple or clear, but we don't get much call for blue."

"But you do carry it, right?"

"Oh, yes. A color like that would probably be used for a custom piece."

He pulled aside a leather curtain to reveal a small room with several rolls of fabric mounted on the wall, a cutting table and a sewing machine. "We do most of the custom work in here," he said.

Calleigh stepped past him and into the room. She leaned over and inspected one of the rolls; it was a shiny, almost iridescent blue, somehow reminiscent of fish scales. "This looks like the stuff," she murmured. "Mind if I take a sample for comparison?"

"Help yourself," Archer said. "Latex is an interesting substance. As a natural polymer, it's one of the few rubber compounds that's nontoxic in a solid or liquid state."

Calleigh blinked. *Did he really just say that,* she wondered, *or have I slipped into some kind of wish-fulfillment daydream?*

"Except for the allergy problem, of course," he continued. "They still haven't pinned down the exact protein responsible, but I understand one with a molecular weight of 14,600 is a likely suspect."

She straightened up, turned around and gave him a smile tinged with suspicion. "Really. You're extremely knowledgeable for someone working in a sex shop, Mister Archer."

"It's just Archer. Or Mister Bronski, if you'd prefer."

"Mm. Well . . . Archer, you're quite right. Latex is an unusual substance. Are you this well versed in all the materials here?"

"I know a few things. I'm curious by nature, and I have a good memory. So does latex—have a good memory, I mean; it can return to its original shape without distortion. It does shrink while it's curing, though, between three and four percent. The latex molecules polymerize by forming bonds between sulfur molecules over a period of several months, gradually hardening it into one of the strongest rubbers there is. And one of the most sensitive."

"How so?" she said, taking a sample envelope from her bag.

"It can stretch up to a thousand percent of its resting length, but it's easily damaged. Oils, ozone, even ultraviolet light can degrade it. It's one of the reasons we keep it so dark in here."

Calleigh looked around, then picked up a pair of sewing scissors from the table and used them to snip off a corner. "And here I thought it was just for the atmosphere."

He shrugged. "The crowd we cater to does appreciate a certain amount of theater. Nobody wants to buy fetishwear under fluorescent lights and a sign that says 'Clearance Sale!' in big orange letters."

"I guess that's why I have a problem with it," Calleigh said, sealing the sample inside the envelope and slipping it into her purse. "I mean, the hardest people to take seriously are the ones who demand you do."

This time, his smile was more of a grin. "I agree. And believe me, there's no one more desperate to be taken seriously than a two-hundred-pound woman trying to fit into a skintight catsuit."

"Oh? So you laugh at customers behind their backs?"

"Not at all; I just try to maintain a balance. Kink without a sense of humor is like watching people dance without music—kind of absurd and pointless."

"The watching or the dancing?"

"I'm more of a dancer than a watcher, myself . . . what about you?"

"I . . . guess I prefer to watch," she said, smiling. "After all, observation is my job." She put the barest emphasis on the last word.

He took the hint gracefully. "Well, watching is one way to learn."

"And asking questions is another," she said. "For instance: do you keep a list of the people you do custom work for?"

"Not exactly."

She frowned. "What do you mean, 'Not exactly'?"

"Despite the fact that the fetish culture has moved more and more toward the mainstream, it's still a sensitive subject for some of our clientele. Even potential blackmail material. So we don't keep official records of people's names or addresses." He put the same amount of emphasis on "official" as she had on "job," but the look on his face wasn't confrontational. More like challenging . . .

"So if there's no list, a warrant wouldn't be much use," she said. "A warrant to, say, seize and search your computer files."

"You'd be wasting your time, I'm afraid. If any private information existed, an intelligent person wouldn't keep it in the computer—or anyplace on the premises, for that matter."

"No, I suppose they wouldn't," she said. "They'd stash it someplace secure but accessible—like an email account. Too bad email accounts can be traced."

"Not if you know what you're doing. And install the right precautions."

"Automatic file deletion? You'd be surprised what you can pull off a wiped hard drive."

"When the hardware's in Singapore?"

She sighed. "Okay, okay. So I can't force you to give up the information."

"Actually, you can't prove the information *exists*."

She narrowed her eyes. "Claiming I can't prove something," she said, "is a *mistake*."

"I apologize," he said. She searched his face for any trace of mockery, but he seemed sincere.

"Well, all right," she said. "Look, Archer, I appreciate the fact that you're trying to protect your customers' privacy, but I'm trying to protect people's lives. The information you provide could very well prevent a homicide."

It was his turn to study her. After a long moment, he nodded. "You know, a lot of people have a very negative image of the fetish scene; they think that anyone who indulges in extreme sexual behavior must be evil or sick. It's the same kind of attitude that used to prevail about homosexuality.

"But I see these people every day. Sure, some of them are kind of out there, but for the most part they're just people. They don't want to impose their choices on anyone else, they just want to *play*."

"I'm not making any sort of moral judgment—"

He held up a hand and she stopped.

"You know what one of the most common elements of kinky sex is? It's not whips or chains or leather ball-gags—it's *trust*. We like to play with restraints and spanking and dressing up, but none of that happens unless the people involved feel safe enough to take those kinds of risks in the first place. You have to trust someone to let them tie you up, or hurt you, or even see you in certain outfits. Trust is something this community takes very seriously . . . and I'm one of the people they trust on a daily basis."

"I understand," she said. "I have the same attitude toward my work."

"A little information is a dangerous thing. If you were to acquire the information you were looking for, it would no longer belong to you—it would become part of your investigation. And at that point, all sorts of other people would have access to it. People who might be less than sympathetic to the people who've put their trust in me."

He wanted to help her. Calleigh knew it, could see it in his eyes, in the open posture of his body. Just as surely, she could tell he wouldn't—not unless she offered some sort of guarantee.

"The information I need is very specific," she

said carefully. "Almost certainly a male customer, who ordered a custom piece made from blue Pearlsheen Supatex. There can't be that many of your customers who match."

"Trust is about more than just asking and receiving," he said softly. "It's a deeply personal exchange. I know what you need—but what are you offering?"

She met his eyes levelly. "What do you want?"

He smiled, but it was a thoughtful smile, not a lecherous one. "Good question. I think what I want is some reassurance—but I'm going to have to give a little thought to what form that should take."

She sighed. "Okay. I'll give you my email. When you reach a conclusion, get in touch." She pulled out a business card and held it out, but it slipped from her fingers as he reached for it, landing on the plastic-sealed mannequin in the red latex suit. Calleigh bent down to retrieve it—and as she grabbed the card, she noticed the mannequin's chest move.

She straightened up abruptly, and realized there was a pair of eyes regarding her calmly behind the goggles of the gas-mask. "That's—a person," she said.

"Yes," Archer said. "Most people like to experience the vacuum bed nude, but she's into heavy rubber—multiple layers."

"Is this a—service you provide?"

He chuckled. "Not exactly. Latex is expensive, so she offered to put in a certain amount of hours as a living display—in return, she gets to keep the suit. Frankly, it's a better deal for her than us—she gets to live out a fantasy *and* keep some high-quality merchandise."

"So why not just use a dummy?"

He shrugged. "Because she's one of us. 'If we don't hang together, we will all hang separately,' you know?"

"Community spirit."

"Yes," he said simply.

She handed him the card and he took it. "I'll be in touch, I promise," he said.

"Okay, then," she said. She had the feeling that once he made a promise, Archer Bronski was unlikely to break it—and that he expected the same in return.

Doctor Nicole Zhenko is going for a swim.

This is where she feels the most alive, the most at home. She has spent a large percentage of her life in the water, and she feels a kinship to its denizens that makes her human relationships seem awkward and unfocused—not that she's ever been what you'd call a people person. She's tried to belong, to have friendships and romances—with both sexes—but she's always had trouble connecting; it's as if the air is too thin to carry the intention of her words, as if the space between her and the rest of humanity is a vacuum, a dead void that can't be crossed. She's tried, but every bridge she builds is eventually set aflame by her anger.

But there are no flames underwater, only cool blue and murky green, only quiet infinity. Even the predators here are sleek and graceful, more like works of art than biology. This is where she belongs; this is her true home.

For she is a predator as well.

She learned her skills in a Spetsialnoye Nazranie, *a troop of special purpose, attached to a Soviet naval division that dealt with the training of dolphins and beluga whales as weapons. She is well versed in all aspects of combat diving, from underwater demolitions to the operation of small, short-range submarines intended to deliver divers to their targets. If needed, she can emerge from the water, slit a sentry's throat and submerge again in seconds, making less noise than a stone skipping across a pond.*

Or she could, before she lost her legs.

Now, her transition from the wet to the dry is a slow, ungainly process. She requires technology to move through the world, technology to even raise her high enough so people aren't continually looking down on her. Now, she's angry all the time; even the deeps of the Atlantic aren't enough to quench the fire in the pit of her belly.

Strangely, she isn't angry at the tiger shark that tore off her right leg above the knee and then came back for the other one—it was only doing what it was meant to do, what millions of years of evolution had honed it for. In devouring her legs, it had made her an integral part

*of a complex chain of life; it had been a rite of passage,
one she felt deeply honored by. She hadn't been handi-
capped by a loss, she'd been given an opportunity, offered
a chance to transform. To become something more than
human.*

And she had accepted.

*The ankles on her prosthetics could be locked in a sev-
enty-degree plantigrade flex position, giving her an ease
of underwater motion greater than before. Her new legs
didn't bleed, didn't cramp, were immune to blisters and
athlete's foot and even broken bones. Carbon fiber composite was stronger and lighter than bone, and the
curved design stored and returned ninety-five percent of
the energy put into it.*

*That had been the second phase of her transforma-
tion. It had led her, inevitably, to consider further
changes. Changes in her values, in her career, in how she
viewed herself. Her very shape had changed, and she no
longer fit in her own life. Her new form had new priorities, new needs . . . or perhaps they weren't so new after
all. Perhaps they were as old as the urges in a shark's
backbrain, as old as the desire to hunt and kill and eat.*

*Or maybe they weren't primitive urges at all, but
something more evolved: a sense of responsibility, of duty.
The moral imperatives of a new life-form, better developed than the squabbling, selfish apes it was descended
from. A life-form that understood that the ocean was the
blood of the planet . . . and that blood called to blood.
That it called for blood.*

She slips over the edge of the boat and into the water.

The latex suit she wears is of a very special design; it incorporates a rebreather in the hump on the back that allows her to stay underwater for extended periods, while the mouthpiece, the air hoses, all the external technology has been internalized, hidden beneath a layer of shimmery blue latex that is now her second skin. Her legs aren't her only prosthetics: the carefully sculpted mask, the fins that jut from her limbs, the gloves with their razor-sharp embedded blades in the fingertips—these are all part of her now. And the artificial phallus that projects grotesquely from her groin is more than a symbol; it's a weapon, one that lets her mete out punishment in kind, raping those who rape the sea . . .

"No," Horatio muttered. "Only the women were raped. And why the elaborate staging of the car?"

"Sorry to interrupt, H," Wolfe said, standing in the doorway to Horatio's office. "But I think I can answer that."

Horatio pushed his chair away from his desk and stood. "Just thinking my way through a possible scenario," he said. "What's this about the car?"

"Take a look at this." Wolfe handed Horatio a printout. "This is a blowup of a frame from the movie *Creature From the Deep.*"

The black-and-white picture showed two teenagers in the front seat of a car in a grove of trees. Though it was obviously shot at night, the car was immediately recognizable to Horatio—a 1957 Chrysler 300C, the same make and model as the vehicle Janice Stonecutter's body was found in.

"Well done, Mister Wolfe," Horatio said with a smile. "I take it your foray up the coast was worth the trip."

"Eileen Bartstow was telling the truth. She was attacked by someone in an exact replica of the suit from this movie—one so realistic she thought she was facing a genuine monster."

"She was," Horatio murmured, studying the picture. "So the scenario our merman is trying to recreate is cinematic, not historical. Have you found any other parallels?"

"Well, the cove where Bartstow was attacked is one of the places that scenes from the movie were shot—but that's not all. Remember the submarine mock-up the chain was attached to? There's a scene in the movie where the Sea Creature attacks a Navy sub and sinks it."

"Which means we need to take a closer look at that wreckage. I'll get Delko on it." Horatio pulled out his cell phone.

"Uh—H?"

"Yes?"

"You mind if I tell him?"

Horatio paused, then snapped his phone shut and grinned. "Go ahead. Just don't waste too much time gloating . . ."

The email was waiting for Calleigh when she got back to the lab.

Dear Ms. Duquesne:

I've given your request a great deal of thought. My main concern, I've come to realize, is not with the dissemination of private information; you are obviously intelligent enough to conceal your sources if the situation demands it. I'm more concerned with your attitude.

Please don't take offense. For the most part, you treated me with the utmost respect and courtesy. As long as our discussion was limited to the hypothetical, you appeared willing to have an open mind, as befits a scientist and investigator. But alternate modes of human sexuality is a subject that cannot be discussed dispassionately; indeed, passion is its essence.

Your reaction to R's presence in the vacuum bed was both honest and disheartening. It is disturbing to be confronted by an unusual sexual situation, especially when it is unexpected. However, as a seeker of knowledge, you know that a single instance is hardly a representative sampling of data, and I would hate for all your future opinions to be based on one example.

Therefore, I would like to invite you to broaden your base of experience by attending a cultural event—strictly as an observer, not a participant. The nightclub Szexx hosts a weekly fetish night; explorers of every stripe are welcome, but the crowd leans heavily toward those of the rubber and latex persuasion.

Spectators are ordinarily not allowed. This is a celebration of our community, not an aquarium—but I believe that the value of increasing the understanding of a public servant outweighs any voyeuristic concerns. Proper attire is required; however, a revealing (or expensive) outfit is not. Medical fetishists will also be in attendance— therefore, a simple lab coat over street clothes will suffice.

Please accept this invitation in the spirit in which it is offered. Doing so will not only demonstrate you can encounter my community without prejudice or suspicion, it will grant you knowledge I'm sure you'll find invaluable—knowledge that will, I promise, be forthcoming as soon as you RSVP.

Yours,
Archer Bronksi

Calleigh read it over twice. Then she sighed, and hit REPLY. "The things I do for my job," she muttered.

She wondered where she could borrow a stethoscope.

13

THE PILE OF RUSTING, corroded metal on the floor of the crime lab's garage bore little resemblance to a submarine. Horatio paced around it slowly, hands on his hips, trying to envision it lying on the ocean floor.

Delko, in a set of coveralls, knelt beside the wreckage, taking measurements and recording them in a PDA.

"Can't believe I missed this," Delko muttered.

"Don't blame yourself, Eric," Horatio said. "It looks like just another piece of debris—one that's obviously been down there a long time."

"Not as long as you might think," Delko said glumly. "I've been documenting barnacle coverage and seaweed, and now I don't think it was on the bottom for more than a couple of months. The surface corrosion fooled me, but I think it must have already been in that shape when it was dumped."

"Not a lot of reason to use high-end materials when your project is destined for the ocean floor."

"Rivets are new, but most of this probably came from a scrapyard."

"Maybe the same place he got the barrels he used to float the car?"

Delko nodded. "Could be."

"I'll let you get to work, then."

Horatio would have preferred to jump in and get his hands dirty—but he knew that at the moment Eric was kicking himself, and any assistance from his boss would feel like a vote of nonconfidence. If he just left the CSI alone, Delko would push himself twice as hard—and, Horatio had no doubt, produce results.

I could point out that he was the one who spotted Janice Stonecutter's final message, Horatio thought. But a little wounded pride could go a long way . . . so he kept his thoughts to himself.

He took the elevator up to the next floor, where he stopped in on Wolfe and Calleigh in the computer lab.

"Where are we at, people?"

"Checking military records against licensed scuba divers," Wolfe said.

"Isn't that more up Eric's alley?" Horatio asked mildly.

"He's busy," Wolfe said with a grin. "Thought I'd take up the slack."

Calleigh sighed. "I—not possessing the requisite

amount of testosterone—am sadly reduced to just doing my job."

Horatio ducked his head and smiled. "Well, a little competition is a good thing . . . so what are you working on?"

She paused, then reddened slightly. "I'm waiting for a—resource to get back to me. With, you know, information."

"Okay . . . I take it this has to do with the source of the latex?"

"Yes. My contact was a little reticent, but I think I convinced him to cooperate."

"Good to hear. While you're waiting, do me a favor?"

"Sure, H."

"See if you can find any military or scuba reference to the Cyrillic symbol found on Janice Stonecutter. It was important enough that she gouged it into her own flesh as her last living act; let's not forget that."

She nodded. "Of course. I'll get right on it."

"Good. I'll be in my office . . . watching a movie."

Wolfe and Calleigh exchanged a look.

"After all," Horatio said, "why should Mister Wolfe have all the fun?"

"Man, there are a lot of scuba divers in Florida," Wolfe said. He stifled a yawn. "Excuse me."

"Uh-huh," Calleigh said absently, staring at her

computer screen. "Ryan, do you know a nightclub called Szexx?"

"Sounds familiar. Over on . . . Lincoln, I think. Never been there, but I've driven past it. Why?"

"Oh, nothing. Someone mentioned it to me, I was thinking about checking it out."

"Any luck on the Cyrillic front?" Wolfe got up from his workstation and stretched.

"Lots of Russian websites, most of which seem interested in selling me porn, Viagra, or introductions to single women from Vladivostok. Nothing that seems relevant, so far—how about you?"

"Like I said, there's a lot of scuba divers in Florida. There's also a lot of military and ex-military personnel—I think every surviving veteran since Korea has decided to retire here." Wolfe shook his head. "There's no way we can check out each and every person on this list—we've got to narrow it down."

"Have you tried cross-referencing with environmentalist groups?"

"Those membership lists aren't public. We'd need a warrant, and I don't think a judge is going to grant us access to every ecological group in the state because we think one of their members *might* be a psycho."

"No," she said, "but we might be able to get access to something else. Something a little less reputable and a lot smaller in scope."

"Such as?"

She hit a few keys in quick succession. "Theme nights are popular in a lot of clubs. They'll bring in DJs to play a particular kind of music, or sponsor events or even products. It's all about targeting a specific market—and you can't do that without advertising."

Wolfe leaned over her shoulder and studied her screen. "So?"

"So clubs have mailing lists to inform their clientele of upcoming events. If our guy is into latex, he's not just a serial—he's a demographic."

Wolfe nodded. "Makes sense. It should be a lot easier to get a warrant for someplace perverts hang out than the Sierra Club."

Calleigh glanced at him and frowned. "Let's stick to calling it a theme night, okay?"

"Huh? What, did I say something politically incorrect?"

"Probably."

"Well, what am I supposed to call them? Rubbersexuals? Full-body condom enthusiasts?"

"Look, they're just people, all right? A preference for latex is no more relevant than how often 'Wayne' pops up as a killer's middle name."

"All right, all right, I'm sorry. Sometimes I open my mouth without thinking."

"That's all right. Just keep it in mind."

"I will, I—wait a minute."

"It's interesting, though, isn't it? The Wayne thing?"

"That's the website for Szexx. The club you asked me about."

"John Wayne Gacy, Elmer Wayne Henley— there's this guy on the Internet who's compiled a whole list—"

"The club you said you were going to check out."

"Supposedly it's because they all had overly macho fathers who named them after John Wayne and then mistreated them as children, but that's only a theory—"

"Hmm. 'Bounce and Squeeze, a fetish night for latex, uniform and leather enthusiasts.' Interesting."

Calleigh turned slowly and looked up at Wolfe. Her smile froze his on his face.

"Ryan," she said. "Do you know how many firearms I own?"

"Uh—no."

"Would you like to hazard a guess?"

"Uh . . . a lot?"

"That is correct. Would you like to know how many of them it would take to make your life very, very difficult?"

He swallowed. "How many?"

"Not a single one," she said. She turned back around.

"Right," he said. "So . . . you think we can get a warrant for Szexx's mailing list?"

"That depends," she said. "I'm hoping we won't have to."

"Still waiting on that lead you got on the latex source?"

"Yeah. If it doesn't pay off, I'm going to have to get more aggressive."

"In that case, I feel sorry for your source . . ."

Delko carefully examined both sides of every piece of rusting, corroded metal. He removed one of the rivets and studied it; he took measurements, photographed tool marks where the metal had been cut, removed samples for metallurgical analysis.

Nothing.

The rivets were commonplace. The metal was cheap tin, with no serial numbers conveniently stamped on it. He might be able to match the tool marks to a tool—but first he had to find the tool.

He went back to the piece he'd originally removed from the scene, the fake periscope. He repeated the process, with similar results: It was a common lead pipe.

The problem is that it's been underwater for a while. Not years, like I first thought, but long enough for the ocean to wash away any prints or transfer on the exposed surfaces.

A sudden thought struck him. He leaned over and took a good look at one of the seams where two pieces of sheet metal had been riveted together. *Exposed surfaces, sure . . . but what about between surfaces?*

He used a Dremel cutting tool to carefully sever

each rivet, until he could pull two of the sheets apart. Sure enough, there was a thin strip where the pieces had overlapped that appeared unaffected by the salt water.

He disassembled the entire structure, then went over every inch. He didn't find what he was hoping for—a print, latent or otherwise—but he did find something else.

Something he recognized.

Dear Ms. Duquesne:

Here is the information you requested. I fear you will find it less than helpful, but please believe me when I say it was all I was able to obtain. Some of our customers are even more circumspect than myself, and if this person is a suspect in a crime he has even more reason to conceal his identity.

The only name he gave was "DeVone." His measurements were taken by himself—which is not unusual—and mailed to us. He came in personally only once, when he picked up the order. He paid cash.

I must confess, from the choice of material alone I quickly recognized who you must be looking for. From his secretive demeanor, I assumed he was in a sensitive position—possibly in the public eye—and therefore his privacy was important to him. I can give you only the roughest of descriptions: he wore dark glasses and a cap

*the entire time he was here. Around five-nine or
so, with short brown hair. From the measurements I would say he has a slender build, but his
clothes were too baggy to evaluate his physique
firsthand. A beard that I'm fairly certain was
false. He had a somewhat unusual gait, as if both
his knees were stiff.*

*I'm afraid he also took his measurements and
the design for the latex piece with him; however,
I've duplicated it as best I can from memory. If
you would like to discuss this further, I look forward to seeing you at Szexx tonight.*

Yours,
Archer Bronski

"Hello?" Delko called out, knocking on the frame
of the screen door. "Anybody home?"

"Just me," came a familiar throaty voice. This
time, when Bonnie Pershall came to the door, she
wasn't dressed in her underwear—barefoot, she
wore a short, tight skirt and a halter top that
showed a lot of cleavage. On reflection, Delko realized that ounce for ounce she was probably
wearing fewer clothes than last time.

"Oh? Where's Brutus?" Brutus was Bonnie's pit
bull; it hadn't taken long for Delko to make friends
with him.

"Out in the backyard, doing his impression of a
side of beef in a coma. I think I could probably buy a
narcoleptic sloth with more energy . . . come on in."

He opened the door and stepped inside. "Well, I think I have something of his."

"Yeah? He's had all his shots, so it probably isn't fatal." She picked up a pair of high-heeled stilettos and slipped one on, then reached out and put a hand on his chest to steady herself as she put on the other.

"You look like you're going out, so I'll make this quick," Delko said. "What I have is this." He held up a small, plastic envelope. "One of Brutus' hairs."

She frowned. "I don't get it. Did you find it in the car?"

"No. I found it on another piece of evidence, trapped between two layers of sheet metal. Didn't I see a bunch of that stuff in your backyard?"

"Yeah, leaning against the house. Brutus likes to sleep beneath it for the shade."

"Okay if I take a look?"

"Sure, go ahead."

He found Brutus asleep in the shade, in a little lean-to formed by a stack of sheet metal resting at an angle against the wall. "Hiya, pal," Delko said, kneeling down. The dog blinked at him, decided it was too much effort to get up and settled for licking Delko's hand.

Pit bulls were a short-haired breed, but even so Delko could see clumps of fur sticking to the edges of the sheet metal where they jutted out. "You probably rub up against here all the time, don't you?" Delko murmured. "Where there's smoke, there's fire . . . and where there's friction, there's transfer." He took out another sample bag and took some of the fur for comparison.

When he returned to the house, Bonnie was just putting in a pair of earrings by feel. "So?" she asked. "Does he have a solid alibi, or do I have to start looking for a good pet lawyer?"

"I think he's in the clear," Delko said. "Listen, did you get rid of some of that sheet metal a while ago? Say, three months or longer?"

"Yeah, actually. A guy bought some of it off me, said he wanted to build a tool shed or something. More of my ex's junk, so I was happy to get rid of it. I think he took five or six sheets, maybe more. Why?"

"He leave you a name, a number, anything?"

"No. I was having a yard sale, he was just one of the people who showed up."

"Can you remember what he looked like?"

"Not really. It was a while ago, and it didn't seem real important—oh. Wait a minute."

"What? You remember something?"

"No, I just figured out what this is about. It's the same guy, isn't it? That's how he knew about the car. He saw it in the yard and came back."

Delko hesitated, then said, "It looks that way, yes."

"Shit," she said. "What did you tell me about him? 'Be extremely careful,' you said. Little late, I guess."

"I'm sorry," he said. "But it still looks like he's more interested in your scrap metal than you."

"That's it," she said. "I'm selling that damn dog and buying an alligator. Know any good places to buy an alligator?"

"Actually," Delko said, "I really wouldn't go with anything aquatic . . ."

Szexx was in the basement of the building, down a flight of stairs carpeted in a rich, thick purple, with a barred gate at the foot and an imposing bouncer in front of it. He stood at least six foot ten, and obviously divided his time between pumping iron and practicing his scowl. He wore a pair of shiny black PVC shorts that laced across the groin, and black combat boots; inky black tattoos of flames curled and coiled their way across the bulging muscles of his chest, legs and arms. His face was flat and broad, his hair so short it was no more than a dark shadow across his scalp.

The line of people waiting to get in extended all the way up the staircase and outside; outfits ranged from the outrageously revealing to a surprising preponderance of people in long coats or dressed like they were going to a workout: sweatpants, baggy shirts, gym bag.

Calleigh herself was dressed as Archer Bronski had suggested, a white lab coat over street clothes. She bypassed the line, flashed a smile at the bouncer, and tried to show him her badge as surreptitiously as she could. He glared at it and her, but waved her in.

She discovered quickly that the people in loose clothing didn't keep it on for long, and what they wore underneath—or brought in their gym bags—was usually even more provocative than what was on display in the line. Men and women went top-less, or covered their nipples with strips of black electrical tape; there were thongs made of latex or leather, or more elaborate outfits with holes strate-gically cut in the material. People came in uniform, too; she saw cops, marines, firemen, nurses, and enough Catholic schoolgirls to give a nun a heart attack.

The club's dance floor was to the left, a sunken area with a staircase on one side leading down-ward to another floor. There was a simple, hand-lettered sign in black over the stairwell that read DUNGEON. Sweating bodies swayed and bounced to the sound of Nine Inch Nails throbbing from chest-high speakers, bathed in red, blue, green and pink from the lights that spun and flashed on the ceil-ing.

Past the dance floor was a large central area, with a pool table in one corner and a bar at the back. She found Archer Bronksi there, dressed much as he had been the last time she saw him, with the addition of a leather vest over his black silk shirt. He smiled and raised the glass of beer in his hand in greeting.

"I'm glad you agreed to come," he said.

"Don't be too impressed with yourself," Calleigh said. "I'm still working and there's a high possibility my suspect either *is* here or has been."

"Of course. I'm sorry the information I gave you wasn't that helpful."

"I'll have a club soda, please," she told the bartender, then turned back to Archer. "Oh, it was more helpful than you might think. The drawing you submitted matched another description from an eyewitness, so at least we have corroboration. The measurements gave us his approximate height and build, and the detail about how he walked might prove the most useful of all. Do you remember what he talked about?"

"I've been racking my brains trying to remember, actually. After all, I did tell you I had a good memory . . . but he didn't say that much. The only thing that might be significant was he asked about the effect salt water might have on latex. I told him it'd be fine, but he might want to rinse it off before it dried because it would leave salt crystals behind. I also suggested a silicon-based polish."

"Well, we found traces of silicon on our latex fragment, so that makes sense." She sipped her club soda. "You know, Archer, I've been doing some thinking, too." She took a deep breath, then let it out. "You've been very . . . forthcoming, all things considered. Your objections to sharing private information are based on ethical grounds, which I respect. But you have to understand that when I'm conducting an investigation, I'm very focused."

"You like to be in control."

"Well, yes. But I'm also part of a team, and I know the value of drawing on other people's experience, other people's insight. The CSI lab uses outside experts all the time, and we have a very professional relationship with them. I would never dream of threatening another lab with a subpoena if they didn't produce results fast enough."

"But you didn't hesitate to do so with someone working at a fetishwear store?"

"I apologize. I should have viewed you as a resource instead of a hostile witness."

"Your apology is accepted." He took a sip of his beer. "Does this promotion have any beneficial results, or was it solely to soothe your conscience?"

"Of course it does. See, a resource is someone I *share* information with, instead of just demanding it."

He laughed softly. "Okay. What are you planning on sharing with me?"

"For one thing, I thought I'd tell you *why* the information I'm after is so important . . ."

Calleigh had already told him she was working on a homicide investigation; now she told him about the *Creature From the Deep* angle. "We think our guy has a fixation on the monster, and is actually re-creating some of his attacks. The suit he had your shop make is just the foundation of his outfit; he's obviously added to it himself since then."

"That's—bizarre," Archer said, frowning. "Even for some of the people I know."

"That's why I'm telling you this," Calleigh said. "You know this crowd, you hear and see things I have no access to. I was hoping that if I shared a few more details of the case with you, it might jog your memory about something or someone."

"So—you want me to be your snitch?" His tone was more amused than annoyed.

"Oh, come on. This isn't the criminal underworld and you're not a lowlife with shifty eyes. We're both trying to do the same thing—protect your community from a predator. Or do you think the people here *want* a serial killer coming to their parties?"

"Some of them, you might be surprised . . . but you're right. Role-play is one thing, rape and murder are another." He took another drink of his beer, then set it down. "You know, I wish you'd mentioned the underwater aspect before. Stay here—I'm going to circulate and talk to a few people. I might be able to find someone who knows more."

"All right. Uh—I'm not really sure of the protocol, though."

He raised his eyebrows.

"I mean, I don't want to offend anyone—but I don't want to accept any offers, either."

Archer smiled. "I wouldn't worry about it. Most people that come here to play bring their own partners." He hesitated. "But if someone invites you to go downstairs . . . you should probably decline."

He moved off into the crowd. Calleigh glanced around, trying not to look nervous. The bartender, a young woman with multiple piercings in both eyebrows, leaned forward and peered at the name stitched on Calleigh's coat. "So, R. Wolfe—you want another drink?"

"No, thanks," Calleigh said. "I'm fine."

"That's an impressive list," Horatio said, paging through the thick sheaf of paper Wolfe had just laid on his desk.

"I know, I know," Wolfe said ruefully, rubbing the back of his neck. "I limited it to men between twenty and fifty with a military background, but it's still massive. I need some other factor to narrow it down."

"How about using the film?" Horatio suggested.

"I thought of that, but I can't figure out how to define the data. I mean, there's no way to tell who's seen it and who hasn't—we don't even know if our perp saw it on TV or the big screen. I'm sure he owns the DVD, but he could have bought it off the Internet from any one of a thousand sources."

"I was thinking of a more personal connection. Didn't you mention a local fan club?"

"Yeah, I've got an appointment with their president first thing in the morning."

"Good. You might want to check in with some of the people involved in the making of the film, too—I understand that one of the actors who did the underwater scenes is local and still does public appearances."

Wolfe frowned. "I hadn't thought of that. I guess I just assumed everyone involved was dead or in Hollywood."

"You mean there's a difference?"

Wolfe grinned. "Good night, Horatio."

"Good night, Mister Wolfe . . ."

"Calleigh Duquesne, I'd like you to meet Samantha Voire," Archer said. "I believe she has some interesting information for you."

Samantha Voire was a striking redhead, towering over Calleigh by at least a foot—much of that due to the extremely high-heeled boots she was wearing. Her outfit was similar to the one Calleigh had seen on the woman in the vacuum bed, but Voire's was black instead of red, with no hood. It also had holes cut in interesting places; Calleigh found herself focusing on the woman's face and trying not to let her eyes wander anywhere below that.

"So are you a cop or a doctor?" Voire said. Her voice was curious, not hostile.

"I'm an investigator with the Miami-Dade crime lab," Calleigh said. "Pleased to meet you."

"Ooh, a mad scientist," Voire said with a wicked grin. "Archer, you know the *best* people."

"Samantha is into breath control," Archer said. "She met someone a while ago you might—"

"Archer says you're looking for a bad person," Voire cut in. "I trust Archer, which means I'll trust you. You're not going to make me regret that, are you?"

"No, ma'am," Calleigh said.

"Good. I met a guy named DeVone here, a few months back—Archer wasn't here that night, or I'm sure he would have mentioned it himself. Anyway, the outfit he wore immediately caught my eye, because it was *extreme*. I see head-to-toe latex suits all the time, but not in Pearlsheen blue—and *not* with a diving mask and regulator. He even had a small tank of oxygen on his back. And he *moved* like he was underwater, the whole time—in slow motion, right? Like he was drifting through an underwater wreck instead of a bar . . ." She shook her head. "At the time, I thought it was cool. Thinking about it now, it seems pretty creepy."

"So you talked to this DeVone?"

"Not much, I'm afraid. Some people get totally into their own heads when they have a fantasy, and he was one of those. He kept the mask on and the regulator in his mouth the whole time. When I realized he was trying to pick me up—and *still* wouldn't take it out, even to talk—well, I was impressed with his dedication. Also, I wondered just how far he'd go."

"And how far did he?" Calleigh asked.

"All the way to the deep end of the pool," Voire said. "We went back to my place to play, and it was like he was underwater the whole time. Pretty surreal experience, even for me."

"I don't mean to be indelicate, but—exactly what do you mean by 'play'?"

Voire laughed. "Indelicate—I *love* that. Look, you might have noticed I gave you my full name when we were introduced—that's because I'm not ashamed of what I do or who I am. You don't have to worry about embarrassing me . . . though I might embarrass *you*."

"I can take it if you can," Calleigh said.

"Okay. Well, we started out in the tub, which is no surprise . . ."

Calleigh listened attentively as Voire detailed the encounter. DeVone had never removed his headgear, hadn't left a phone number, hadn't even spoken. Calleigh nodded her head from time to time, but waited until the woman was finished before asking any questions.

"Samantha, would you mind if I took a look at your place and anything he might have come in contact with?"

"I guess not—but it's been a few months, and I keep my toys clean."

Calleigh nodded. "I'm sure you do—but this definitely sounds like our guy, and if there's any chance of getting a sample of his DNA I have to take it."

Voire gave Calleigh her address and arranged to meet her the next day. "Oh, there's one more thing you might be interested in," Voire said. "He had a tattoo, just above his pubic hair."

"Wait a minute. I thought his suit covered his whole body?"

"He had a hole cut out at the groin. I don't think I was supposed to see the tattoo, but the hole ripped a little while we were going at it."

"What did it look like?"

"Give me something to draw on and I'll show you."

Calleigh pulled a pen and pad from her pocket; it only took Voire a moment to sketch a diagram.

"Now, that *is* interesting," Calleigh murmured. She thanked Voire, then watched her stride away into the crowd. "I don't know how she can walk in those things," she said, then turned back to Archer.

"Archer, I want to thank you again, too. This was invaluable, it really was."

"I hope so. Even though Samantha wasn't hurt, members of my community are particularly vulnerable to this sort of danger; I sincerely hope you catch him."

"So do I . . ." She hesitated, then said, "Look, there's something else. I know you've given me all the information you have on DeVone, but if he attends events like this one there's a chance he's put his name on a mailing list. I've got a warrant for any such list the club may have—assuming they haven't been as smart as you were."

He studied her calmly, then nodded once, slowly. "I understand."

"I'm sorry. I promise I'll do my best to keep the information on the list as contained as possible. I— I've got an associate waiting outside in a car. If you like, I can have him serve the warrant instead."

His eyes narrowed, and then he smiled. "Ah. Because you've been seen talking to me, right? You don't want to blow my cover as your informant. How thoughtful."

She reddened. "I thought you might appreciate a certain amount of—anonymity."

He picked up his glass of beer, took a last swallow and set it down again, carefully. "Go ahead and serve your warrant. I won't hide what I've done—I believe in dealing with consequences, not denying them. What I don't believe in is taking that choice away from other people."

"You haven't—"

"No," he said. "You have."

He turned and walked away.

14

HORATIO STUDIED THE CRUDE drawing Samantha Voire had made. "So this is what Janice Stonecutter was trying to tell us," he said.

"She must have gotten a look at it during the rape," Calleigh said. "Voire said it was tattooed just above his groin."

"The Cyrillic version of Z, inked in a very private place," Horatio said. He looked down at the other objects on the light table and raised his eyebrows. "Along with some items that have also seen their share of private places . . ."

"Samantha Voire called it her toybox," Calleigh said. She picked up something that looked like a rabbit riding a carrot. "Which she apparently keeps well stocked. She says that the toys used internally she keeps scrupulously clean, but I thought I might get lucky on some of the others."

"So to speak," Horatio murmured. "Good work. And this is the mailing list from the club?"

"Yes. We had to confiscate their computer, but Anderson managed to get into their system and retrieve the file this morning. DeVone *is* on the list— but it's a PO box."

"Our boy is careful—but not careful enough. He's proud of what he is, and it chafes him to have to conceal it."

"Why do you say that, H?"

"The name. In the film, the Sea Creature is supposed to have evolved during the Devonian age; the fact that he used it as an alias tells me not only how deeply he identifies with the character, but that he considers it an expression of his true self." Horatio shook his head. "What I don't understand is why he let Samantha Voire live. She was vulnerable, nobody at the club could ID him, and he was wearing the suit. And his behavior shows he was deeply immersed in his fantasy . . ."

"Maybe not deeply immersed enough. According to Samantha, she invited him back to her place because her apartment complex has a pool; when they got there, she found out it had been drained for maintenance. They made do with a bathtub, but apparently he was quite disappointed."

"I'll bet," Horatio said. "So it wound up being— if you'll pardon the expression—a dry run . . ."

*   *   *

The president of the *Creature From the Deep* fan club lived in North Miami, but Wolfe got only voice-mail when he called. He left a message, then decided to take Horatio's advice and look up someone that had actually been in the movie.

Brett Rosamond wasn't hard to find; he had his own website for people who wanted to contact him for personal appearances or signed photos, with a phone number at the bottom of the page. Wolfe called it, and the gruff but friendly voice on the other end agreed to meet him at a coffee shop in Miami Beach in half an hour.

Wolfe found him in a red-leather–upholstered booth, staring out the window at rollerbladers skimming past, and enjoying a milkshake. He was a big man, in his seventies, with white hair combed back and the sort of build that reminded Wolfe of a sack of potatoes that's settled over a long period of time. "Mister Rosamond?"

Rosamond beamed with a mouthful of spotless white dentures and held out a big, meaty hand. Wolfe shook it, then slid into the booth across from him.

"Thanks for agreeing to talk to me," he said.

"Always glad to help out the authorities," Rosamond said. His voice was just as hearty and robust as the rest of him. "Although I don't see what possible interest you could have in an old frogman like me."

"Believe it or not, it concerns an old role of yours: the *Creature From the Deep*."

"Gilly?" Rosamond laughed. "Why, does the Policemen's Ball want him to put in an appearance?"

"No, sir, I'm afraid it's more serious than that.
We believe that someone with a fixation on the
character may be involved in several homicides."

Rosamond's eyes widened. "Homicides? You're
kidding."

"I wish I were. It's also possible this person may
have tried to contact you—is there anyone you can
think of that stands out as unusual?"

Rosamond shook his head. "Most of Gilly's fans
are just ordinary people, usually ones that saw the
movie as kids and have fond memories. I've gotten a few crazies over the years, but never anything that worried me. Not until now, anyway."

"How about someone who just seemed a little
too interested? Maybe somebody who asked questions you felt were inappropriate?"

"Well, that certainly widens the playing field.
I've had people ask me how I went to the bathroom in the suit, if I had sex with any of the actors, if I ever wear the suit around the house . . .
I mean, there are fans, and then there are *fans*. I
met this one guy from Tennessee, he had seventeen different model kits of Gilly, all perfectly
painted and posed on his mantelpiece. I can't say
he struck me as dangerous, though."

"Can you recall his name?"

"I don't think so. But if you want that sort of
information, I'm not the person you should be

talking to; you want someone from the fan club. They have their headquarters right here in Miami, you know."

"I know," Wolfe said. "I'm going to be talking to them next. So, about the suit—do you still have it?"

Rosamond chuckled. "No, no, that was always the property of the studio. They let me wear it for a few publicity appearances when the movie first came out, but after that it went into storage. Eventually it was donated to a charity auction."

"Do you know who bought it?"

"Sure. Oliver Tresong. He's—"

"—the president of the fan club," Wolfe said. "Do you know anything else about him?"

"Well, he's a diver. One of the reasons he was so interested in the suit is the mechanics of how it worked."

"I was wondering about that myself."

"It had a built-in air tank," Rosamond said, leaning forward. He reached over his shoulder and tapped his own back. "Sat right about here, concealed under the rubber. It's what gave Gilly his distinctive humpbacked appearance. Tank didn't hold that much air, but it was good for about fifteen, twenty minutes. Between takes I'd stay on the surface, breathe through my nose."

"When was the last time you talked to Mister Tresong?"

"Last week. We were talking on the phone

about a local festival—we're doing an appearance together and he wanted to go over some notes."

"Did he sound normal?"

"Well, he was sort of excited, but with the anniversary coming up and all . . ." Rosamond looked troubled. "You don't think he has anything to do with this, do you?"

"I don't know," Wolfe said. "But I guess I better go ask him."

Calleigh surveyed the array of items laid out on the light table. "I feel like the prop manager for a porn studio," she muttered. There were devices intended for penetration, flagellation, masturbation and sheer intimidation. One phallic instrument measured a whopping two feet in length, while another was a mere five inches. Some were realistic, others so bulbous and brightly colored they reminded her of a dog's chew toy.

Other parts of the animal kingdom were represented, too: riding crops, cat-o'-nine-tails and even flyswatters. There was a variety of harnesses and leashes. There were paddles made from leather, wood, rubber and plastic, there were ball-gags and blindfolds and enough rope to rig a tall ship.

There was even technology, in the form of vibrators and several objects she had to experiment with before she figured out what they were for. One looked like a small sports racket—it was a battery-powered bug zapper that delivered a jolt of electricity when something struck its metal strings.

"Tennis, anyone?" Delko asked as he walked through the door and grabbed his lab coat.

"Love, set and match?" Calleigh said. "Not sure about the love part, but this is definitely the entire set. Just about to start on the match—want to give me a hand?"

"Wouldn't miss it," Delko said with a grin. "You want me to tackle anything in particular?"

"Hmm. Here, why don't you start with this?" She picked up something long and beige with a head on either end, and waggled it at him.

"Sure," Delko said. "Uh, just put it down, okay?"

"Whoops—sorry, I think that's upside-down." She spun it around like a floppy baton. "Better?"

Delko laughed. "Not even remotely . . ."

They got to work. They swabbed down surfaces with Q-tips dipped in sterile water, looking for stains that might hold viable DNA. The swabs went into vials for processing.

"Think we'll find anything?" Delko asked.

"Hard to say." She picked up a flogger with a braided leather handle on one end and a bundle of thick leather straps on the other.

"Anything we do find isn't necessarily going to do us any good in court, either. I mean, I get the feeling that more than one person has been on the receiving end of these . . . implements."

"Depends on what it is," Calleigh said. "The

owner told me that DeVone liked it rough—hope-fully, that'll increase the chances of transfer."

"Yeah, but the guy was wearing a full-body con-dom the entire time, right? No contact, no trans-fer."

"Yes, but in this case the container may be as important as the contents . . ." She put down the flogger and picked up a short whip. "Did you know the tip of a whip can travel at over fifteen hun-dred miles an hour?"

"Sure. The crack you hear is the tip breaking the sound barrier."

"That's been the commonly accepted wisdom for the last hundred years," Calleigh said. "But a pro-fessor at the University of Arizona recently proved the tip was actually moving at more than twice the speed of sound when the crack occurred. Turns out it isn't actually the tip that makes the sound, it's the loop that travels the length of the whip when it's cracked."

Delko thought about that for a second. "Makes sense. Like the outside of a wheel is actually mov-ing faster than the center."

"Exactly. A whip is also tapered, which acceler-ates the loop traveling along it by a factor of ten; the tip also weighs less, which contributes as well." She took the whip over to the microscope and po-sitioned it carefully. "In some whips, the tip can wind up moving more than thirty times faster than its initial speed . . ." She peered into the eyepiece and adjusted the focus. "Which is more than fast enough to damage latex. Take a look."

She moved aside and let Delko take a turn. "Looks like something adhering to one of the strands," he said. "Something a very familiar shade of blue."

"I'll get it to Trace," Calleigh said.

"Mister Tresong," Wolfe said. "Thank you for seeing me."

Oliver Tresong was a tall, thin man in his thirties, with scraggly blond hair and a cigarette dangling from his lips. "Uh, no problem," he said. He was dressed in a pair of baggy shorts, a T-shirt with a faded picture of the Sea Creature on it, and flip-flops. "Come on in." He stood aside and motioned Wolfe inside.

Tresong's house looked like a shrine to old horror movies. Shelves lined the walls, filled with cast-resin models of every imaginable type of monster: vampires, werecreatures, bug-eyed aliens and giant radioactive lizards. A gleaming chrome statue of the Terminator aimed a large-caliber gun at the head of a zombie, who was too busy eating someone's brain to notice. A large flatscreen dominated most of one wall, with a comfortable leather recliner positioned in front of it.

And beside the TV, the Sea Creature.

It stood inside a glass case that reached to the ceiling, its base a foot or so high so that it seemed to tower over any observer. Blue-tinted spotlights gleamed off its wet-looking skin. The webbed claws of its hands were placed flat against the glass of the front panel, as if it were trying to get out.

Tresong sank down onto the recliner. "What's, uh, all this about?" he said. He sounded like he'd just woken up.

"Well, it's about—*him*, actually," Wolfe said, pointing at the display.

Tresong suddenly seemed a lot more awake. He sat up straighter in the recliner. "Excuse me?"

Wolfe walked up to the display case and studied it. "It's in really good shape," he said. "I would have thought the rubber would show more signs of wear after all this time."

"I'm—really careful with it," Tresong said. "What is it you want, exactly?"

Wolfe turned to face him. "I'd just like to ask you a few questions, if that's all right."

"I guess so. What do you want to know?"

"First of all—how long have you owned this suit?"

"I bought it six—no, seven years ago. It's never been out of that case. I mean, not as long as I've owned it."

"Really. You've never been tempted to—you know."

"What?"

"Try it on."

He shook his head. "No way, man. That thing is

valuable. Who knows what I might tear by accident? I mean, old rubber can get pretty brittle."

"Valuable, huh? *How* valuable?"

Tresong hesitated before answering. "I don't know, exactly. I put it up on eBay, I could probably get a few thousand for it."

"Only a few thousand? For a one-of-a-kind item like this?"

"Maybe as much as nine or ten. If I found a collector who was interested."

"Considering that you're the president of the fan club, I guess you'd know who to ask."

Tresong abruptly stood up. "Look, I'm kinda busy right now. Can you get to the point?"

"All right. When was the last time you went diving?"

"I don't know—a few weeks ago, I guess. I don't remember, exactly."

"Ever been swimming in Poker Cove?"

"Sure. Lots of times."

"How about the night of March twenty-fourth, this year?"

"No. No, definitely not. I was in New Jersey, at a collector's convention." He wouldn't meet Wolfe's eyes.

"Can you prove that?"

"Well, I used my credit card, so there's a record of me being there, yeah."

"I'll need to see those records. I also need to know where you were on the following dates . . ."

Tresong, it turned out, had virtually identical alibis for the times the Stonecutters were attacked and when Gabrielle Cavanaugh was killed: He was out of town.

"One last thing, Mister Tresong," Wolfe said. "I'd like to take a closer look at the Sea Creature suit."

"What? No. No way," he said. "I told you, that thing is valuable. You think I'm going to let a bunch of cops turn it inside out and cut off samples and who knows what else? Forget it. You want to touch Gilly, you show me a warrant."

"If that's what it takes," Wolfe said. "But it may not be necessary. Would it be all right if I just took some pictures, through the glass? I won't touch it, I promise."

Tresong thought about it for a moment. "Well . . . I guess. But that's it—after that, I'm *done*."

I wouldn't be so sure, Wolfe thought as he went out to his car for his camera. *Gilly may have more to say to me than you think . . .*

"Well?" Calleigh asked.

Delko straightened up from the microscope and sighed. "Multiple epithelials," he said. "You were right, the floggers picked up skin cells on impact. Problem is, we don't know how many donors we're looking at, or which one is our guy's. If he kept the suit on, maybe none of them."

"So we process them all," Calleigh said.

"Oh, Valera's gonna *love* us . . ."

"I'll tell her," Calleigh said.

Calleigh ran into Horatio on her way to the DNA lab and told him what they'd found. "It looks like the suit he wore while he was with Samantha Voire was just the basics; he didn't go for the full fishman getup until he attacked Eileen Bartstow."

"Which fits his pattern of continually evolving his methods," he said, walking alongside her. "I've been doing a little deep background research, myself."

"Oh? How deep?"

"Four hundred million years, give or take a century or two."

She smiled. "The Devonian era? You never struck me as the paleontology type, H."

"I'm not. But forewarned is forearmed . . . did you know the Devonian Age is commonly known as the Age of Fishes?"

"Sure. It was the period where vertebrates first moved from the sea to the land—from an evolutionary standpoint, it was a highly significant time. I think the only other animal life on land back then were bugs and spiders—or their great-to-the-nth-degree-grandparents."

"But that wasn't true of the oceans," Horatio mused. "They were home to all sorts of unusual life-forms—including predators. Take a look at this." He reached into his breast pocket, pulled out a piece of paper and handed it to her.

She unfolded it, studied it for a second, then nodded. "I see the resemblance."

"It's called a placoderm. It was armored with thick scales, and had a bony ridge in its mouth instead of teeth. In fact, it was one of the first creatures to evolve a jaw. There's no telling what color this thing's scales were, of course . . ."

"But they could have been Pearlsheen blue," she said, finishing his thought. "And the detail about the jaw might tie in to the dolphin-jaw device he's used."

"The same thought occurred to me," Horatio said. "The most important theme that crops up concerning the Devonian Age is transition. Transition from jawless bottom-feeders to predators, transition from one environment to another. I think our merman views himself as going through the same process."

"Which is why the details have changed with each attack," Calleigh said. She nodded, and pushed a stray tuft of blond hair behind one ear. "The question is—transition to what?"

"I don't know. But we do know his starting point—the one he's getting further and further away from."

"Yes," Calleigh said quietly. "Human."

Wolfe took his pictures of the Sea Creature suit and clipped them to the wall. He stood back, slid his hands into the pockets of his lab coat and studied his work.

In every shot, he'd also placed a marker that documented the size of his target. Thanks to the way the suit was posed with the outspread gloves against the glass, he'd managed to get a pretty good measurement of the space between each of the claws.

He compared them to the measurements he'd taken from Eileen Bartstow's slashed bathing suit.

They matched.

"Horatio."

"Emilio." Horatio pulled up a chair and joined the Cuban at the little sidewalk café where he was sitting.

"Twice in one week, my friend? What are the odds?"

"Do you have what I asked for?"

"If some third party were to see us together again after so short a period of time, they might draw all sorts of inferences," Emilio said, unperturbed. "Inferences surely unfounded, but perhaps troublesome. For both of us."

Horatio sighed, took off his sunglasses and pinched the bridge of his nose. "I'm sorry," he said quietly. "There are lives at stake, and the clock is ticking."

"That is the nature of your profession," Emilio replied. "Not mine. I *have* no profession, Horatio, as I believe you are well aware. And I have no desire to be drawn into anyone else's."

He paused, took out a cigar and took his time lighting it. When he was finally satisfied that it was smoldering to the right degree, he leaned back and blew a careful, rippling smoke ring before continuing. "I may have learned something that you will find interesting. But before I impart this knowledge to you, I need to know that you take my reservations seriously."

"Emilio," Horatio said, "you know I wouldn't ask for a favor unless it was urgent—and I've *never* asked for two in a row."

"What I know is that you and I are very different men," Emilio said. "Men who respect each other, yes, but different things matter to us. If it would save a single life, you would sacrifice our friendship in an instant."

Horatio regarded him levelly, but said nothing.

"That is nothing to apologize for," Emilio said, "nor would I expect such an apology. Your convictions are one of the reasons I hold you in such high regard."

He fixed Horatio with an amused stare, but now there was something deeper and colder below it. "They are not, however, *my* convictions. Do not mistake my assistance for a soft heart."

"I wouldn't dream of it," Horatio said.

"That is good. While I do possess such an organ, I have been assured that mine is a black and shriveled thing, able to keep the blood coursing through my veins more through pity than anything else . . .

and that is hardly the basis for a reliable relationship. It is, I suppose, why I find myself alone in my declining years."

Horatio smiled despite himself. "Then I won't appeal to your better nature."

Emilio smiled in return. "A wise choice. In fact, you would do better to appeal to my sense of the absurd—it is far better developed, and in today's chaotic world more applicable as well. For instance, the detail you asked me to research."

Horatio leaned forward intently. "You've found something?"

Emilio took another long, lazy drag on his cigar. "Indeed I have. The particulars are here." He reached into his breast pocket, pulled out a thin envelope and handed it to Horatio. "It was a most peculiar request, but not beyond my talents."

"Thank you," Horatio said. "I owe you, Emilio. I won't forget."

"I am sure," Emilio said, blowing another smoke ring, "that you will not . . ."

15

"THANK YOU FOR COMING in to talk with us again," Horatio said.

Malcolm Torrence stared at him contemptuously from the other side of the table. "Believe me, I'm not here because I want to be," he said. "But you made it very clear you could cause the Alliance a lot of trouble if we didn't cooperate."

"I'll try to be brief, then," Horatio said. "I'd like to talk to you about the Navy's Marine Mammal Program."

"What about it?"

"You worked on it, didn't you?"

"After I'd already left the Navy, yes. The company I worked for had a contract with the Defense Department to do reclimatization testing on their animals."

Horatio nodded. "Reclimatization—that means getting them ready to return to the wild, correct?"

"It was supposed to. We had to teach them how to fend for themselves after years of being trained to come when whistled for. When we got them, they wouldn't even eat live fish, let alone catch any themselves."

"So your job was to ensure they could survive once they were freed."

Torrence snorted. "So they told us. But really, the whole thing was all just about politics—the only reason they hired us in the first place was to appease the animal-rights organizations."

"The company you worked for . . . that would be the Aquarian Institute, correct?"

"That's right."

"Under the supervision of Doctor Nicole Zhenko?"

"Yes."

"But you aren't there anymore. What happened?"

Torrence began drumming the fingers of his left hand on the table. Horatio couldn't tell if it was out of agitation or boredom. "You want to know what happened? Zhenko *lost* it, is what happened."

Horatio settled back in his chair. "Lost it how?"

"She just went over the edge, man. She was always a little strange, but the closer we came to releasing the dolphins the stranger she got. Finally, she just snapped. Refused to release them, said they belonged with her, not running free."

"How did the Navy take that?"

He laughed once, bitterly. "It played right into their hands. See, it turned out they didn't really want to release them at all—and she gave them exactly what they wanted. Wrote a report saying that further study was needed, that the dolphins wouldn't survive on their own."

"It sounds, Mister Torrence, as if you don't exactly approve."

"I'm a cool breeze compared to Hurricane Nicole. Afterward, we all quit—none of us could work with her. She wasn't rational. Spent all of her time in the water, and even when she wasn't she talked more to the fish than any of us."

"Any of you? Who else was employed by Aquarian?"

"Anatoly Kazimir, Fiodr Cherzynsky and Ingrid Ernst."

Horatio raised his eyebrows. "All members of the ALA," he observed. "Funny that an organization with such extreme views would refuse to work with someone like Doctor Zhenko."

Torrence pursed his thin lips. "The ALA, despite what you may think of us, is not a terrorist organization. We have enough public-image issues without having a psycho on our roster. You know what I caught her doing once? She was *licking* a dolphin. I love animals, but that—that was just *sick.*"

"Uh-huh. Tell me, have you ever seen this?"

Horatio pushed a piece of paper across the table.

Torrence picked it up, glanced at it and said, "Sure—it's a tattoo. Anatoly, Ingrid, Fiodr and Nicole all have the same one. It's some kind of Russian bonding thing—I never really understood it."

"Well then," Horatio said mildly, "I guess I'll just have to ask someone who does . . ."

Doctor Zhenko refused to come in to be interviewed. Horatio went to talk to her, instead.

She was out by the pool again, perched on the tiled rim next to her Levo chair. The night breeze off the ocean was cool, but she was dressed only in the same one-piece black bathing suit she had been the first time they'd met. Underwater lights threw rippling blue patterns over her face as she bent over the dolphin floating placidly at the pool's edge.

"Doctor Zhenko," Horatio said, stopping a few feet away. "There's a few things we need to discuss."

"I'm very busy," she snapped. "Whaleboy has some sort of fungal infestation."

"I've been getting contradictory information from some of your former colleagues," Horatio continued. "Specifically, from your former associates in the ALA."

She snorted. "So? Whatever they have to say, I'm not interested. I told you what I think of those *mudilos* already."

"What they say is that they used to work for you. And when you refused to return the Navy dolphins in your care back to the wild, they resigned in protest."

"What?" She clambered onto her chair, not bothering with the pretense of needing help; Horatio noted the strength in her arms, in how easily she pulled herself into a sitting position. "Those *niegadzai podonok svolotch! Hooy tebe v zhopu zamesto ukropu* . . . that is *not* what happened. Those idiots wanted to release them before they were ready, and when I objected they released them anyway. And you know what came next? The dolphins wound up chasing charter boats around, begging for fish. One got chopped up by a propeller. The Navy came and blew their damn whistles, and the dolphins swam right back into their pens like good little soldiers. What did those *zalupas* expect, that suddenly the bottlenoses would forget what had been drilled into them for the past twenty years? *Paltsem delanniy!*"

Horatio approached the edge of the pool, squatted down and looked Whaleboy in the eye. The dolphin made a high-pitched sound and dove under the water. "So the Navy returned them to you?"

"Only after I fired Anatoly and all his cronies. Even so, they didn't stay—the dolphins were moved to another facility in California. The Navy, they thought maybe I got a little too attached to them."

Horatio straightened up. "Did you?"

She rolled right at him, but he didn't step back. She stopped inches from his foot. "Of course I did. You think I'm some kind of heartless monster, that I would feel nothing when beings I have cared for, beings I have *healed*, leave me? I cry for them, Horatio; I cry more for their loss than that of my own limbs."

"And does someone have to pay for your tears, Doctor? Pay with tears of their own?"

"We all pay, sooner or later." She glared at him, then made a dismissive gesture and wheeled away again. Horatio followed her.

"You don't understand," she said. "I am Russian. I know I am dying from the moment I am born. Losing what you love, that is simply the way of things. That does not mean you don't love; it means you embrace the flames and don't curse the fire. You Americans, you always act as if everything should be free, as if the world is a big birthday party just for you. You take and take and do not see the price you will one day be asked to pay."

"Some of us," Horatio said, "are more aware of that price than you might think."

She rolled slowly to a stop. She paused for a long second before speaking again. "*Da*. Maybe so. You know how it feels, to lose something you love—I can see it in your eyes. But that doesn't make us friends."

"I'm not asking for your friendship," Horatio said, putting his hands on his hips. "I'm asking for your honesty. In return, here's a little of mine . . . every time I turn around, something else points toward you. You hate the Navy, you work with dolphins. Despite your earlier coyness about whether or not cetaceans could be trained as weapons, that's exactly what you used to do in Russia— where you also received training in underwater demolitions and combat diving.

"Despite all that, I don't think you're the killer—but I do think you're involved. You and someone else from the ALA. Someone else with a Cyrillic *Zhe* tattoo in a very private spot."

"The tattoo? What does that have to do with anything?"

"Why don't you tell me?"

She wheeled around, frowned at him. "It is from my time in the Soviet Navy. We all got one, in a grungy little parlor in Novobirsk."

"I know. I also know why you got it, and why you chose that particular letter."

"You must have good sources."

"I make do. And apparently, so did you."

She gave him a venomous look. "I did what I was ordered to. If it hadn't been me, it would have been someone else. At least I could make it quick."

"It must have been . . ." Horatio trailed off.

"Horrifying? Monstrous? An atrocity? Yes, to all of them. You want to know the details? I did it with explosives. Got the entire group in the same pool and set off an underwater charge. Hydrostatic pressure killed them all, instantly." Her eyes grew distant. "When I dropped the bomb in the water, they thought I wanted to play. One of them was pushing it along the bottom with his nose when it went off."

"Couldn't you have just released them?" Horatio asked.

"No. They were weapons, you see. My superiors were afraid you Americans, or maybe the Chinese, might capture one and study it. They couldn't have that, and there was no money for 'special projects' after the wall came down—so they all had to be destroyed."

"I'm sorry," Horatio said. "That's a terrible thing for anyone to have undergone."

Her shoulders jerked in a quick, angry shrug. "So? You think we're the only ones to do such things? You Americans love your pets, your cats and dogs. In Vietnam, you used German shepherds to find mines, sniff out traps. They saved many lives. And when the war was over, did those dogs come back to a well-deserved reward? No, they were all exterminated, just like my dolphins. Why? Because it was *cheaper*." She spat the last word out like it was laced with poison.

"And the tattoos were a way of honoring your dead."

"It was the code letter for our unit. We swore we would never forget."

"Janice Stonecutter didn't forget, either—because the person that raped and killed her had the same tattoo."

"And you think it was one of us. One of *them*."

"I do."

"All right, you are too tough for me. I confess." She threw her arms up in mock despair. "I did it all, with a big rubber *yelda*. Clever of me, hah? No one suspects the legless woman of being the rapist!"

"While you're making jokes, another woman could be dying," Horatio said. "Would you like to know how Janice Stonecutter died? She was chained inside a sunken car for most of a day, kept alive with a tank of oxygen while he brutalized her with a homemade set of claws. She was raped repeatedly. When she finally bled to death, he disemboweled her."

The look she gave him was stony. "Is that supposed to shock me? Even with your sources, you have no idea what I've seen, what I've done. I'm no angel, Horatio."

"No, but you're not a monster, either. And he is. Do you really want this guy loose in the same water you swim in?"

"Why not? It's a big ocean," she said. She rolled over to the old fridge, yanked it open and reached inside the freezer compartment. She pulled out a bottle of Stolichnaya vodka and a small glass, rimed with frost. "You think he's the only predator in there? There are over two hundred seventy species of shark. Okay, so very small number of species ever attacks humans—three percent, maybe. You know how many kind of man-eaters that is?"

"I can do the math."

"Math, pfah. I can tell you their names." She balanced the glass on the arm of her chair, uncapped the vodka and poured a shot. "The great white, the oceanic whitetip, the bull. The hammerhead, the mako, the nurse; the blue and the grey and the blacktip reef. Even the ones with the ridiculous names: the spitting shark, the wobbegong, the porbeagle." She raised the glass. "And let us not forget my favorite, *Galeocerdo cuvier*. The tiger shark. Up to eighteen feet long, weigh as much as a ton. They eat almost anything: fish, rays, marine mammals, turtles, birds, sea snakes, even other sharks. And of course, tasty Russian divers."

She tossed the shot back in a single, convulsive movement, then continued without pausing for breath. "The native Hawaiians call them *Awna Kua*. They believe they hold the spirits of their ancestors. A hell of a thing to believe, eh? To have as your last thought, 'I wonder if that's grandmother chewing on my liver.' You want some of this?" She held up the bottle.

"No."

"Of course not. In Moscow, a cop wouldn't even

hesitate." She poured herself another. "It was my own fault, you know."

"What was?"

"Losing my legs." She laughed once, a harsh bark with no mirth in it. "English, it's such a stupid language. My legs are not lost; I know exactly where they are. You want to see?" She threw back the shot, then wheeled around, bottle in hand, and headed for a laptop glowing dimly on a table beside the pool. She tapped a few keys, cursed, then tapped a few more. "See, I was helping tag tiger sharks as part of a research program. Tigers swim in a very certain way, from the bottom to the surface and back again, like a yo-yo. I knew this. Tigers will also not attack prey that sees them coming; the best defense, believe it or don't, is to look them in the eye. I knew that, too. Ah, here we go. Look."

Horatio came over. On the laptop's screen was a murky green background. "What is this?" he said.

"The work we were doing, it was to track the movements of tiger sharks, figure out their behavior, see how far they ranged in search of food. We used two methods: one, we implant ultrasonic pinger in peritoneal cavity, gives off beeps we can detect with hydrophone. This is other method." She indicated the screen. "Sharkcam. Clipped to dorsal fin. Data uploaded via satellite, sent to Website via miracle of Internet."

Horatio leaned in, squinted at the screen. He

could make out a few jerky details now, silvery flashes he supposed were fish. "Are you telling me this is—"

"Was *my fault*," she repeated. "Wasn't paying attention. Sharks never attack from above, did you know? Bodies aren't built for it. So all I have to do is look down and around every once in a while to keep from being supper. That's all . . ."

"So you blame yourself."

"They wanted to kill it, you know? Afterward. It was one of the ones we'd already tagged, so it wasn't hard to catch again. But I wouldn't let them. I told them to put a camera on it, to see what it would do next. An invaluable chance for research, I told them. And they did as I said."

Horatio rubbed his chin. He stared at the screen, then glanced at Zhenko. The look on her face was equal parts fascination and longing. "I come out here, sometimes, late at night when I can't sleep," she said softly. "I watch another world through a hunter's eyes. I used to wonder if it changed him—consuming part of me. But I realized that was foolish . . . sharks don't change. Millions of years of evolution had no effect, so why should I? No, it was I who was transformed, not him . . ."

"So you're no longer part of the human race, is that it?" Horatio asked softly. "No connection, so no obligations? What does that make you?"

"I don't know," she said. "Tired. Alone. Frustrated. *Mne vse ravno.*"

"What does that mean?"

"It means, I don't care." She put the bottle of vodka to her lips and took a long drink.

"I don't believe that," Horatio said. "If nothing else, you still care about dolphins."

"So? If your killer starts going after them, give me a call."

"You know, I've known a number of people that work closely with animals. Sometimes their social skills are a little off, but few of them are actually misanthropic. The reason most of them choose to become vets or zoologists or members of the K-9 squad isn't because they hate people; it's because they see the best qualities of humanity expressed in another form of life. Loyalty, intelligence, playfulness, even love . . . those are the aspects they recognize, and those are the aspects that draw people to a lifetime of caring for and communicating with a different species. I don't think you're any different."

She slammed the bottle of vodka down on the table. "Look, what do you want from me? I told you, I don't know anything about your damn killer! You say he's one of *Zhe* unit? Fine! Go talk to Anatoly or Ingrid or Fiodr!"

"I will," Horatio said calmly. "But before I do, I wanted to ask you one question."

"Go ahead," she growled.

"David Stonecutter was killed with a unique weapon, a Soviet underwater pistol called an SPP-1.

It's exactly the sort of thing a Russian expat might take with them, as a military souvenir or to sell later." Horatio locked eyes with her. "Would you have any knowledge of such a weapon?"

She met his gaze without blinking. "*Da*. We were all trained to use them, but only Anatoly decided to take his with him. He used to think it was funny to set up a bull's-eye in the deep end of a pool."

"Thank you," Horatio said.

"You are so welcome," she said acidly. "Now get out. I have some serious drinking to do." She grabbed the bottle of vodka and turned back to the laptop. "Just me," she said, raising the bottle to the murky green screen, "and my brother . . ."

"I've got your results," Maxine Valera said. The DNA tech had a sheaf of papers in one hand—a sheaf of papers, Delko noticed, that was entirely too thick for his liking.

He liked what she said next even less. "Twelve donors. Seven male, five female. Apparently the owner of Sex Toys 'R' Us was an equal-opportunity deviant."

"Or she liked to share," Delko said. "Thanks, Maxine. Hopefully, we'll have something to compare these results to soon."

"If you do, you'll know where to find me."

Delko left the DNA lab, deep in thought. DNA on the sex toys would help identify DeVone, but it didn't definitively link him to any of the crime scenes; the scrap of blue latex would, but only if they found the suit with his DNA on it. What they needed was a piece of evidence that tied DeVone himself to the murders.

It bothered him that they'd never been able to track down the Farallon shark dart. Weapons were Calleigh's forte, but diving was Delko's; he felt as if he'd missed something, somehow.

Maybe I'm going about this wrong. Maybe I should be looking for the ammunition, instead of the weapon . . .

Carbon dioxide, ordinary CO_2. Available in small aluminum canisters, usually sold in boxes of ten, they were sold for a variety of uses, seltzer bottles and air pistols being the most common. But Delko didn't know anyone that used an old-fashioned seltzer bottle anymore; it was far more likely that DeVone had picked them up at a place that sold paintball supplies.

There were a number of shops that fit the bill in the Miami area. Even though gas-powered weapons were still dangerous, they weren't classi-fied as firearms and therefore no license was re-quired to own or sell one. That meant there wasn't any official database he could search—but maybe he could find a different source of information . . .

"Care to go for a ride?" Delko asked.

Calleigh looked up from the paperwork she was mulling over. "I guess so. What's the occasion?"

"Search warrant," Delko said, holding up a piece of paper. "For the post office box DeVone was using as a mail drop."

Calleigh frowned. "You really think we'll find anything there? I mean, I guess we could get lucky with a fingerprint, but most likely it'll just be stuffed with pornographic junk mail."

"Maybe—but I'm hoping some of that junk mail might have a different slant. See, our guy seems to have a thing for esoteric weapons: the shark dart, the dolphin-jaw trap, the underwater pistol. He's already signed up for one mailing list. If he's on another—say, for paintball equipment, or rare guns—maybe we can backtrail him from there."

"Worth a shot," she said. "Especially considering what I had to go through to locate that PO box."

"You'll have to tell me about that sometime," Delko said with a grin.

"Sure," Calleigh said, slipping off her lab coat and hanging it up. "Let's make it sometime around the turn of the century . . ."

16

"Apparently," Horatio said mildly, "we can all stop working so hard. Mister Wolfe has single-handedly managed to not only track down, but incarcerate our prime suspect."

Frank Tripp nodded, his arms crossed and a thoughtful expression on his face. "Y'know," he said, "I thought he'd be . . ."

"Taller?" Horatio suggested.

"No—*damper*," Frank said.

They were in the lab, staring at the object Wolfe had just wheeled in on a handcart. Inside its glass prison, it stared back.

Wolfe buttoned up his lab coat and grinned. "The Sea Creature himself," he said. "You should have heard the guy when I showed up with the warrant. You'd think I was taking away his first-born."

"First-spawned, more like," Tripp said. "I've

seen some ugly suspects in my day, but he's got a mug even Frankenstein couldn't love."

"Now, Frank, don't be so superficial," Horatio said. "It's what's inside that's important—right, Mister Wolfe?"

"Absolutely, H," Wolfe said, snapping on a pair of gloves. "Specifically, what—and who—has been inside that suit."

"Hang on," Tripp said, frowning. "I thought you said the second vic had been slashed with home-made claws. The ones on this guy don't look sharp enough to cut butter."

"That's because this isn't the murder weapon," Horatio said. "It's the original suit worn in the movie, which makes it an important icon in the merman's personal mythology."

Wolfe produced a small key from an evidence envelope. "Right. The fact that the claws on it are the same size means the killer duplicated the dimensions of the suit's gloves—which means he either had very good information, or access to the suit itself."

"And you think our killer might have left a little something behind?" Tripp asked.

"Only one way to find out," Wolfe said. He unlocked the back of the case and opened it up.

The store was called Bullseye Accessories. It specialized in paintball guns and supplies, carrying everything from body armor and full-face masks to the latest fully automatic paintball assault weapon.

"Boy, this place has everything," Delko remarked as they walked in. Calleigh rolled her eyes.

"Yeah," she said. "Except for any signs of intelligence."

"Oh? You don't approve of paintball? Kind of strange, considering."

"Really? Would you think it's strange that a classically trained chef doesn't appreciate all the subtle nuances of a Betty Crocker EZ-Bake oven?"

Delko chuckled. "That's a little snobbish, don't you think?"

She sighed. "I'm sorry, I don't mean to come off all high-and-mighty. It's just that I take guns very seriously, and it offends my sensibilities to have it turned into something so—fake. If people want to shoot guns, they should go to a firing range and learn how to do it properly, not run around blasting away indiscriminately at each other. It just seems *wrong*."

A man with a military haircut, a reddish orange handlebar mustache and a substantial beer gut ambled up to them. He was dressed in baggy camouflage shorts, a khaki vest covered in Velcro-sealed pockets, and a T-shirt that read KILL 'EM ALL—LET GOD SORT 'EM OUT. "Help you folks?" he asked. "Got a special today on the Diablo Mongoose—electronic trigger frame, multi, turbo, semi and full-auto firing modes, custom anodizing and milling, low-pressure volumizer—it's one helluva gun, you ask me. Buy one today and we're throwing in a forty-five-hundred psi tank for only a hundred bucks more."

"Actually," Delko said, flashing his badge, "we were wondering if we could talk to you about one of your customers."

The man raised his eyebrows. "Depends. My customers depend on me for a certain amount of discretion, y'know."

"Your customers are fifteen-year-old boys with Rambo fantasies," Calleigh said. "Which you indulge by selling them expensive toys that do nothing to teach responsible firearm ownership—"

"—Uh, Calleigh?" Delko said. "A word, if you don't mind?"

He pulled her aside. "Look, we don't have a warrant. If you don't ramp down the hostility, this guy is going to tell us to take a hike."

"All right, all right," she said irritably. "You deal with him. I'm going to take a look around."

Delko returned with an apologetic smile on his face. "Sorry about that—my associate is a little touchy on certain subjects. But I'd greatly appreciate your help, Mister . . . ?"

"Caldicott. Andrew Caldicott." The man seemed more bemused than offended. "Boy, she really goes off, doesn't she?"

"She can," Delko said agreeably. "My name's Eric Delko, by the way. We're with the Miami-Dade crime lab, and we're investigating a homicide."

Immediately, an intrigued smile bloomed on Caldicott's face. "Oh? What sort of homicide?"

"I can't really discuss the details, but I can say you don't have anything to worry about as far as your stock goes. We know none of these guns were involved."

Delko heard a muffled "hmmph!" from behind him, and chose to ignore it. "We found admail from your store in a post office box rented by our suspect, indicating he's on your mailing list. We were wondering if anyone here might have talked to him in person."

"I suppose I could ask my staff. What was the name?"

"DeVone."

"Oh, yeah—*that* guy."

"You remember him?"

"Sure. He came in here and asked some weird questions—wanted to know if our guns would work underwater. I told him I'd never tried, but probably not. Pellet wouldn't go very far, anyway."

"Did he fill anything out—a form, maybe?"

"Nah. Anybody wants to be put on our mailing list, we just enter them directly into the computer."

"Can you tell me what he looked like, how he was dressed? How about his voice—did he have an accent?"

Caldicott held up his hand. "Whoa, slow down. I can do better than that—I can show you." He pointed to the ceiling over the till. "You can't see it, but we have a camera up there. I can get you a shot of him."

"Really? How long do you keep footage on file?"

"Only a few days—but he was just in here yesterday. Bought a box of CO_2 canisters, I seem to remember . . ."

Calleigh strode up. "How's it going?"

"You're not going to believe this," Delko said.

Delko told her what happened, while Caldicott hurried away to get the security tapes.

"Let's hope we get a good shot of his face," Calleigh said. "And that he isn't in disguise the way he was in the fetishwear shop."

"Every perp makes a mistake sooner or later," Delko said. "Hopefully, this is when our merman commits his . . ."

Caldicott was back within minutes. "Here you go," he said, beaming as he handed over a videotape.

"Thank you," Calleigh said graciously, taking it from him. "And I'm sorry if I bit your head off before."

"Oh, that's all right," Caldicott said. "A lot of women don't really get our sport. Guns tend to be more a guy thing."

Delko glanced at Calleigh and took a step backward.

"A guy thing?" Calleigh said coldly. "Right. Do you know how many deaths have been caused by air-powered guns? Thirty-nine between 1990 and 2000—thirty-two of them children. In the year 2000 alone, there were over twenty-one thousand injuries reported from air-powered weapons."

"Those were all from BB guns. Paintball guns are perfectly safe if you know what you're doing—"

"Is that so? Most handguns deliver a slug at between 750 feet per second and 1450 feet per second. A .22-caliber bullet only has to reach 245 feet per second to penetrate skin. Piercing an eye can happen at velocities as low as 130 fps—and the guns you sell can propel a pellet at up to 250 feet per second."

"Look, there's a big difference between a bullet and a plastic ball filled with dye—"

"Yes, there is. Tell me, do you require any sort of safety course before people buy your products?"

"Well, no—"

"Then I guess most of your customers never learn that difference." Calleigh gestured toward a group of boys in their early teens at the counter, admiring a futuristic-looking pistol. "Are you aware," she said, "that in Florida it's a second-degree misdemeanor for anyone under sixteen to use an air-powered gun unless an adult is supervising the possession and the minor's parent has consented to such possession?"

"Of course I am."

"Well then, I'm sure you never sell your products

to boys like that without their parents' permission. Because you certainly wouldn't want to find yourself in court, facing a teenager wearing an eye-patch and an angry parent with a million-dollar civil suit. Would you?"

Caldicott swallowed. "No, I guess I wouldn't."

"Good. Because if I ever hear about such a case, I'll be more than happy to testify as an expert witness—for the prosecution. Thank you for the tape." Calleigh turned and stalked away.

Delko grinned and followed her. "Talk about shooting your mouth off," he said. Calleigh muttered something in return, which he didn't quite hear.

He didn't ask her to repeat it.

"Mister Kazimir," Horatio said. "Glad to see you're feeling better."

Anatoly Kazimir stared at him blearily from the crack of the open door. His eyes were rimmed in red, he was unshaven and dressed only in a pair of boxer shorts. "Detective Caine," he said. His voice, no longer warped by a decompression chamber's effects, was phlegmy and rough. "To what do I owe the pleasure? You have more paperwork for me?"

"As a matter of fact, Anatoly," Horatio said, "I do." He held up a search warrant. "If you wouldn't mind stepping outside, please."

"Can I put on some pants, first? Or would that be too much to ask?"

"As long as there's an officer present when you do so, I have no objection."

Kazimir opened the door and let Horatio and the uniformed officer with him inside. The officer followed Kazimir to the bedroom, while Horatio took an initial look around.

Kazimir's place was about what he expected: small, cluttered, not terribly clean. Take-out containers clustered on the countertop and dining table, magazines and old newspapers formed untidy stacks on chairs, clothes were draped over furniture. The kitchen sink seemed to be used mainly as an ashtray.

Kazimir reappeared at the door to the bedroom, now dressed in jeans and a T-shirt so faded it was illegible. "Whatever you're looking for," he said, scratching the stubble on his neck, "why not just ask me?"

"I'll do that," Horatio said. "If we don't find it . . ."

Kazimir and the officer went out into the hall. Calleigh showed up at the door a moment later, slightly out of breath. "Sorry I'm late, H—but I think we may have a major break in the case." She told him about the videotape. "Delko's taking a look at it now. I haven't seen it yet—I came right over as soon as I got your call."

"Excellent work," Horatio said. "Now, let's see if we can add a murder weapon to today's list of accomplishments . . ."

*   *   *

The first thing Wolfe did was remove the suit itself, piece by piece. It came apart in sections: the head, the breast-plate, the torso, the arms and leggings, the clawed hands and feet. Without the blue-tinted spotlights on it, the surface of the skin appeared a dull, slightly greenish grey.

The mannequin that had been wearing the suit came next. It was bolted to the floor of the case through the soles of its feet; Wolfe removed the bolts carefully and set them aside, then pulled the figure itself out.

He dusted the exterior of the case for prints and wasn't surprised when he found none; Tresong obviously wiped the glass down thoroughly on a regular basis. He was hoping he'd have better luck with the interior.

He used a ten watt argon ion laser to sweep the glass and highlight any possible latents. He got lucky near the base; there were a couple that looked promising. He decided to fume the entire case, from the inside.

Superglue fuming was a method used for bringing out latent prints. Although often credited to a British police officer in 1979 who noticed that fingerprints on a heater he'd repaired had become much more visible, it was actually discovered two years before by a lab tech working for the Criminal Identification Division of the Japanese National Police Agency. It was imported as an investigative technique to the U.S. by the Bureau of Alcohol, Tobacco and Firearms, and was now used nationwide.

There were a number of different kinds of super-glue: Methylcyanoacrylate or ethylcyanoacrylate were the most common, but butylcyanoacrylate or isobutylcyanoacrylate were occasionally used, too. The technique was quite simple: The object to be fumed was placed inside an enclosed space—a fish tank, or sometimes just a cardboard box—with a small heating unit placed beneath a container holding a few drops of superglue. Once the heater was turned on and the container sealed, the glue was heated to its boiling point, somewhere between one hundred twenty and one hundred fifty degrees fahrenheit, generating gaseous cyanoacrylate.

The main ingredient in most fingerprints was sweat. Once the water evaporated, what was left behind was a mix of the organic—glucose, ammonia, riboflavin, lactic acid, peptides, amino acids and isoagglutinogens—and the inorganic—chlorine, sodium, potassium and carbon trioxide. The concentrated glue vapor reacted with the chemical traces and the moisture in the air to produce a visible, sticky white material that formed along the ridges of the fingerprint.

Ordinarily it could take several hours for the procedure to finish, but Wolfe knew a few tricks to speed up the process. First, he unscrewed the two blue spotlights set into the base, and replaced one of them with a higher-wattage, plain white bulb. He rigged a simple, cup-shaped container out

of tinfoil and fitted it over the bulb, then added
the superglue to the foil.

He screwed a plug adapter into the other socket,
and plugged in a small electric fan to help circulate the fumes. Then he used the lab microwave
to heat up a large flask of water, which he placed
next to the fan. It would increase the humidity and
speed up the chemical bonding process.

Lastly, he closed the case door and switched on
the power. He monitored the process closely; if it
ran for too long the latents could overdevelop, the
chemical buildup on the ridges overlapping each
other.

When the prints seemed ready, Wolfe used a
tape-lift to pull them off the glass. Oliver Tresong's
fingerprints were already on file, the result of a
marijuana possession charge ten years ago; most of
the prints Wolfe had lifted matched his.

But one didn't.

"Who are you?" he murmured. "And whoever
you are, did you leave more than a fingerprint behind . . ."

The suit itself was next. The exterior produced
several more prints, some of which matched
Tresong and others the unknown donor. He
swabbed the interior surfaces of every piece for epithelials; he didn't have a DNA sample from
Tresong for comparison, but if the evidence
pointed the right direction he could get one.

The head of the Sea Creature stared at him

blindly from where it sat on the light table. Illumination from below made its bulbous eyes glow weirdly.

"What are *you* looking at?" Wolfe said. His own voice sounded strange to him, echoey and nervous in the empty lab. "All right, stop acting like you're victim number three in a bad horror movie," he told himself. "It's just a rubber mask." He paused. "That you're *talking* to . . ."

The Sea Creature had nothing to say in return.

But maybe, Wolfe thought, *its skin does . . .*

Horatio smiled at the Russian sitting across from him. The room that Horatio generally used for interviews was a far cry from the interrogation cells of the movies, with their single bright light overhead shining into the subject's eyes, the questioner a threatening silhouette looming in the shadows. No, the interview room of the Miami-Dade crime lab was full of light, the metal honeycomb grid over the windows diffusing the bright Miami sunshine into a kind of golden haze. This wasn't the kind of room you could hide in; this was a room where you could see clearly, where everything was out in the open.

Everything but the freedom to leave. That was a privilege Horatio made you pay for . . . and the only coin he was willing to accept was the truth.

"So, Anatoly," Horatio said. "I must admit, I was surprised by what we found. Somehow, I never figured such an ardent activist for the ecology to be involved with this kind of contraband."

Anatoly Kazimir's eyes were bleak. He'd fallen back on stoic Russian fatalism, accepting the fact that he'd been caught but not really seeming to care. "What can I say?" he said brusquely. "We all have our vices."

"Vices are one thing," Horatio said mildly, "but thirteen cases of hand-rolled *Cohiba* cigars, signed by Castro himself? A box of those goes for a thousand dollars a pop . . . that's not an addiction, my friend. That's a business enterprise."

Kazimir shrugged. "You think it's cheap, running an activist organization? Donations aren't enough to pay the bills, to buy fuel, to maintain equipment. Money has to come from somewhere."

"And for an ex-KGB agent with Cuban connections, a little smuggling goes a long way . . . too bad it's against federal law."

"KGB? Detective, you have me all wrong. I was Soviet Navy, yes—but KGB, never. You've seen too many spy movies."

"I stand corrected. I guess I was confused," Horatio said carefully, "by the clever toys you like to play with." He pushed a photo across the table toward Kazimir.

Kazimir glanced down, then back up. "You want to know what that is, you just had to ask. I'm happy to share my expertise with you."

"I know what it is, Anatoly. It's an SPP-1 underwater pistol. What I want to know is—where's yours?"

A cautious smile was breaking its way through the wintery expression on Kazimir's face. "So that's what you were looking for, hey? And, of course, did not find."

"Don't play games with me, Anatoly. I know you brought one with you when you emigrated, and I don't think you'd get rid of such an item casually. So where is it?"

Kazimir gave a single grunt of laughter. "You Americans—so sentimental. You don't think I'd just sell it on eBay?"

"I know you didn't," Horatio said evenly. "But maybe you made a more private deal."

Kazimir shook his head. "I wish I had. But, foolish and trusting soul that I am, I neglected to keep it properly locked up. It was stolen from me—six, seven months ago. Why, did someone use it to stick up a Seven-Eleven?"

"No, Anatoly. Someone used it to commit murder. And if you expect me to believe some flimsy story about it being stolen, you don't know me very well."

"Don't I?" Kazimir's voice turned cold. "You don't think I know a hardass when one is sitting on me? I know you very well, Horatio Caine; I have dealt with your type before. You don't make threats you can't keep."

"That's right, Anatoly. When I go after something, I get it—and I want that weapon. You'd better rethink your story in a hurry, because I have absolutely no problem with throwing you to the wolves. Those cigars will net you a quarter-million dollar fine and ten years incarceration—and blowing up fishing trawlers isn't going to buy you a lot of street cred behind the bars of a federal prison."

Anatoly sighed. "Look, what do you want from me? I don't have the gun, I don't know where it went. I can't even prove it was stolen, because it was never registered in the first place."

"And you expect me to believe that a piece of hardware like that just wound up being part of my investigation? That doesn't wash, my friend. You want to know what I think?"

Anatoly gazed at him stonily, but said nothing.

"I think," Horatio continued, cocking his head to one side, "that you're telling the truth."

Anatoly blinked.

"I think your gun *was* stolen. Because if you still knew where it was, you'd just deny ever having it in the first place. But I also know that gun is responsible for a homicide, and the evidence puts it in the hands of someone you know. Someone you know very well . . . so here's what I want from you."

Horatio leaned forward, his eyes intent. "I want details, Anatoly. I want to know where the gun was stolen from, I want to know who had access,

I want to know who you think took it. And God help you if you waste my time."

Anatoly considered this for a long moment. He reached up, scratched the underside of his jaw. At last, he said, "Hokay. You want me to point a finger, I will point a finger. I kept the gun at the ALA offices; it was no secret it was there, we all knew. It was for self-defense, you know? In case some junkie came in, tried to steal our donation box. So yes, it was one of us."

Anatoly met Horatio's eyes, held them. "I even think I know who . . ."

Delko played the security footage for his boss again. Horatio leaned in and studied the screen, a satisfied smile tugging at his lips. "Well, well, well," he said. "I certainly recognize *that* face."

"No beard, no hat, no disguise at all," Delko said. "First serious mistake DeVone's made."

"No, Eric," Horatio said. "DeVone's first serious mistake was thinking he could outsmart my team. Good work."

"We know who he is, but we still can't link him directly to any of the murders," Delko said quietly.

"Not yet," Horatio said. "But we've got enough for a warrant to search his residence. And he's got to keep that suit somewhere . . ."

Wolfe walked through the door, brandishing a sheet of paper in one hand. "The suit," he said, "is a *fake*."

"The one you confiscated from Tresong?" Delko asked.

"Yeah. I thought it was in far too good a condition, so I ran some tests using NMR."

"Nuclear magnetic imaging?" Delko asked.

"Yeah. Rubber is fairly sensitive to environmental degradation, but until recently, the only way to really measure wear and tear has been inspecting the surface visually."

NMR used atomic nuclei in which at least one proton or neutron was unpaired; the imbalance spun the nuclei, making them act like magnets. When exposed to a strong external magnetic field, the nuclei tried to align their axes along the lines of magnetic force—but the alignment wasn't exact, resulting in an uneven rotation different for each kind of nuclei. If the nuclei in a sample were also hit with a radiofrequency pulse, they'd absorb and re-emit energy at specific frequencies according to individual rotation rates. An NMR spectrum displayed the frequencies as spikes of varying height; the spikes were used to identify the constituent nuclei of the sample.

"Good idea," Delko said. "I know the tire industry has been experimenting with NMR techniques to predict blowouts. Lets them detect changes in polymer length, cross-linking, and the presence of degradation products."

"Well, it's also pretty handy for telling how old a piece of rubber is. This suit has yet to celebrate its first birthday."

"You get anything else?" Horatio asked.

"Epithelials from two donors. One's from an un-known—the other's a match to one of the samples we pulled off the sex toys."

"Meaning DeVone's worn that suit," Horatio said.

"I also found some prints, one set belonging to Tresong, the other unknown. I ran it through AFIS and got a hit from a Navy database, for—"

He stopped when he noticed the video screen. "—him," he said. "Guess I'm a little behind the curve."

"All right," Horatio said, "here's how we're going to play it. I'm going to a judge to get a war-rant for our friend's residence, and you, Mister Wolfe, are going to have Mister Tresong come in and give us a DNA sample. While you have him here, you might want to ask him a few ques-tions . . ."

"Got it, H," Wolfe said.

Oliver Tresong looked like he didn't like police sta-tions much. He shifted nervously in his seat, sweated despite the air-conditioning, and generally acted like he had a kilo of contraband hidden in a body cavity.

Wolfe studied him. He didn't say a word, just smiled and glanced down at a sheet of paper he held, then looked back at Tresong. He was trying his best to produce that combination of quiet benevolence and simmering anger that Horatio could project, but from the looks Tresong was giving him it was probably coming off closer to barely repressed lunacy. Wolfe was about to give up and just tell him what was going on when Tresong suddenly blurted, "Look, I really needed the money!"

Wolfe blinked. "Excuse me?"

"For the suit. It's a fake, I know it's a fake, but I *swear* I wasn't trying to defraud anyone—it was only five hundred bucks anyway, okay? That's not, like, a felony, right?"

"That depends," Wolfe said, pretending he knew what Tresong was talking about. "I need to know the whole story, from the beginning."

Tresong shook his head miserably. "Okay, okay. The Sea Creature festival said they'd give me five hundred bucks if I'd let them display the original suit in the lobby of the Verdant Springs theater during the event. I really needed the cash, so I said sure, fine, no problem. But there *was* a problem, because I didn't have the suit anymore. What I had was a replica."

"A really good one, too," Wolfe said.

"Yeah, I got this buddy of mine in LA to make it. I didn't even have to pay for it."

"What, it was a favor?"

"No, it was part of the deal. Another member of the fan club offered me twenty grand plus he'd pay for a replacement—no one else would ever have to know, he said. For me, owning the suit is a status thing—I mean, not only do you own a piece of history, but you get bragging rights, too. But this guy, I think he got off more on the idea that not only did he have the real thing, but it was his own little secret. Nobody else in the club—in the world—knew what he had. Except me, of course."

"And if you died, the suit might be exposed as a fake," Wolfe said. "You may not realize this, Mister Tresong, but you are a very lucky man. Not only are you alive, but I'm not going to charge you with anything—and all you have to do is tell me the name of the man who bought the suit from you."

Tresong didn't even pause. "Torrence," he said. "Malcolm Torrence."

17

MALCOLM TORRENCE WAS the merman.

It was his face on the footage from the paintball store, his DNA on the replica Sea Creature suit and Samantha Voire's toys, his fingerprint on the inside of the suit's display case. Like Tresong, he hadn't been able to resist trying on the suit—even though it was a fake, even though he now owned the real thing. According to Kazimir, it had been Torrence working behind the counter of the ALA store the day the SPP-1 disappeared . . . and he'd suffered a mild case of the bends a few weeks ago. It had mainly affected his knees, causing him to walk with a somewhat stiff gait for a while.

Horatio led the team that stormed his house, a run-down shack hiding behind a pair of half-dead palms in Hialeah. It looked as if the windows had all been boarded over in preparation for some long-ago hurricane, and never taken down; Horatio was willing to bet the interior of the house saw barely a photon of light on even the sunniest of days.

Calleigh and Delko took the back, while Horatio and Frank Tripp took the front, backed up by two uniformed officers. "Malcolm Torrence!" Horatio called out. "This is the Miami-Dade police! Open up, *now*!"

No response. "Break it down," Horatio said.

The battering ram knocked down the cheap door with a single impact. Horatio was inside an instant later, Glock leveled in front of him. The place was as dark as he'd expected, the air as heavy and damp as the breath of a swamp. He found the light switch on the wall, flicked it on.

The place wasn't large, the front door opening directly onto what seemed to be the living room. The decorating scheme was odd, to say the least; the floor was lined with some sort of black rubber mats, the walls covered with a large photo mural of an underwater scene. Big chunks of coral adorned rusting, barnacle-covered shelves that must have been scavenged from wrecks. The furniture, a couch and two chairs, were made of transparent, inflated plastic; they gleamed in the blue and green light from the tinted bulbs overhead.

Horatio didn't spend much time admiring the décor. He moved quickly and efficiently from one room to the next, checking the bathroom, the kitchen, the bedroom. The first two were unremarkable—though the bathroom featured an oversized shower that was clearly a custom job—but the bedroom, behind a closed door, was even stranger than the living room.

It had no overhead light source. It was illuminated by the fluorescent bulbs of dozens of fish tanks, stacked against the walls from floor to ceiling. They were stocked with every kind of marine predator: cold-eyed sharks, eels with gaping jaws, razor-toothed barracuda and nervous schools of pirhana. In one tank the long, poisonous spines of a lionfish swayed idly; in another, a small yellow octopus clung to the glass, bright blue bands visible on its tentacles. Horatio recognized it as a species that secreted a toxin ten thousand times as potent as cyanide.

A king-size waterbed dominated the center of the room. It had no bedding, only a frame holding a large, transparent, water-filled mattress.

Horatio took a cautious step into the room. The air was even thicker here, wet and salty and warm; it was like wading through blood. Beads of moisture instantly formed on Horatio's skin. A warm rivulet slowly made its way down his cheekbone, his jaw, his throat.

As he got closer to the bed, he saw that it, too, held an occupant. Something flickered in the shadowy depth of the mattress, something he couldn't quite make out.

It wasn't until he was directly over it, looking down, that he realized what was inside.

"There's no one here," Horatio told Delko and Calleigh. "But there's something I want you to see."

He led them into the bedroom. Calleigh stopped to study the tanks, while Horatio took Delko straight to the waterbed. "Care to identify that for me?" he said, pointing down.

Delko pulled out a flashlight and shone it into the mattress's interior for a better look. The bottom initially seemed to hold nothing but sand— but after peering at it for a few seconds, Delko nodded and said, "Ah." There was a face looking back from the sand, one with bulging, speckled white and brown eyes, and a large mouth full of jagged teeth. Its face was so flat it looked as if it had been run over by a steamroller.

"Eastern stargazer," Delko said. "Some people call it the ultimate ambush predator. It hides just under the sand, with only its eyes sticking out— and when something tasty swims past, it zaps them with an electrical charge."

"This guy sleeps with an electric fish?" Calleigh said. "That's so far past weird I don't even know how to classify it."

"An electric fish in a big plastic bag," Delko pointed out. "Keeps him from getting zapped himself. But yeah, this guy and normal parted ways a long time ago."

"Let's not lose our focus, people," Horatio said, holstering his gun. "I want every square inch of this house processed. Torrence is in the wind, and we need to find him before he gets back in the water . . ."

Two of the fish tanks held something other than fish—one contained a small TV and a top-loading DVD player, the other a collection of DVDs. "Airtight lid on both," Delko noted. "Must be to protect them from the high degree of humidity in the room."

Calleigh sorted through the DVDs. *Latex Lovelies, Underwater Sex Party,* a bunch of hard-core S&M— and of course, the special-edition, extended version of *Creature From the Deep*.

"I'm going to check the closets," Delko announced.

He found what he was looking for in a storage room just off the kitchen: scuba gear. Tanks, regulator, mask, flippers and wet suit—but no Sea Creature outfit.

"I've got some liquid latex supplies in here," Calleigh called out. "And some kind of glitter. Looks like he was trying to make his own Pearl-sheen blue—probably for the more private parts of his anatomy."

Horatio was in the living room, thinking. Some men in his position would be micromanaging, making sure his people didn't miss anything; Horatio didn't operate like that. You didn't get in the way of trained professionals—you stood back and let them work. They would relay information to him as reliably as his own senses, supplemented by whatever he observed and learned on his own. He was already thinking ahead, trying to figure out where Torrence would go, what he would do next.

"H?" Calleigh called. "I think I've found something."

He joined Calleigh in the bedroom. She was crouched down in a corner, studying one of the tanks in the bottom row. She shone her flashlight at it, and something disk-shaped shone back prismatically.

Horatio got down on his haunches and peered at it. It was a DVD, lying flat on the bottom. Two words had been scrawled across its face in black marker: HORATIO CAINE.

"Well, well," Horatio said softly. "It seems as if we were expected . . ."

The tank's other resident was sinuous and monochromatic, a sea snake with dark bands down the length of its pale, sinuous body. Sea snakes, Horatio knew, were highly venomous; their primary neurotoxin caused paralysis, respiratory failure and cardiac arrest. "What's black and white and extremely dangerous?" Calleigh asked.

"In this case," Horatio said, straightening up, "our killer's point of view. Which means that tank contains more than one kind of poison . . ."

*　　　*　　　*

They played the DVD on the TV in the fish tank.

It flickered to life with no preamble. At first, Horatio thought he was looking at a scene from the original *Creature From the Deep* film; it was in black and white, a shot of the Sea Creature standing in the shadows of a cave.

But then the monster began to talk, and it became obvious that this wasn't footage from a low-budget horror movie; it was a glimpse into genuine madness.

"I know you will find this," Torrence's voice rasped. "I left it for you so that you might *understand*. Understand what it is I am. Call me *Homo mermanus*, for I am not like you. I am as far beyond you and your pathetic species as a killer whale is beyond a minnow."

The figure shuffled forward a step. Its arms lifted from its sides to waist height, and now Horatio could clearly see the six-inch-long, slightly curved black blades jutting from the end of each finger. They were flawlessly attached, looking like they'd grown there.

"You think I'm some sort of aberration, I know. But it's *you* who are the monsters. You're the ones killing our planet, poisoning our oceans, fouling our air. It made me ashamed to be one of you."

Torrence's elbows bobbed slowly up and down, as if there were invisible currents tugging at his limbs. His fingers stayed in constant motion, the length of the claws exaggerating their slow, careful arcs through the air. It was like watching a double handful of cobras.

"But I wasn't one of you. I was something else . . . something *older*. But it took something new, something artificial, to teach me what I was. Technology. It was technology that told me about my prototype, technology that let me embrace my true environment, technology that finally showed me I could become something better than I was.

"Ninety-seven percent of human DNA is junk, with no obvious function—doesn't it make sense that there might be some sort of defense system encoded? An antibody routine, to be activated when something goes wrong? *That's* what I am. An antibody. Swimming through the bloodstream of the ocean. Destroying the infection that you, *all* of you, are . . ."

The screen went blank.

Nobody spoke for a moment.

"Right," Horatio said. "Calleigh, finish processing the house. Delko, get back to the lab with the scuba gear and see what it can tell us. I'm going on a little road trip."

"Verdant Springs?" Calleigh said.

"That's correct. If our guy thinks he's a fish, he may return to the place he thinks spawned him . . ."

"Okay," Delko muttered. "Now you're in *my* backyard, pal."

He had the scuba gear spread out on the light table. *Twin Faber high-pressure tanks, FX series— chromium molybdenum steel, rated to 3442 pounds per square inch. 3500 PSI Sherwood DIN valve. Self-balancing Poseidon Xstream Deep 90 regulator, good for technical dives up to six hundred fifty feet. Henderson titanium neoprene Hyperstretch wet suit.*

The flippers were unusual, but Delko had seen them before; a set was on display at the New York Museum of Modern Art. *Tan Delta Force Fin.* Opentoed, made of high-rebound polyurethane with a slightly offset, split-V design, they were far lighter and more graceful than the clunky, heavy fins he had grown up with.

Opaque skirt Halcyon face mask with one-way purge valve. Wing-style air cell with stainless-steel backplate. 12-volt Nickel Metal Hydride, 4-amp battery, connected to a wrist-mounted power head with a ten-watt High-Intensity Discharge bulb. All high-end, sophisticated components, but there was one significant piece missing: a dive computer. Any diver that had invested this heavily would surely have a good one, and the good ones always had a dive log feature. Delko could have used it to figure out where Torrence had dove recently—but it looked like the merman had taken it with him.

It didn't matter. There were other ways.

The tanks were covered in a black protective plastic mesh. He went over it carefully, looking for transfer; he knew from experience that one of the ways a diver was most likely to brush up against something without realizing it was with the tanks on his back.

The mesh was marked in several places; it looked as if the tanks had scraped against something hard and rough. On closer inspection, he found a tiny yellowish white pebble lodged between the mesh and the tank. He examined it and thought he knew what it was.

Delko put the pebble in a glass petri dish, then added a single drop of diluted hydrochloric acid. Immediately, tiny air bubbles foamed on the surface, confirming his hypothesis.

Limestone—extremely common in Florida. And finding it on a piece of underwater gear can mean only one thing.

A cave.

As Horatio drove down the main street of Verdant Springs, he realized why Malcolm Torrence had chosen now to abandon all pretense and leave him an explicit message. It wasn't because he thought Horatio was close to catching him; it was because—in Torrence's mind, anyway—the merman's time had arrived.

It was the first day of the *Creature From the Deep* Seafest.

Brightly colored pennants hung in lines across the street; blue and green balloons clung to lampposts like gigantic clusters of fish eggs. There were booths lining the sidewalk, selling T-shirts and food and various kinds of memorabilia. One was hawking gingerbread versions of the Sea Creature; another let you stick your head through a hole in a life-size plywood cutout of the monster, then took your picture. It was hard to tell exactly how large the mass of people ambling along, taking in the festival in all its kitschy glory, was; but Horatio estimated it at a few thousand, at least.

He parked the Hummer in front of the festival's box office, the local movie theater. There was a man standing outside, giving away cardboard masks to children. Each one bore the visage of the Sea Creature, held on with a thin strip of elastic. Two kids wearing them ran past Horatio as he opened his door, screaming and moaning how they were going to kill each other.

He went inside, flashed his badge to one of the harried-looking volunteers behind a long table and got directions to the office. As Horatio made his way up the red-carpeted stairs, he felt a bit like Roy Scheider's character in *Jaws*—only it wasn't the town's political leaders he was here to talk to, and he didn't think closing down the beaches would necessarily do any good. A great white shark deprived of tasty bathers couldn't just book himself into a Motel 6 and wait.

On the other hand, Horatio thought as he knocked on the office door, *a shark doesn't care about festivals or old movies or even mankind ruining the environment. It just wants to swim and feed. Malcolm Torrence wants a lot more; no matter what he may claim, he wants what all serials want: recognition. And he'll never have a better chance to get it than right here and right now.*

"What?" an irritated voice called out in response. Horatio opened the door to see a balding man behind a desk, wearing a bright red T-shirt with a *Creature From the Deep* Seafest logo on it. He frowned and said, "I'm sorry, I'm really too busy for *anything* right now—"

Horatio held up his badge. "Not for me, you're not," he said calmly. "Mister Delfino, my name is Horatio Caine—I believe you spoke with one of my investigators earlier this week?"

Delfino sighed. "Yeah, sure. What happened? Did you catch the guy?"

"Not yet. But we have identified him, and he's someone I believe you know: Malcolm Torrence."

"What? You're kidding . . ." He stopped, and a thoughtful, disturbed look crossed his face. "Oh. That—okay, maybe I can see that. Malcolm always was sort of . . . *intense.*"

"He's a little more than that. He's killed at least three people, and if I don't stop him he'll kill more."

That stopped Delfino cold. He stared at Horatio and his mouth opened, but no sound came out.

"I need your help," Horatio said. "I don't mean to alarm you, but Malcolm Torrence is an extremely

dangerous man in an unstable frame of mind. He
has a fixation on your pet monster, and so far has
managed to produce a pretty good imitation of
same. There's no doubt in my mind that he'll attack
another swimmer . . . and there's no way he'll ignore this festival."

"Oh my God," Delfino whispered, his voice
trembling. "This is horrible. This is . . . we have to
close the beach. We have to—I don't know, get police divers or the Coast Guard or something to patrol. We can't let him . . . we can't, we just *can't*—"

"Mister Delfino." Horatio's voice was soft, but
there was an edge to it that snagged the man's attention like a fishhook. "Listen to me. I promise
you, *no one else will die*. I will not let this man take
another victim. Nobody at your festival—nobody
from this *town*—is going to suffer at his hands. All
right?"

Delfino stared at him, swallowed, then nodded.
"All—all right. What do you want me to do?"

"Just stay calm, and talk to me. Anything you
can tell me about Torrence will be helpful."

"I didn't really know him that well. I mean, he
went to the meetings, and I corresponded with
him by email, but he mostly kept to himself. He
was the kind of guy that just sort of sat in the corner and watched everyone else."

"Okay . . . are there any conversations the two
of you had that stand out in your mind? Any particular subject he seemed unusually interested in?"

"Well, we talked about Gilly, of course. Malcolm was always very detail oriented—wanted to know exactly how the suit was made, all the locations the film was shot, that sort of thing."

"Right. Would you have a list of such locations?"

"Sure. Actually, there's a tour happening as part of the festival." He checked his watch. "Leaves in about twenty minutes. Some of the movie was shot on a soundstage in LA, but a lot of local places were used, too: the diner, a local park, the beach of course, the caves—"

"Hold it," Horatio said. "Caves?"

There were plenty of things Florida had in abundance, and Delko was familiar with most of them: freshly squeezed orange juice and strong Cuban coffee, brilliant sunshine and relentless hurricanes, beaches overflowing with white sand and night clubs overflowing with beautiful women.

And caves.

Florida was a vast karst area, a region where the underlying structure was mainly carbonate rock, either dolomite or limestone. Ground water and carbon dioxide combined to produce a weak solution of carbonic acid, which over long periods of time ate away at the rock, forming numerous cavities. A thousand-foot-thick limestone bedrock underlay the entire state, some of it buried deep below the surface, some exposed—and much of it honeycombed with caves.

Many of which were underwater—in fact, there were more freshwater caves in Florida than anywhere else in the world. They transported more than eight billion gallons of fresh water to the surface every day, to over six hundred natural springs throughout the state—and every now and then they killed a diver who hadn't been quite careful enough.

Cave diving was one of the world's most dangerous sports, combining the most hazardous elements of spelunking and diving. Even among experienced open-water divers, cave diving was considered high risk; it required a combination of clear-eyed intelligence, methodical preparation and self-assured bravado usually found only in elite military personnel.

Or sociopaths, Delko thought.

His cell phone rang. "Delko."

"Eric," Horatio said. Delko could hear the rumbling of the Hummer's engine in the background. "Torrence may have gone to ground in a cave."

"Like the one he filmed the DVD message in," Delko said. "Yeah, I just came to the same conclusion. The scuba gear we found is definitely a cave-diving rig. Question is, which one?"

"The most likely suspect is a complex near Verdant Springs, where some of the movie was actually shot. I'm on my way there now—I need whatever background on the place you can find. My source tells me the place is fairly large; even if he's there, we may have a hard time locating him."

"I'm on it," Delko said.

The cave system's entrance looked a lot like an overgrown sinkhole—which, Horatio supposed, it was. Moss and weeds had overgrown the rim of the hole, which was no more than twenty or so feet across, with a rusted steel railing encircling it and a wooden staircase leading into the interior. A large wooden sign with the words VERDANT SPRINGS CAVE carved into it hung from the railing from two sturdy, obviously new chains. Horatio wondered how often the sign had been stolen.

He'd beaten the tour group here by a few minutes, but there were still a few middle-aged sightseers milling around, taking pictures and muttering to each other in German. Despite the festive appearance of their brightly colored tropical shirts, they didn't sound happy; apparently the cave didn't live up to their standards for a hole in the ground. *Maybe it's the absence of bats,* Horatio thought. *Or maybe that's just what German tourists sound like when they're discussing the relative merits of geologic features.*

He looked around, hands on hips, and tried to envision Torrence coming here. He'd need a vehicle to haul his equipment around—but the only car in the small parking lot was a rented Mazda that the German tourists had obviously arrived in.

It's not like he can put on the suit and call a cab, either—though it's possible he could have been dropped here while carrying it with him.

Then what? Slip into the bushes and get dressed, then try to maneuver those steps while wearing fins?

He strode over to the top of the stairs and looked down. He could see a barred iron gate at the base, open now but obviously used to seal the cave at night. He went down the steps and took a close look at the lock. It didn't appear to have been tampered with, but if Torrence had been able to obtain a key . . .

"Can I help you?" The question came from a young blond woman in jeans, hiking boots and khaki shirt, as well as a white construction helmet with a Verdant Springs Cave logo on it. She stood on a wooden boardwalk in a natural foyer, an impressive display of stalactites over her head. Light came from several posts along the boardwalk.

"Yes, you can," Horatio said, showing her his badge. "Are there any other entrances to this cave system?"

"Yes, but none of them accessible unless you're a bat, a snake or a bug," the woman said. Her plastic name tag read *My Name Is STACY!* Horatio guessed she was a student making some extra tuition and possibly academic credit doing cave tours.

"You're sure? No other possible way in?"

"I'm sure. This cave has been completely mapped since the seventies. Why?"

"I'm looking for someone who may think this is a good place to hide."

Stacy frowned. "Well, that'd be an impressive trick. The tour covers the whole place, except for the stuff that's underwater."

"Uh-huh. Tell me, are there any rooms accessible *only* via water?"

"Rooms, no. There's probably a few places where there are air pockets, but—"

Horatio's cell phone rang. "Just a moment," he said, holding up his hand. "Caine."

"He's not there, H," Delko said.

"I had just come to the same conclusion myself."

"But I think I know where he is. I ran the gas in the scuba tanks through an analyzer, and came up with a mix of oxygen and helium. That's only used for technical dives deeper than a hundred and sixty-five feet."

"And the Verdant Spring cave system doesn't go down that far?"

"No. Deepest pit is a hundred and twenty three feet. Actually, there are only four cave systems in Florida that run deeper than a hundred sixty-five—and one of them is inside the city limits of Verdant Springs. It's a sinkhole in a wooded lot at Twenty-third Street and Vargas Avenue."

"Get your gear and meet me there," Horatio said.

18

SINKHOLES WERE A MAJOR problem in Florida. Even though they were an important part of the aquifer system, they caused hundreds of millions of dollars of damage. The process that formed them was the same as the one that formed caves: Acidic groundwater ate away at the soft limestone beneath the surface, forming large cavities that filled up with H_2O. As long as the water table stayed high, there was no problem; but once the water level dropped, the upper part of the cavity could no longer support the weight of the ground—often composed of heavy clay and sediment—above it, and collapsed. There were more sinkholes in Florida than any other place in America; Horatio had once heard a geologist compare the state to a gigantic incisor jutting from the edge of the continent, with a permanent case of tooth decay.

Sometimes this caused surreal effects. When a sinkhole formed underneath an existing body of water, the collapse was like pulling the plug in a bathtub. Entire lakes—including fish, vegetation, birds and alligators—could suddenly find themselves swirling down an immense natural drain. There were even places that did this periodically, known as "disappearing lakes"; Lake Jackson in Tallahassee was one of them, having suffered sudden, massive drainings four times in the twentieth century, the most recent in 1999.

Sometimes, unfortunately, they were also used as garbage dumps. More than one Florida sinkhole had become the final resting place for old appliances, mattresses, tires, even cars. Horatio wasn't sure the operative principle at work was "out of sight, out of mind," or some sort of collective resentment—a means of retribution, perhaps, against a natural phenomenon that wrecked houses, highways, even destroyed fishing spots.

It didn't matter. No matter how much junk people threw into them, sinkholes would continue to open like unexpected, hungry mouths, swallowing up whatever they could.

Horatio was closer and got there first. It was a wooded lot on the edge of town, only a few blocks from a school; from the cigarette butts, broken bottles and junk-food wrappers, it looked like it had seen its share of bored teenagers. The sinkhole itself resembled a small pond, no more than thirty feet in diameter, with only the blackness of the water hinting at its depth.

Horatio walked the perimeter of the pond carefully, scanning the ground. He'd been able to park the Hummer quite close and in such a way that it was hidden by trees; Torrence would have been able to do the same. If he came and went late at night, especially during the week, he could probably do so undetected.

He found what he was looking for right at the water's edge, in a little patch of damp, claylike earth. A footprint—one that didn't look human.

When Delko arrived in another department Hummer twenty minutes later, Horatio had finished casting and lifting the print. "What did you find?" Delko asked.

"Evidence that something with large, webbed feet has been here recently," Horatio said. He sealed the cast up in a cardboard evidence box and put it in the back of the Hummer.

Delko glanced around. "No vehicle."

"I know, but he could have been dropped off by a cab, or even parked on a nearby street and hauled his stuff here by hand," Horatio said. "I've contacted local PD and they're going to do a search of the area. In the meantime, I want you to go down there and see what you can find."

"Right," Delko said. He was already pulling tanks and gear out of the back of his Hummer.

"And Eric—be careful. This guy has a whole repertoire of ways to kill underwater."

"I know," Delko said grimly. "It's why I brought this."

He pulled out a sleek-looking speargun with a black plastic finish. Around thirty inches long, with two molded handgrips and four long, thin barrels tipped with flared black triangular sights, it resembled a cross between a German Luger and a Gatling gun with anorexia.

"Johnson submarine gun," Delko said. He loaded each of the four barrels with a short, razor-tipped spear quickly and efficiently. "Four shots, twenty-two-caliber load."

"Don't think I've seen one of those before."

"It's a vintage piece from the early seventies— borrowed it from a friend of mine. A pole spear isn't much good in close quarters, and a regular speargun only lets you fire once before you have to reload. This way, at least I'll have as many shots at my disposal as he does."

Delko suited up quickly. Cave diving equipment, to the untrained eye, was the same as a regular diving rig, but there were several important differences. The wet suit Delko wore was warmer than he'd use in the ocean, to compensate for the lower temperatures found in caves. Valves, hoses, lights, anything that might catch on a guideline or outcropping of rock was either strapped closely to his body or eliminated entirely. The current inside caves could be intense, so a streamlined profile also helped reduce drag. He used a full-face mask with a built-in hands-free radio unit and an opaque skirt around the edge; while communication was important, light leaking in from the side was an unneeded distraction inside a cave.

He didn't need a snorkel, so the strap of his mask went on the inside of his hood, instead of the outside. His light source was a wrist-mounted unit connected to a battery on his waist, and he carried two backups.

Unlike the stylish Tan Delta Force Fins Torrence owned, Delko used springheel-strapped fins with a solid webbing design. Split fins could easily get caught on a guideline, and even though the V shape of the Force Fins was fairly open, Delko preferred safety over appearance.

Accurate instrumentation was extremely important. The submersible pressure gauge on the high-pressure hose of his tanks was an ultra-precise, brass Bourdon tube model calibrated in 100-psi increments. An open-water diver would usually wear a wrist-mounted dive computer, sometimes with a wireless connection to their regulator's first stage; cave divers didn't bother with the second part, as wireless signals sometimes malfunctioned inside caves. Delko used a wrist-mounted multi-gas computer that functioned as both a bottom timer and digital depth gauge, backed up by a conventional dive watch.

Open-water divers generally used a single aluminum tank, but cave divers in Florida preferred double steel cylinders, with a dual-orifice isolation manifold and a secondary regulator. Short hoses connected the tanks to the diver's buoyancy control unit, a wing-style device that provided a quick fifty to sixty pounds of lift when inflated. An open-faced guideline reel holding four hundred feet of thin, braided nylon line went into the thigh pocket of his wet suit, instead of being clipped to a D-ring—anything that dangled was to be avoided.

Cave divers didn't generally use weight belts, since the additional equipment they required was more than heavy enough already; still, Delko had added one fairly weighty piece most cave divers didn't need.

A bulletproof vest.

Delko handed a surface transceiver to Horatio. "I don't know how well this will work when I get in there," he said. "The rock may interfere with the signal."

"Be safe," Horatio said.

Delko nodded, slipped his mask on and walked over to the edge of the water. He dove in.

"H? Can you hear me?"

"Loud and clear, Eric."

"Good. I'm down around a hundred feet . . . water's pretty clear. Not much to see except rock walls and the occasional fish . . . I'm going deeper."

"Understood." Horatio paced back and forth, one hand cupped to the tranceiver's headset. He hated being a passive observer, hated the fact that

Delko was down there alone—or worse, not alone.

"Getting deeper . . . down around a hundred forty feet. Turning on my lights. I can see the bottom now. Lot of junk down here—I think I may have found where old shopping carts go to die."

"Any sign of our friend?"

"Not yet. I'm doing a check of the perimeter . . . huh."

Horatio's pulse leapt. "What is it?"

"There's a current down here, flowing toward the north wall. It seems to be directed toward an old set of rusty bedsprings propped against one wall . . . hold on. I'm going to try and move them out of the way."

Horatio bit down on the urge to tell him to be careful. Delko knew what he was doing.

"I thought so," Delko said. "The bedsprings were concealing a natural tunnel entrance. This has to be it, H. I'm going in."

"All right, go ahead. Stay in contact as long as you can."

"Will do . . . I'm attaching a guideline to the bedsprings. Tunnel's narrow, no more than four feet in diameter. Walls are smooth and rippled. It's angling downward—*kkkkkkkk*—to the right . . ."

Delko's transmission began to break up. "Say again, Eric?" Horatio said.

"—*kkkkkk*—still descending—*kkkk*—widening, but—*kkkkkk*—"

"Eric? Eric!"

All Horatio could hear was the dead hiss of static.

All children go through phases where they become obsessively interested in one particular thing, and for a while, a ten-year-old Delko's thing was tunnels. It all began when he saw *The Great Escape* one rainy Saturday afternoon on TV, and grew from there. Not content with trying to dig his own, he also read as much as he could find on the subject— from big engineering projects to the homemade kind favored by prison convicts.

And the Vietcong.

The intricate system of tunnels dug beneath tropical jungles during the Vietnam War fascinated him. There were the equivalent of whole towns down there, complete with hospitals, kitchens, living quarters and wells. They were begun in 1948 to provide refuge from the French military, starting beneath individual villages and slowly connecting to each other over time; by 1965, a network of over a hundred and twenty miles of tunnels had been dug from the hard clay beneath the Vietnam countryside.

The tunnels were an impressive feat of engineering, on both a physical and social scale; they housed up to ten thousand people, who lived, worked and slept underground, sometimes for weeks at a time.

At the moment, though, Delko wasn't reflecting

on how the Vietnamese cleverly constructed baffled vents to get rid of their cooking smoke, or even the concealed underwater entrances they sometimes built.

He was thinking about traps.

The Vietcong favored pits filled with *pungi* stakes, sharpened lengths of bamboo contaminated with human feces to cause infected wounds. They also connected tripwires to grenades or mines. Sometimes, they even used animal sentries, tethering a poisonous snake like a Krait in a tunnel, or rigging a box of scorpions to be dumped on an intruder's head.

Delko thought about the tanks of marine predators in Torrence's bedroom. He hoped none of them was missing an occupant.

The Cong also employed underground ambush techniques, stationing guards in hidden spots just inside a tunnel entrance. An enemy soldier venturing inside could find a wire garrotte or knife against his windpipe so quickly he would never have time to cry out.

The cave wound and twisted its way forward, angling down and then up again. He swam against a current that was steady but not strong; over centuries, it had polished the walls of the tunnel into a channel as smooth as the inside of a gigantic throat. The floor of the cave was covered with sediment of varying shades, a many-colored tongue lining the maw of the beast.

"—*kkkkk*—Delko, are—*kkkkk*—"

Horatio's voice was lost in a rush of static. *Sorry, H. Guess I'm on my own.*

The tunnel began to angle upward. Delko kept going.

He wasn't surprised when his head abruptly emerged from the water and into air. He turned off his light and listened intently; all he could hear was the slow, echoing drip of water. It was completely, totally dark.

Delko brought his wrist light up and turned it back on. It showed him a small chamber, with a ceiling ten feet or so overhead and a smooth-lipped rock shelf six feet away, about a foot high. Beyond that, he couldn't make out how deep the chamber went.

He swam over to the shelf, peered over the lip, then pulled himself up and onto dry ground.

He tried his radio link one more time. "Horatio?" Nothing.

The chamber had an exit in the far wall, an opening about four feet high. Delko shrugged out of his gear and took off his flippers; he didn't want to try negotiating the narrow confines of a tunnel with tanks strapped to his back. He kept the light strapped to his wrist and the battery clipped to his belt.

Holding the speargun ready, he crouched down and stepped through the opening. The smooth, rocky floor was cold against his bare feet.

On the other side was another, larger space; the ceiling was twenty feet overhead, lined with yellowish stalactites like long, decaying fangs. The chamber itself was at least fifty feet in diameter.

And it wasn't empty.

A head broke the surface of the water. Horatio's gun was out and trained between the figure's eyes even before its shoulders became visible.

Delko spat out his regulator. "H, it's me," he said. "Sorry, the radio cut out on me and I couldn't get it to come back on."

Horatio lowered his Glock. "What did you find?"

Delko clambered out of the water. "Plenty," he said. He held up a sealed plastic evidence bag, with a grim contraption inside: an artificial set of jaws, wired to what appeared to be a steel bear trap. "I brought this back to show you, but it's not all that's there. I also found the remains of the original suit—looks like he cannibalized it for a newer version."

"Grafting on bits of the old, like passing along the DNA of an ancestor . . . what else?"

"H, the place is—it's like the nest of some kind of animal. He's got food and water stashed in there, a chemical toilet, some kind of neoprene mesh rigged up as a hammock, rechargeable batteries for power . . ."

"But no Torrence."

"And no other exit. What I did find were two snorkels, probably belonging to Gabrielle Cavanaugh and the Stonecutters—and photos."

Horatio nodded. "Trophies."

"Yeah. I guess he used an underwater camera when he had Janice Stonecutter captive. I found the chemicals and equipment you'd need to develop film—it must have taken him a while to haul all that stuff down there."

"But once he did, he had a perfect darkroom, didn't he . . ."

Delko shook his head. "He had them stuck all over the walls, dozens of glossy eight-by-tens. They were pretty gruesome."

"But excellent evidence. Good work, Eric. But if he isn't here," Horatio said, putting his hands on his hips, ". . . where is he?"

There was only one answer that made any sense: underwater. But in a coastal state like Florida—which also contained hundreds of bodies of water like lakes, rivers, streams and canals—that wasn't an answer that was very useful. And if Delko was right and Torrence had built rebreather technology into his suit, he could literally stay submerged for days.

Horatio had returned to Miami. He'd reinterviewed Anatoly Kazimir, several other members of the ALA, Oliver Tresong and Leroy Delfino, even Samantha Voire. All of them knew Malcolm

Torrence—in one way or another—but none of them well; he had never talked about his family to any of them, rarely engaged in small talk, tended to devote himself obsessively to any task assigned him.

Horatio had gleaned one useful piece of information; having seen the Cyrillic tattoo on several of his dive buddies and inquired about it, Torrence had been so affected by the story of its origin he had gone out and gotten one himself—after Doctor Nicole Zhenko had already left the ALA.

And now, the only person left to talk to was Doctor Zhenko herself.

He'd tried to do it over the phone, but she had only cursed at him in Russian and hung up. Horatio had sighed, slipped on his sunglasses and gone out to the Hummer.

Horatio's first instinct was always to help people. Occasionally he ran into people who didn't want or appreciate his help, but he'd never met someone who resented it as bitterly as Nicole Zhenko.

Not that he'd been particularly helpful to the doctor herself—he'd come to her for information, starting with the technical and progressing to the personal. No, what Zhenko seemed to resent was Horatio's caring itself—she reacted to his natural compassion like it was salt in a wound. She'd convinced herself that all human beings were basically selfish, and anyone that contradicted that point of view irritated her immensely.

She didn't care about other people's losses. She was too involved with her own.

Perversely, this touched Horatio deeply. He had recognized, a long time ago, that pain could take you down a very, very dark path. He had seen other cops take that path; it had different branches, but all of them led down. Alcohol, drugs, violence, sex—they were all just ways of shutting out the suffering. He'd taken a different path himself, one much harder, accepting his pain and using it to make himself stronger. In a way, Nicole Zhenko had done the same thing—but where Horatio used his pain like fuel, she used hers like a suit of armor. A suit bristling with razor-sharp edges, the better to cut anyone who got too close. She wasn't exactly likeable, but she was a survivor . . . and Horatio respected that.

He pulled up in front of the Aquarian Institute, parked the Hummer and got out. A single halogen light burned on a tall pole outside the front door, circled by a shifting swarm of bugs and slashed by the occasional swooping bat. He could see the glow of the pool lights coming from beside the building, but the windows of the structure itself were dark. *Probably out by the pool, or in it.*

The front door was unlocked. As soon as he stepped inside, he knew something was wrong.

There was nothing out of place, no obvious sign of a struggle or break-in. Horatio just knew. Some subtle collection of clues had instantaneously been processed by years of cop experience, causing the back of his brain to scream DANGER! at the top of its subconscious lungs.

His gun was in his hand before he was even aware of reaching for it. He made his way quickly, silently, through the darkened foyer and down the hall. The door at the end was slightly ajar. Horatio peered through the crack, but he didn't have a view of the pool from this angle, just the deck and part of the ramp. He could hear a voice, but it was speaking too quietly for him to make it out clearly.

He opened the door and moved onto the deck. From the railing, he could finally see down onto the pool area.

The merman had one finned arm tightly around Nicole Zhenko's throat. She stood in front of him, on her prosthetic legs, in a white bathing suit. He held a single forefinger with a black, curving blade extending from it to the corner of her eye.

"Hold it, Torrence!" Horatio snapped. *Damn it, I don't have a shot.*

The merman looked up. Horatio understood immediately how someone could be fooled into thinking he was some sort of actual aquatic creature; there was no sign of any equipment, no hoses or tanks, just the rounded bulk of the hump on his back. His eyes were wide, glassy orbs, unblinking and dark. The twin rows of needle-like fangs that lined the open jaws of his mask looked like they'd come from an actual fish—a barracuda, maybe.

The illusion was spoiled when Torrence spoke—
the jaws didn't move at all. "Lieutenant Caine," he
said, his voice only slightly muffled. "Please come
down and join us."

"Let her go, Torrence, or I'll put a bullet right
through that fancy mask."

"No, Lieutenant. You come down here, right
now, or I'll stick this claw through her eye and into
her brain."

For once, Doctor Zhenko seemed to have nothing to say. The look on her face wasn't terror,
though; it was fury.

Horatio moved slowly down the ramp, keeping
his gun leveled at the merman the entire way.
When he reached the bottom, Torrence said,
"That's close enough. Lower your gun."

"It's over, Torrence. Let the doctor go—"

The claw pressed against her skin moved, ever
so slightly. She made no sound, but a single drop
of blood welled up and rolled down her face like
a crimson tear.

"Would you like me to take her eye to prove
my sincerity?" Torrence snarled. "How much more
do you want her to lose?"

Slowly, Horatio lowered his gun.

"Good. Now, throw it in the pool."

Horatio hesitated. Losing your gun was a nightmare every officer dreaded, but he didn't see that
he had a choice. He tossed it in; the slight splash
it made seemed abnormally loud to his ears.

"Take out your handcuffs. Cuff your right wrist to the railing."

Horatio did as he was told. "There's no place for you to go, Torrence. We found your little nest at the Verdant Springs sinkhole."

"I was done with that place, anyway. I belong under the waves, not under the earth."

Under a rock, you mean. "Then go. You don't belong up here, fine. Just leave her alone."

"I can't do that, Lieutenant," the merman hissed. "She's too important to me. She was my inspiration, you know. Part of me was always afraid to commit to the Other World, the True World, but then she showed me that it could be done. That our bodies, our forms, are not important, that balancing upright is no more than a clever monkey's trick. That you could still move with grace and ease through our natural home. And just as that tiger shark changed her, so she changed me; just as she accepted her destiny, I accepted mine . . ."

"Malcolm?" Zhenko said, her voice constricted and hoarse.

"Yes, Nicole?"

"If you weren't . . . wearing this damn slippery suit . . . I would have already broken your neck."

Torrence gave a thick, wet chuckle. "Oh, I know that, Nicole. But now you have no leverage, no balance, no weapons. No chance."

"Don't . . . need them. Have . . . something *better*."

"Oh?" Torrence's tone was mocking. "And what's that?"

"*Friends,*" Nicole rasped. "My good friend . . . Horatio . . . is getting ready to kick your ass . . ."

Torrence laughed. He hauled her backward, knocking her off balance so that the heels of her prosthetics dragged along the concrete with a dry, grating sound. "I don't think so . . . in fact, I think just the opposite." He shoved her onto her wheelchair, then wrapped a length of chain around her, binding her to the frame. He finished by securing the chain with a heavy padlock, his long, clawed fingers having some difficulty getting it closed. The Levo itself had already been immobilized, a broomstick shoved through the spokes of its back wheels.

Horatio caught a flicker of movement from the pool while Torrence was occupied. Something grey and sleek swam just below the surface.

Torrence moved toward Horatio. His hands came up, fingers flexing, blades clicking against each other like castanets. "Killing you underwater would be so much more pleasurable . . . but I suppose sometimes we just have to settle for catching what we can . . ."

Nicole grabbed a whistle hanging off the Levo's arm by a lanyard. She blew two quick, short blasts.

Torrence swiveled back toward her at the same moment Whaleboy's head popped up. Horatio clenched his free hand into a fist, raised it in the air and brought it down in one quick motion.

Torrence glanced at the pool, but Whaleboy had already submerged again. "What was the point of that?" he snapped.

Whaleboy's head popped up again—with Horatio's gun in his jaws.

"Backup," Horatio said.

The dolphin tossed the gun to Horatio with a snap of its head. The Glock spun through the air . . . and into Horatio's outstretched hand.

Torrence let out a howl of pure rage and lunged for Horatio, his arm drawn back for a murderous swipe.

Horatio shot him. Once, twice, three times.

One of the bullets punctured his oxygen reservoir. As Torrence collapsed to the concrete, the last sound he made was the bubbling, whistling noise of air being forced through blood . . .

Calleigh, Wolfe, Delko and Trippall came down to the Aquarian Institute after Horatio called it in. There was no need, he tried to tell them—he was fine and Torrence was history.

But they came anyway.

"Hell of a thing, Horatio," Tripp said as Torrence's body was being loaded onto a stretcher. "Guy really thought he was some kind of monster."

"He was," Horatio said mildly. "He just got the particulars wrong."

Wolfe and Calleigh walked over. "I can't believe you got a dolphin to retrieve your gun," Wolfe said, shaking his head.

"I can," Calleigh said with a smile. "Obviously, Horatio had a much better line of fire than he did."

Horatio smiled back, but his eyes were on Nicole. She was at the other end of the pool, perched in her Levo with a blanket around her shoulders, talking to Delko. He couldn't quite hear what they were saying, but from the venomous glances she was giving Torrence's body and the bemused look on Delko's face, he thought he understood the gist of it. She was going to be fine.

"H?" Calleigh asked. "You okay?"

"Yes, I am . . . you know, Malcolm Torrence thought of himself as a species of one. The ultimate predator. But even the deadliest predator has natural enemies . . . and *that*, my friends," he said, looking around at his team, "would be *us*."

PC GAME
AVAILABLE NOW

Featuring the likenesses
of the entire CSI Miami cast

CSI: MIAMI and elements and characters thereof © 2002–2004 CBS Broadcasting Inc. and Alliance Atlantis Productions, Inc.
All Rights Reserved. Software © 2004 Ubisoft Entertainment. All Rights Reserved. Ubisoft, ubi.com, and the Ubisoft logo are
trademarks of Ubisoft Entertainment in the U.S. and/or other countries. CSI: Miami, CBS and the CBS Eye design are TM CBS
Broadcasting Inc. Company logos are trademarks of their respective owners. No celebrity endorsement implied. Developed
by 369 Interactive. All Rights Reserved. Software platform logo TM and © IEMA 2003.

CSIM-ubi.01

As many as 1 in 3 Americans
have HIV and don't know it.

**TAKE CONTROL.
KNOW YOUR STATUS.
GET TESTED.**

To learn more about HIV testing,
or get a free guide to HIV and
other sexually transmitted diseases.

**www.knowhivaids.org
1-866-344-KNOW**

09620

THE DNA OF GREAT DVD

CSI: NY

CSI: MiaMi

CSI: CRIME SCENE INVESTIGATION

OWN THEM ALL

TM CBS Broadcasting Inc. © 2004, 2005 CBS Broadcasting Inc. and Alliance Atlantis Productions, Inc.
CBS Broadcasting Inc. and Alliance Atlantis Productions, Inc. are the makers of but program for the purpose of copyright and other laws. All Rights Reserved.
Paramount logo and artwork design TM, ® & Copyright © 2005 by Paramount Pictures. All Rights Reserved Cover, availability, and artwork subject to change without notice.

www.paramount.com/homeentertainment